THE DEMI-WOLF AND THE HUNTER

THE FAIRY GODMOTHER TALES
BOOK 2

AMBERLEY MARTIN

CAVELINE PRESS

A catalogue record for this book is available from the National Library of New Zealand

ISBN 978-0-473-62876-5 (Softcover - POD)

ISBN 978-1-0670325-1-7 (Softcover – POD 2nd Edition)

ISBN 978-0-473-62877-2 (Epub)

Cover by Miblart

www.miblart.com

Caveline Press

www.amberleymartin.com

Content guide at end of book

As hounds and greyhounds, mongrels, spaniels, curs,
Shoughs, water-rugs, and demi-wolves are clept
All by the name of dogs. The valued file
Distinguishes the swift, the slow, the subtle,
The housekeeper, the hunter, every one
According to the gift which bounteous nature
Hath in him closed, whereby he does receive
Particular addition, from the bill
That writes them all alike. And so of men.

—Shakespeare, *Macbeth*, Act 3, Scene 1

CHAPTER ONE

ONCE UPON A TIME, there was a girl who dreamed of a better life. Donella had worked day and night in her father's tavern from the time she was old enough to carry a flagon of ale without spilling a drop. She learned how to balance a tray of dishes while weaving around the tables, memorized the menu since she wasn't very good with her letters, and mastered the art of summing prices in her head and calculating change.

When she was thirteen summers old, and her body had begun the long, slow shift from a child's to a woman's, she acquired an extra skill: avoiding the roaming hands of the patrons who treated her like an item on the menu.

She had no money of her own, no skills other than waitressing, and no friends to lighten her load. But she had her dreams, and her favorite way to imagine escaping her life of drudgery involved a gallant prince arriving on a white steed to declare his love and whisk her away to a life of luxury.

Whenever her father caught her daydreaming, he would cuff her over the head, or smack her with his spatula, and tell her to get her head out of the clouds. Cowed, she would throw herself into her work and tuck her dreams into the back of her mind, knowing they would never come true.

Then, one day, her dream walked into the tavern.

He wasn't a prince on a white steed, he didn't declare his love or whisk her away, and he was barely older than she was, but none of that stopped Donella from immediately falling in love, the way that only a thirteen-year-old can.

The boy was incredibly handsome, with brown hair and gray eyes, and was dressed in a fitted black vest and trousers. Donella felt frumpy and awkward in comparison. She had too many freckles, could never wrangle her red curls, and her dress fitted poorly because her father bought her clothes without consideration for her changing shape and she didn't have the sewing skills to adjust them.

When she attempted to take the boy's order, her words got tangled on her tongue. He'd come in with an older man, who was also dressed in black, and the boy gave that man a disdainful look as if to ask why he'd brought him to a place where the waitress was clearly incompetent. Heat flared in Donella's cheeks, and as much as this boy was her heart's desire, she hoped that since this was the first time he'd patronized the tavern, he was merely a traveler passing through and wouldn't be back to patronize her a second time.

But he did come back. At least once a month. And he became a regular participant in Donella's dreams of escape. On nights when the patrons were being particularly handsy, she survived on the hope he would kick down the tavern's door, tell her father no one would ever treat her like that again, and sweep her into his arms.

Two years passed, her feelings didn't wane, and the times the boy and his companion would arrive for lunch were the only bright spots in Donella's otherwise dull life. Bright spots that quickly faded ... until the boy turned up alone. He ordered the same bowl of chowder and flagon of ale he always did and sat down at a table away from the other patrons, his chin propped glumly on his fist.

Donella's chest ached to see his distress.

She delivered his meal, turned away, hesitated, turned back, and finally, for the first time since they'd met, overcame her shyness to speak to him of something other than his order. "Where's your companion today, sir?"

He blinked as he looked up at her, his lost expression causing the ache in her chest to deepen. "He has gone, my lady."

My lady.

Donella was about the furthest thing from a lady she could imagine, but regardless, to hear him speak the words made her heart sing.

She cast a wary glance toward the kitchens, but her father was out of sight, so she slipped into the seat opposite the boy. "You don't mean dead?"

He shook his head. "No, he's gone home. At least, I hope he made it."

"Maybe you could visit him there," she suggested.

"I don't know where *there* is."

"Oh." Donella knew she should get back to work—her father had a way of only noticing her when she was idle—but she couldn't bear to leave the boy alone with his misery. "Where is *your* home?"

He looked at her as if the question confused him.

She shouldn't have asked him something so personal. It was a common occurrence for her cheeks to heat in his presence, but the blush felt particularly strong this time, and she knew, with her pale, freckled complexion, it would stand out like rot on a potato.

"I don't really ..." he said, then, "I mean, I stay places, but I wouldn't call them ..." He floundered before finally offering, "Bretland."

Considering that here, in the north of North Lynnborough, they were about as far away from the principality of Bretland as anyone in the Seven Realms could get, his Lynnbrovian was excellent, and Donella could have listened to him speak all day.

Before she could think of something else to keep him talking, her father bellowed her name from the kitchens. She jumped to her feet, her heart pounding at the thought of being caught slacking.

"Wait," the boy said, before she could rush back to her work. "Donella? Is that your name?"

If her blush had been bad before, it came back with a vengeance at hearing her name on the boy's lips. "Yes," she murmured. "Named for my father, Donel."

His lost expression was replaced by the most charming smile she'd ever seen.

Her heart pounded for an entirely different reason.

"It's nice to meet you." He offered her his hand, and she stared at it for a long moment before slipping her fingers into his. His touch was everything she'd ever dreamed: his skin warm, his grip firm but not crushing, and his lips soft as he pressed them briefly to her knuckles. She floated like a piece of driftwood on a wave, washing ashore in the kitchens before she realized she hadn't asked *his* name.

Her father was as angry as a pot bubbling over on the stove. "Why are you lingering with that rogue when there are other customers to serve?"

Donella glanced back at the boy. She'd never considered him, nor his companion, to be a rogue. He did dress in utilitarian black and carry a dagger at his waist, but she'd always thought rogues spent their time selling their services to manor lords who wanted devilish deeds done without dirtying their own hands. She couldn't imagine this boy hurting anyone.

"He was sad," she murmured.

"Sad? Rogues are more likely to murder you out of spite than shed a tear over anything." He grabbed her arm in his meaty fist and gave her a good shake. Her skin burned and she let out a whimper of pain. "Focus on the customers who are freer with their coins."

Donella babbled promises that she would do as he asked, until he seemed satisfied and released her arm. She backed out of the kitchens and turned to face the crowded dining room. There was a flicker of movement from the boy's direction, as if he'd been watching her through the kitchen doorway but had quickly glanced away.

She rubbed at her arm and returned to work, hoping he hadn't seen her humiliation.

THE ONLY TIME DONELLA truly had to herself was after her father kicked out any remaining patrons and closed the tavern each night. Depending on how the ale had been flowing and how free the patrons had been with their coins, this usually happened an hour or so before midnight.

Her father would leave Donella to clean the last of the tables, wash the last of the dishes, and sweep the last of the mess out the door. Then Donella would hang up her apron, pull on a shawl, take any leftovers that would only be given to the pigs in the morning, and slip outside.

Leyton was a fishing village, nestled on the ocean's edge in a sweeping bay. It wasn't a pretty place. The beach consisted almost entirely of mudflats that stretched for miles when the tide went out, the air was perpetually permeated by the scent of salt and fish, most of the buildings were small hovels held together by the same gray mud, and the people eked out livings that generally revolved around fishing.

The thing that made the people especially grim, and which no one liked to talk about, was the dragon that lived in the side of the cliff that loomed at one end of the bay. The villagers were afraid of the dragon. Not that it would eat them—they kept the meadow on top of the cliff stocked with sheep or calves to avoid that—but that word of the dragon's existence would spread, thus scaring off the merchants and travelers that came through. For her part, Donella felt only jealousy. The dragon could do as she pleased, when she pleased, and didn't need to please anyone to keep a roof over her head and food in her belly. Being feared wouldn't be so bad a price for freedom such as that.

A blanket of sleep lay over the village, and Donella felt no fear as she walked through the darkness to a small hut that stood alone on the shore. Warm light snaked between the slats of the shuttered windows and under the door, on which she rapped three times.

"Come," a voice called from inside.

"It's me, Grandmother," she said as she let herself in.

The hut was home to an old fishwife. She was bent with age, her thin gray hair failed to conceal her mottled scalp, and deep troughs wrinkled her face. From the first time they'd met, the fishwife's slightly addled mind had left her convinced that Donella was her granddaughter, Greta, and since attempting to disabuse her of that notion always upset the old woman, Donella kept up the charade.

Though it looked like nothing much from the outside, the single-room hut was cozy enough on the inside. It was lit by a few carefully positioned candles and had a bed in one corner, a thickly padded chair in another, and a rickety table and chairs in a third. The walls were decorated with torn nets, tangled fishing lines, and fish skeletons. A fire pit sat in the middle of the floor, where the fishwife crouched over a cauldron suspended above the embers.

"Come, child, come," the fishwife said, beckoning Donella forward. "The tea's almost ready."

Donella didn't visit every night, only when she had food to share, but the fishwife always had tea ready to offer in return. Donella laid her package on the table—carefully wrapped mussel fritters that had been returned to the kitchens by a picky patron who didn't appreciate the fact they were burned on one side—and went to help serve the tea. The old fishwife paused in her stirring to grasp Donella's shoulders and kiss her thrice on the cheeks. Donella hugged her thin frame—taking a moment to enjoy the loving embrace, even if she wasn't actually the person the old woman loved—then held the earthenware mugs while the fishwife ladled the tea with quivering hands.

When they were seated, Donella shared out the fritters and they ate in a silence only broken by the smacking of the fishwife's lips. The tea was rich and earthy, and simply partaking of a cup always soothed Donella's suffering. No matter how bad a day she'd had, she always slept better on the nights she visited the fishwife.

"Those weren't bad." The fishwife sipped at her tea and gave Donella a mournful look. "Though I've been hankering lately for fried flounder. I haven't had one for so long."

"I know," Donella murmured through a twinge of guilt. She had no idea how the fishwife fed herself when Donella couldn't. "We don't often have any to spare."

Flounder were plentiful in the mudflats, and a common staple for the villagers, but they weren't a popular item on the tavern's menu. Her father only ever bought as many as he thought he could sell in a day, and if Donella tried to keep one aside, he would berate her for wasting money.

"Well, no need to feel bad." The fishwife reached over to pat Donella's hand. "Maybe next time."

They chatted idly as they drank the remainder of their tea. The fishwife told the same stories she always did, and Donella listened as if it was the first time she'd ever heard them. When the fishwife asked after her mother, Donella said she was well, wondering briefly if Greta's mother had been better than her own, who had abandoned her as a babe. And when she asked after her father, Donella said he was as busy as ever, pondering whether Greta's father ever raised doubts about her parentage when he was angry, like hers did.

When their cups were drained, the fishwife shuffled around the room to douse the candles.

Donella stayed in her seat for a moment. Her visits with the fishwife were always too brief, and she was never ready to return to her small room above the kitchens.

"I'll come back soon," she said, as the light in the room faded to almost nothing. "Maybe I'll have some flounder for you then."

The fishwife gazed at her kindly. "Good night, my dear Greta."

THE BOY DIDN'T RETURN to the tavern the next week or the week after that. Donella blamed herself, revisiting their final conversation in her mind, attempting to figure out if she'd offended him somehow. When she found nothing obvious, she started to wonder if he truly was a rogue, as her father claimed, and had been injured—or worse—during one of his villainous ventures.

She considered, briefly, searching for him—he'd visited so often that he must reside nearby, and surely one of the villagers would have seen which direction he hailed from—but she dismissed the idea. With no money, she wouldn't get far. Not to mention that if she'd been far too timid to even ask his name, there was no way she would be able to demand answers from anyone.

After six long months, when she'd come to accept that she would never see him again, he walked through the door.

Their time apart had been very kind to him—he'd made great progress in his journey to being a man while she still dragged her feet—and again she found herself flustered in his presence.

This time, there was no disdain in his expression as he waited for her to say something. In fact, his face bore the same heavy look as when his companion had left, and she wondered who he'd lost this time.

She licked her lips. "What can I get you, sir?"

He smiled faintly and ordered his usual chowder and ale.

She remembered her father's warning not to spend too much time with him and was polite when she delivered his meal, but didn't attempt to engage him in conversation.

Unfortunately, he hadn't been appraised of the situation.

He started to turn up with alarming regularity. Monday was their quietest day of the week and, with no pressure to vacate his table for another patron, he would linger over his lunch. He didn't come every week but often enough that when he didn't appear, Donella was hit by the cudgel of unfulfilled anticipation. If she was in the kitchens when he arrived, he would rap his knuckles on the bar in a rhythm she soon came to recognize. When she took his order, he would give her his charming smile and murmur, "Thank you, Donella," in a way that made her heart grow wings and fly to the heavens. He asked if she was well. He inquired about local gossip and warned her when he'd spotted the dragon, which made her think he must live toward the cliff. When he came in wet, he groused about the weather. When he arrived covered in scrapes and bruises, he commented wryly that he needed to run faster.

He never did more than that.

He didn't glance lasciviously at the hemline of her frock. He didn't squeeze her rump like he was checking a loaf of bread for freshness. He didn't pull her to him and ask if there was something else he could get in exchange for his coins. He might not be a prince, but he was clearly a gentleman.

One Monday, after another year had passed, the rogue stayed long into the afternoon, entranced by the pages of a small book and ordering the occasional ale. When Donella delivered a flagon to his table, she paused to read over his shoulder, but she hadn't gotten any better with her letters and couldn't decipher any of the words.

"It's Brettish," he said without glancing up.

"I'm sorry, sir." Her cheeks flamed at being caught, and she hastened to flee.

"Wait, please," he said softly, and she did. He gave her a curious look. "I've been coming here for over three years. I think we're past you calling me 'sir.'"

"Of course—" She caught herself before she called him 'sir' again, but she didn't know what else to call him. Even though he'd given her the perfect opportunity, she'd never been brave enough to ask his name before, and she was too embarrassed to ask it now. Yet she couldn't walk away from the chance she might finally learn it.

She felt as stuck as a speared flounder.

When she didn't say anything more, he spoke instead. "You could call me Rory, if you'd like."

"Rory," she murmured, and his name was the sweetest thing that had ever passed her lips. She glanced over her shoulder, but her father was nowhere in sight. And surely, after so many months, he must've realized that the rogue wasn't here to cause trouble and his rule no longer applied. "What are all those words in your book?"

"They tell a story of a knight who travels to a tournament in a far-away realm." He winced, as if embarrassed by what he was about to say. "It looks like he'll have to choose between winning the prize and wresting the queen away from her villainous husband."

The only books in the tavern contained recipes that her father had long since stopped referring to, and the idea that a book could contain a story as delightful as that one brought a smile to Donella's lips. But she was even more charmed by Rory's chagrin. "You know, you could have lied. I would have been none the wiser."

His mouth sagged open. "I didn't think to lie to you."

Donella edged closer and peered at the page again. The etchings still meant nothing to her. "Could you teach me?"

"Brettish?"

"To read. So I can read this story one day and find out what the knight chooses." She regretted her boldness as soon as she'd spoken. He would likely say no and mock her ignorance. What reason did he have to waste his time teaching her to read in a language that she would likely never have the opportunity to speak?

Instead of making her dire predictions come true, he murmured, "Of course, my lady," and gestured to the seat next to him.

"Now?" she squawked.

"Unless you have duties to attend to."

She shook her head, swallowed hard, and eased down into the chair.

Once the shock wore off, Donella enjoyed sitting close to him, with a perfectly reasonable excuse to focus intently on his face, as he began to teach her Brettish. His eyes were not merely gray but encircled by dark rings. A small scar curved through his right eyebrow, and another sat on the left of his chin. Reddish hints appeared in his hair when the light hit it just right, and for as long as she had known him, it had been cut in the same short style.

The black outfit he always wore consisted of a hooded vest and a pair of bracers on his wrists but no shirt sleeves, which made Donella wonder if he felt the cold, though she certainly didn't mind being able to contemplate the tone of his biceps. The underside of his left was dotted by what looked like scars from three puncture wounds, neatly lined up in a row. A marred patch of skin on his right shoulder peeked out from his vest whenever he reached for his ale. It made her wonder if there were more scars he kept hidden. All in all, it was a miracle she had any capacity to focus on what he was teaching her.

When he finally left, Donella practically floated to the kitchens, and, like a doomed fly, flew directly into the spider's web.

"What did I tell you about that rogue?" her father demanded, placing himself between her and the door.

Donella glanced around, but there was no escape. "I thought …" she started, attempting to come up with a lie. "It's been so long—"

Her father lunged forward and jabbed her in the chest to emphasize his words. "Don't think I don't know what keeps him coming back. It's not the quality of the ale."

Donella wasn't sure what he meant, but she agreed about the ale.

His gaze drifted over her, as if he were seeing her for the first time in years. "If *talking* is what it takes to keep him from causing trouble, you do whatever he asks. But don't think that means you can slack on your other work."

Donella stood mutely, afraid to speak unless she woke herself from this dream. For, surely, this could not be real. If it was, her father had just given her permission to spend time with Rory.

"Got it?"

She bowed her head to hide her smile, and murmured, "Yes, Father."

Rory returned the following Monday, and every week after that, to give her another lesson. In order to keep her father happy, for every hour Rory was there, Donella would fill a flagon with ale and place it on his table. Some he drank, others he ignored, and still more he nudged in her direction, though she didn't have the taste for it herself. Regardless of their fate, he paid for every one.

She made sure that he'd gone before the dinner rush began, and she worked twice as hard to complete all her usual tasks. Occasionally she would catch her father watching them, but she made sure never to give him an excuse to raise the matter.

In the time between Rory's visits, she practiced dutifully. Instead of daydreaming about a prince, she fantasized about nouns and verbs, commas and quotation marks, conjunctions and contractions.

It took a year before Donella felt ready to attempt Rory's book. She gave up after barely making it through the first page. The next time he visited, she handed the book back.

"Finished already?" he asked.

She struggled to contain the churning maelstrom of shame that she felt at having to admit her failure. "It was too hard," she said tightly. "I'll try again in another year."

She turned to go back to her work, but again Rory asked her to wait and gestured to the chair beside him. When she eased into it, he opened the book and laid it between them. "Let's read it together," he said. "I'm eager to find out what the knight decides."

"You didn't finish it?" she asked, unable to keep the surprise from her tone.

The corner of his mouth quirked up. "Not yet."

He read the first chapter aloud as Donella followed along, and his voice brought the story to life. She took over for the next chapter, and it was so much easier with him beside her, helping her sound out the difficult words and explaining the meanings of those she didn't know. It took a few lessons for them to reach the end of the book, where the knight sacrificed the prize to win the queen, and Rory promised to bring her another. She hoped it wouldn't be too easy, so she could ask him to read it with her again.

Brettish lessons weren't the only thing Rory gave her.

One week, when he paid for his meal, he handed her too many coins. She didn't notice until he'd already taken his seat, so when she brought his meal out and sat down beside him, she set the extra coin on the table.

"You paid too much, sir."

"Did I?" he murmured. "I apologize."

Which seemed like a strange thing to say. They carried on their lesson as normal, but when she cleared the table after he'd gone, the coin was still there. She slipped it into the pocket of her apron, intent on returning it to him.

The next week, when she delivered his meal, she set the coin on the table once again, but when she cleaned up after he'd left, not only was the coin still there, it had been joined by another.

She stopped attempting to give the coins back.

It was the first money she'd ever had of her own. She couldn't spend it, of course. She'd gotten away with spending time with Rory, but if her father caught her with new clothes or special treats, he would most certainly accuse her of stealing from him. But she made a small purse out of an old scrap of fabric and kept it hidden under her skirts at all times.

And she started to imagine a new dream.

Rory was a rogue, not a prince, and whatever his job entailed, rescuing her wasn't part of it, but if she managed to save enough coins, she might be able to follow him out of the tavern one day and make herself a new life.

By the time she turned eighteen, Donella and Rory spoke to each other exclusively in Brettish, and she devoured every book he brought her. Her language was still a bit stilted, as he was the only person she was able to converse with, but she felt confident enough that if someone plucked her out of the tavern and dropped her in the middle of Bretland, she would get along just fine.

One autumn day, she heard his familiar rap on the bar, though it wasn't a Monday. The thrill of a surprise visit stirred in her stomach, and she ran her fingers through her curls quickly before rushing out to see him. When he ordered two servings of chowder, her gaze swung to his companion, thinking that the older man must have returned after all these years. But instead it was a woman, not much older than Donella herself. Despite looking travel-worn in a simple shift dress, and with her long auburn hair tied in a thick braid, she was undoubtedly pretty.

Donella's traitorous heart continued to beat.

During all their time together, she'd never asked Rory if he had a sweetheart. She'd never really asked him anything personal. He told her stories about Bretland, about how the people lived and what she should expect if she ever went there, but he never mentioned how he'd grown up or anything about his family. She'd spent so long dreaming of escaping with him that she'd forgotten it was a fantasy.

Though she was flustered, she could at least conceal it better than her younger self, and she forced her tone to be polite. "No lesson then, today?"

"Not today, sorry, Donella," Rory said. He passed her the coins for their meals, and though she tried to remain cool, the touch of his fingers warmed her.

It was late for lunch and the tavern had only a few patrons, but unfortunately for Donella, one table contained Dyson Doon and his band of rowdy fishermen. Dyson was one of the most outspoken men in Leyton. He had a fishing boat that he worked himself, but he made most of his money by renting boats to other fishers and taking a cut of their catch. It might have been the action of a generous man, but he charged the fishers extra for maintenance and mooring, failing to fulfill their quota, or using the boats when the tides were right. None of that was relevant to Donella's situation, but something else was. Despite the fact that Dyson had a wife and children at home, he was one of the most handsy patrons she had, especially on days like today, when he'd been drinking with his friends for hours.

She avoided Dyson's table as she took Rory and his new companion their meals.

"Tell me," Rory murmured. "Does the dragon sleep?"

Donella's breath caught, and her gaze flicked to the woman. No one spoke about the dragon in front of outsiders. "I'm sorry, *sir*," Donella said pointedly. "I know not what you speak of."

Rory gave her the charming smile that melted her insides. "Don't worry about her. She's my sister. She won't say a word."

His sister! Donella's heart sang, and she had to fight to stop a grin from spreading across her face.

"I didn't know you had a sister," she said as she turned to study the woman. Now that Rory had pointed it out, it was obvious. "I can see the resemblance, though. You have the same hair." She leaned over, positioning her hand on the table so her finger brushed against Rory's, and murmured, "No one has seen it in over a week."

"Thank you," he said as he slipped her another coin.

She tucked the coin into the pocket of her apron and headed back to the kitchens.

There was only one reason Rory would ask after the dragon. He was planning to go to the cliff.

She never asked him about the work he did to keep up his steady stream of coins. She hoped he hadn't been foolish enough to accept a job stealing from the dragon or, worse, attempting to slay it.

Dyson called for another round of ales, interrupting her thoughts, and Donella filled four flagons before carefully carrying them—two in each hand—across the dining room. She'd barely laid the ales on the table when Dyson's arm slipped around her waist. His gaze raked up her form, and his breath was thick with ale. "How old are you now, girl?"

"Eighteen, sir."

"Has your father found you a husband yet?" His gaze dropped. His head was level with her breasts.

"No, sir." She doubted her father had any interest in doing so. If she married and moved out, he would have to pay someone to work as a waitress.

Dyson's other hand grabbed her hip, and he pulled her hard against him. "I could help you with that."

"Better get your wife's permission first," said Cole Treseder, who was sitting to Dyson's right. This caused a raucous laugh from the other men at the table.

Donella tried to pull out of Dyson's grasp, but his hands held her in place like an anchor. She hated the way he looked at her, the way he touched her, and the propositions he made, but he cared not a whit for her protestations, and her father had no interest in protecting her. All she could do was spend as little time in Dyson's presence as possible.

"I have to get back to work, sir," she said.

Dyson glanced around. "I don't see anyone demanding your attention." His hand slid up her side. "If you ever get sick of waiting tables, I'm sure my wife would appreciate having a maid to cook and clean and care for the children. And if you provided a few other services she's not so keen on anymore ..." His creeping fingers reached her breast. "Well, I wouldn't complain."

Donella let out a muted cry and pushed against him, struggling to break free. "Please," she said. "Let me go."

He only gripped her tighter and licked his lips.

"Pardon me, miss. More bread?" Rory's sister called.

Dyson's laughter stopped, and he sent a vicious glare in the young woman's direction before reluctantly dropping his arms. "We'll finish this later," he muttered.

Donella ran to the kitchens, her face hot and tears burning her eyes. She wiped her face on the hem of her apron, grabbed a loaf of bread, and delivered it to Rory's table. She hovered beside them, unwilling to leave the small circle of safety that a needy patron offered. She wanted to hug the woman, or at least thank her, because no one had ever done anything even as small as that to aid her. Rory wouldn't look at her; instead he chose to stare at his sister. He was probably disgusted that Donella let Dyson handle her in such a manner.

"Pay the girl," his sister snapped at him.

He made a small, irritated sound, as if he didn't like her bossing him around, then slapped his hand flat upon the table before pushing to his feet and saying, "Time to go." When he moved his hand to reach for the loaf of bread, Donella saw he'd left her not only a coin, but a small dagger.

He still didn't look at her as he stepped around the table, took hold of his sister's arm, and pulled her to her feet. Donella flinched at seeing him treat a woman so roughly but still slipped both the coin and the dagger into her pocket. The dagger was heavier than she expected for something so small, and the weight of it pulling at the fabric of her apron for the rest of the day made her feel, for the first time in her life, that escape might finally be possible.

WHEN RORY ARRIVED FOR their next lesson, he was alone again and made no mention of his sister, and Donella was too shy to ask after her. He bore the signs of a fight, and Donella wondered if giving her his dagger had made him vulnerable, but she didn't bring that up, either.

Then, a few weeks later, as midwinter neared, Rory made another surprise visit, on a Sunday evening.

"I wasn't expecting you tonight," Donella said, after she'd delivered a tray of plates to a table of hungry patrons.

"I came to apologize," Rory said, his brow furrowed. "I have to go on a journey tomorrow and will miss our lesson."

She fought to keep the disappointment from showing on her face, and she held the empty tray to her chest as a shield between them. "Oh, well, that's fine."

Rory touched her shoulder, and a thrill ran through her. Despite the amount of time they'd spent together, he always kept his hands to himself. She let him guide her across the dining room.

He leaned in and whispered, "For the past few years I've been in someone's employ, not free to do as I please, but one way or another, that ends in two days' time." He hesitated, and the silence was filled by the hammering of Donella's heart. "If I leave, will you come with me?"

"To Bretland?"

"If you want."

She didn't hesitate. She didn't need to think about it. "I would leave with you right now."

Rory smiled, but it faded quickly. "I have no money," he said. "I have no prospects. I have nothing to offer you."

"Donella!" her father bellowed from the kitchens. "Where are you? There are paying customers waiting."

She flinched, and Rory stiffened. His gaze snapped to the kitchens as if he'd finally decided he wouldn't tolerate the way her father treated her. But now wasn't the time to act on those feelings, not if he was willing to take her away.

Donella closed her hand over his. "I'll accept your offer of nothing if it means I get to leave this life behind."

Rory relaxed and handed her a coin. "Give me two days to finish my business, and I swear I'll return."

Donella tucked the coin away before hugging her tray to her chest again. "I'll be waiting."

The rest of the night passed in a happy blur. No one laid their hands on her; when a couple tried, and she smacked them away, knowing she only had two—maybe three—more days to suffer any consequences. She hummed as she scrubbed the dishes and skipped to the fishwife's hut with the fried flounder she had secreted away.

After greeting Donella with her usual three kisses on the cheeks, the old fishwife took the carefully wrapped bundle with glee. She didn't bother dishing the fish onto a plate but merely produced two forks and dove in.

"This might be the last time I see you, Grandmother," Donella said. "I'm going away soon."

"Are you now?" the fishwife asked, not shifting her focus from the food.

She knew the old woman didn't truly care for her—it was her own granddaughter she loved, and she would probably miss the food more than Donella herself—but she felt the need to explain. "I have a friend, and he's invited me to join him on a journey. We leave in three days."

"We'll see."

Donella sat stunned. The old woman got muddled up sometimes, but she'd never been cruel. "What does that mean?"

The fishwife paused with her fork halfway to her mouth. "You've had a hard life," she said, and her voice didn't have its normal absentminded air, "and it makes you think you know how brutal the world can be, but you are still young, child, and you hold tight to your dreams as if they will not be wrested from your fingers. You think this boy will save you from your miserable existence? He will not. Mark me. He will break his promise. He will *not* show up."

"You can't know that," Donella said, but a shiver ran down her spine. She'd never mentioned Rory before, or her dreams that he would rescue her, and she'd said nothing of tonight's promise, she hadn't had time.

"I can indeed." The fishwife's gaze bored into Donella. Her eyes were less rheumy, her pupils large. "And that's not all I know. You will become the liege of a grand manor. You will win the heart of a prince. And you will have your happy ending. But it will all come at a great price."

The fishwife's words should have been reassuring. A grand manor, a prince, and a happy ending all sounded good, but there was such malice behind the prediction that Donella lurched to her feet. "Stop this. Why would you say such hateful things?"

The fishwife's gaze dropped to the fork that had not yet reached her mouth, as if surprised it still hovered there. Her expression glazed over, and she smacked her lips. "Oh, I do like a nice fried flounder. You're a good girl to bring me some, Greta."

A feeling of unease settled in Donella's stomach, and she didn't stay to share the meal, even though the fishwife seemed to have reverted to her old self. She slipped out of the hut into the darkness, her whole body trembling from the fishwife's portentous words. They couldn't be true. Rory *would* show up. He had to. He'd sworn it.

DONELLA SPENT AN AGONIZING two days worrying over the fishwife's words, but there was nothing she could do except wait.

The third day dawned, and Rory didn't arrive at breakfast time.

That was all right, Donella thought. He never came that early.

He didn't come for lunch.

But she didn't expect he'd want to eat.

He didn't show up before the dinner rush.

Donella's worry solidified into a hard lump in her stomach.

Every time the door banged open, Donella turned to see if it was him. She dropped dishes, spilled ale, and bumped into patrons. Her father scowled at her from the kitchens. He probably would have taken the cost of her mistakes out of her wages, but since he didn't pay her, he would take it out in other ways.

The night dragged on, and still Rory didn't come. Her father closed the kitchens, but instead of retreating to his room out the back, he joined Dyson Doon at his table, and Donella had to serve them round after round of ales. It was after midnight when her father finally sent Dyson on his way.

Donella hid in the kitchens and washed the last of the dishes as she waited for him to lock up and retire to his room. She hadn't set aside any food for the fishwife tonight, as she hadn't expected to be here, but there was a little seafood chowder left in the pot.

As she stared into the depths of the creamy mixture, tears tracked down her cheeks.

Rory hadn't come.

He'd sworn it, but he had not come.

And why would he? She may have spent five years completely in love with him and hanging off his every word, but he'd never made any indication he reciprocated her feelings.

He probably visited several waitresses in taverns around North Lynnborough. One for each day of the week.

Her heart broke, and she cursed herself for her foolishness.

"What are you stealing this time?" her father slurred from behind her.

Donella spun around and pressed back against the counter. "What do you mean?"

"Don't try to deny it." He swayed as he stepped into the kitchens, and the room shrank around her. "I don't care about a bowl of leftover chowder or a few burnt fritters, but when you steal a whole flounder, you're stealing coins from my pocket."

"It was just a fish," Donella babbled, grasping for an excuse that his ale-tainted mind would accept. "I have to eat."

"You'll eat what I give you and nothing more."

He stepped closer, and Donella skirted to the side.

"I'm sorry," she said. "I won't do it again."

"No, you won't. But a sorry isn't going to pay me back for what you've taken."

Donella hit the corner and had nowhere else to go. "How am I meant to repay you? I don't have any money. I already work here day and night."

"Luckily, I've had an offer."

"For what?"

"Dyson wants to buy the place."

Donella gasped.

"He's offered me a pretty price, too, enough for me to finally leave this village and the reek of fish behind."

"But where would we go?"

Her foolish heart immediately wondered how Rory would find her. But, of course, there was no reason to think he would even come looking.

Her father snorted. "Oh no, my girl. Dyson needs a waitress. I'm selling you along with the business."

Donella struggled to take a breath, as if an iron band had closed around her chest. "No," she choked out. "You can't. I work so hard. I do everything you ask. I'm your daughter."

His expression darkened. "So your mother said when she dumped you in my lap and went to sea."

Donella lifted a trembling hand to her mouth. Her gaze darted over her father's shoulder to the door.

Please, she thought, *if you're coming, come now.*

But Rory did not come. He did not save her.

Her father lunged forward. Donella shrieked and darted to the side, hoping to slip past him, but he caught her arm and pulled her around.

"You listen to me, girl." His rancid breath washed over her. "You keep your head down and do as Dyson says. He'll have no qualms about tossing you out on the street if you misbehave. And no one will take you in unless they want to get on his bad side."

"No!" She grabbed his fingers, tried to peel them away from her arm, but his grip only tightened. He shook her so hard her head snapped back and her vision swam.

"What was that sound?" he asked.

Donella couldn't gather her wits to ask what he meant before he shook her again. She heard it that time. The rattle of the coins in her hidden purse.

His eyes widened. "Have you been stealing coins too, you little whelp?"

He gripped her apron with one hand and pulled. Donella reached desperately for the pocket, where Rory's dagger still hid, and grasped tight to the reassuring weight through the fabric. Her father yanked again, and the ties scoured her waist before finally snapping. He grabbed at her skirts next, tearing the fabric until he revealed the purse. He caught it and ripped it free. His hand couldn't contain the bulging mass.

He looked at her, incredulous. "How long have you been stealing from me?"

"I didn't steal them." Donella grasped her apron to her chest, her fist tightening around the dagger's handle. "Rory gave them to me."

"Rory?" he growled. "That rogue? If he's paying for your time then that money belongs to me."

"No!" Donella reached for it, but her father lifted it above her head with one hand and kept her at bay with the other.

"If I'd known you were so keen to sell yourself, I would've made a deal with Dyson years ago."

Donella's future played out before her eyes. If Dyson owned the tavern, she would get no reprieve from his roaming hands.

The old fishwife had been right about Rory. So did that mean her other predictions would come true, too? Would Donella become a liege, and win a prince, and live happily ever after?

It all seemed so ridiculous. The life of a manor liege was so far removed from Donella's experience that she could barely contemplate it. But a life she couldn't contemplate had to be better than the one she could. She had no intention of working for Dyson Doon, which meant she had to walk out the door tonight and never look back. And to do that, she needed her purse.

She glared at her father, and though her voice was so choked with fear she could barely force the words out, she said, "Give me my money."

"It's not your money," he growled. Then he raised his arm and backhanded her across the face.

Donella stumbled sideways and hit the wall. When he reached forward to hit her a second time, she threw her hands out to fend him off.

He froze, his mouth dropped open, and he let out a faint whimper of surprise. The handle of the dagger, wrapped in her apron, was still in Donella's hand. And the other end was now buried in her father's gut.

Donella let out a choked cry and yanked the dagger out. Blood clung to the blade, soaked the ripped fabric of her apron, and oozed over her fingers. Her father dropped her purse to clutch at the wound, and Donella caught it as it fell.

He growled her name and reached one bloody hand toward her, and in a panic, she swung the heavy purse. It struck his temple, and he dropped to the ground.

He didn't get up.

Donella tore off the remnants of her shredded skirts and fled out of the kitchens and across the dining room. She fumbled to get the door unlatched, tumbled out onto the street, and stumbled over Dyson Doon, who had gone no more than two steps out the door before falling into a drunken stupor. He grunted, but the ale in his stomach acted like an elixir to keep him asleep.

The night seemed darker than normal. Thick clouds blocked the stars, as if to conceal Donella's foul act of murder from prying eyes. In contrast, the glow from the fishwife's hut seemed especially warm and bright. Donella hammered on the door and thrust it open without waiting for an invitation to enter.

She closed the door behind her and leaned against it, sobbing, her vision blurred.

"He didn't come, did he?" the fishwife asked, her voice more crisp and focused than Donella had ever heard it.

She wiped at her eyes and blinked to clear them, though the tears flowing down her hot cheeks didn't cease.

The fishwife sat at the small dining table. Her back—normally as bent as a fishing pole—was now rod straight. Her hair seemed thicker, her wrinkles shallower, and her gaze sharper.

"No, he didn't," Donella said with a ragged breath. "How did you know?"

"Because I know men. You don't get to be my age without seeing the worst of what they can do."

Donella crossed to stand by the fire pit, shivering in her drawers and blouse, her precious purse and bloody dagger clasped to her chest. "What about the other things you said? Will they come true, too?"

"If you wish it."

"If I wish it?" Donella gasped. "I have murdered my father! I cannot stay here. I would much rather be a manor liege than a peasant on the streets."

"It will not come easy," the fishwife said. She rose from her chair with ease and strode to stand beside Donella at the fire. She leaned over the bubbling cauldron, and served the tea with hands that did not shake. "I warned you there would be a price."

Donella swapped her bundle to one hand to take the offered mug. Warmth bled into her fingers, the intoxicating aroma calmed her panicked heart, and the earthy flavor dried the last of her tears.

"If you want this future," the fishwife said, as they sat down at the table. "You will have to go out and claim it. It will not come to you."

"I have money," Donella said, massaging the purse in her hand.

"And you will need every coin."

"I have a dagger." She remembered the sickening sensation of pulling it from her father's gut. She'd got him with a lucky shot—an accidental shot—that he hadn't been expecting. She couldn't count on that sort of luck if she met other men who wanted to steal from her. "I wish I knew how to use it."

A sly smile spread across the fishwife's lips. "Do you understand what you're asking? There is no point attaining skill with a blade if you're too timid to use it."

Donella nodded. She sipped at her tea, and it steadied her nerves.

"In that case, I will grant your wish, but I require something in return."

The fishwife's hair now had as many black strands as gray, and there were only a few wrinkles left around her eyes. This transformation should have terrified Donella, but she felt calmer than she had in all her eighteen years.

"You're a witch," she said.

The fishwife shrugged. "Some call me that."

"You grant wishes and predict futures?"

"I can see a multitude of futures. Which one comes true depends on you."

Donella drained her mug and set it down. "What do I have to do?"

"It's a simple thing, really." The fishwife leaned across the table. "I want you to hunt down the Dead Prince of Caveline and bring me his heart."

Revulsion twisted Donella's stomach as she imagined robbing a grave to find some long-dead royal's desiccated heart.

"I've never even been to Caveline," Donella said. "I've never heard of the Dead Prince. I don't know where to start looking."

"Well I'm sure I don't know where to *start*," the fishwife said snippily, "but I suggest you stop in Bretland, because that's where you'll find him."

Donella couldn't fathom why a Cavelian prince would be buried in Bretland, but she stood up, ready to begin her hunt. The sight of the bloody bundle in her arms gave her pause. "I'm not exactly dressed for a journey to Bretland. And how am I to get there? I've never even left Leyton."

The fishwife rose to her feet. "Yes, you are quite a sight. Let's see what we can do about that."

The witch snapped her fingers, and light sparkled around Donella. Her tattered clothing peeled away, and a clean white blouse, burgundy vest, and matching leather trousers grew to replace them. Sturdy boots wrapped her feet. A sword belt settled on her hips with Rory's short dagger on one side and a longer blade on the other. The homemade purse slipped from her fingers, and a new leather purse hooked onto her belt, heavy with her coins. Finally, a warm cloak settled around her shoulders.

"Happy?" the fishwife asked.

Donella nodded as she regarded her new clothing. Every item fitted her perfectly, the workmanship was stunning, and it was the most beautiful outfit she'd ever worn.

"Now, about that wish ..."

Donella looked up. Cold determination gripped her. This was what she needed. No more dreaming of being rescued. No more mooning over a boy. It was time to take matters into her own hands. "I will bring you the heart of the Dead Prince."

The fishwife smiled in satisfaction. Her hair was completely black now and lusciously thick, and no wrinkles could be seen on her face. "As for how you will get to Bretland ... Tell me, child, have you ever ridden a dragon?"

CHAPTER TWO

ONCE UPON A TIME, there was a young man who dreamed of a grand legacy. Prince Huxford was the first cousin (once removed) of the Grand Princess of Bretland. He'd been gifted with a head for business, and had taken over the management of his parents' estate from the time he was old enough to realize that they were doing a poor job. He learned how to balance the books, memorized the duties of each of the household servants, and mastered the art of negotiating with the merchants who supplied the estate.

When he was eighteen summers old, he turned his hand to what he imagined would be his greatest business venture: acquiring a wife.

The lady Alyssia was the daughter of an earl and of marriageable age. Huxford's higher rank and growing fortune would keep her in a grander lifestyle than she was accustomed to. She was well-educated and charming and, from what he had heard, fond of children. There was no way to guarantee, of course, that they would be able to produce some heirs, but if not, Huxford was quite open to the idea of adoption. Deciding their partnership made excellent business sense, he set about courting her. He took her dancing and dining, bought her flowers and fripperies, and wrote her poetry and proposals. In short, he did all that should have been required of him, except for one thing.

Alyssia demurred every offer of marriage, saying she didn't feel ready to settle down. Huxford—though finding her reasoning somewhat inexplicable—assured her his offer would remain open until she felt herself ready. After all, what was a few more months when a solid partnership would last the rest of their lives?

So he was rather put out when she announced her engagement to his cousin, Oxden.

Huxford took a horse, rode directly to her house, and demanded answers. Alyssia wouldn't come to the door but passed on a message through the butler.

Oxden loves me.

"But I'm a prince," Huxford protested to the bland-faced butler, who was doing an excellent job of blocking the doorway. "Oxden's only a *count*."

"That matters not to her ladyship," the butler said.

Huxford's mouth dropped open. How could she choose *love* over everything he had to offer? It made not a whit of sense. Marriage was a business arrangement, nothing more. His parents had never done anything so silly as to fall in love, and they were still happily married after more than twenty years. What would happen when Oxden fell *out* of love with Alyssia? Or vice versa. Would they stay together, bitter and hateful? Or would they separate and lose all the gains they had made?

Huxford's parents' manor house was homely if not huge. The estate was fertile if not far-reaching. And the peasants were happy if not hardworking. Thanks to his careful management, his parents made enough income from the land that even after paying their taxes, their fortune was slowly growing.

But that was no longer enough for Huxford. He became determined to make more of himself so the next time he found a suitable bride, she would make the sensible decision.

It was time to put his gift to better use.

He pored over his parents' accounts and started to plan.

The estate's best feature was the river that ran along its northern edge and marked the border between Bretland and its neighbor, Caveline. The river came with fishing rights, which his family had never enforced. Huxford decided it was time to claim what was his.

The peasants complained, of course. They'd never had to pay a tithe on their catch. But as far as Huxford was concerned, they'd had a free ride for far too long to complain now.

He leveraged his fishing rights to buy up the neighboring estates, and won contracts to build bridges across the river where he was able to charge passage to any boats making their way from the coast into the depths of the Seven Realms.

He may not have known how to work a field or build a bridge, but he knew how to hire and manage people to do those jobs for him, and he did that very well. It took the better part of two decades, but eventually Huxford controlled the entire width of Bretland's northern border, about thirty miles. It still wasn't much compared to the other realms, which were all larger geographically, but it made him one of the richest and most powerful people in the principality. And it thrilled him to bump into the now Countess Alyssia at a ball and gloat about his success.

At least, he thought it thrilled him.

When the night ended and he returned to his manor house, the emptiness shocked him. His parents were long dead, he had no siblings, and he was close to none of his cousins, not even Prince Rickett, who was next in line to rule. He thought of Alyssia—still married to Oxden and with three almost grown children—and it saddened him to think he had no heirs of his own. If he died, no one would inherit his estate or benefit from his lifetime of hard work.

But he was not yet forty summers old. He still had plenty of time and plenty to offer. Who would be fool enough to turn down an offer of marriage from the richest man in the realm?

He'd not long made the decision to renew his search for a bride when he received an invitation to the wedding of a minor baron. It wasn't the type of event he would normally bother with, but there would be dozens of nobles in attendance, maybe a widow with a child he could adopt as his own, or a spinster regretting her solitary life.

He took a carriage and rented a two-story house in the nearest town. He dressed in his finery, tied back his long, black hair, and trimmed his beard. He arrived at the wedding with a great amount of pomp and ceremony, though the wedding itself was a rather muted affair. Both the bride and the groom had been married before and had an array of children.

Juliana was the daughter of the soon-to-be baroness, and of marriageable age. She had dark brown hair pulled into a loose bun behind her right ear; olive skin; and a ready smile on her lips. She played perfect host to the wedding guests, had no qualms about giving orders to the baron's sons when she needed assistance, and when Huxford orchestrated an encounter with her, he found she was well versed in current affairs.

Instead of raising the topic with Juliana directly and risking another rejection, he spoke to her parents to gauge her interest, and to his delight, the baroness accepted his proposal on her daughter's behalf almost before he'd finished speaking.

Huxford left the wedding to return to his rented town house a contented man. But as he lay in his luxuriously large bed that night, he realized how much work there was to do. He'd been living alone for so long that most of the rooms in his manor house had been mothballed. He retained only a minimal number of servants. And the grounds had been maintained but not enhanced for years.

Their engagement may not be a love match, but he wanted no reason for Juliana to be dissatisfied with her new lodgings.

He returned home the next morning, leaving a note for the baron and baroness that he would send for Juliana in six months' time. That would be long enough to get the house and grounds into a state worthy of her.

NEVER HAD A PROJECT seemed so worthwhile. He hired gardeners and groundskeepers, butlers and valets, cooks and scullery maids. They opened rooms long closed, dusted off the fine crockery, and filled his bride-to-be's private quarters with lavish furniture in the latest style.

But the grounds came to be his favorite work.

He divided them into small, walled gardens and planted each based on a different theme. Roses and wildflowers, herbs and medicinals, evergreens and topiaries. Everything he dreamed up, the gardeners brought to life. They imported plants from all over the Seven Realms, channeled water from the river to create a wetland for waterfowl, and sourced enough glass for an expansive greenhouse. And when he heard rumors of people calling his home "Huxford's Folly," he made sure to spread rumors of his own that anyone caught using that name would never work anywhere in the north of Bretland again.

Finally, when the six months had passed, Huxford sat in his study, nursing a rousing blend of morning tea as he drafted a letter to Juliana, inviting her and her family to join him at his estate. They would wed as soon as everything could be arranged.

A knock interrupted him and Frida entered. She was a prim woman in her fifties who filled the role of butler judiciously. "Forgive me, my lord, but there's a woman at the door."

"This early? What could she possibly want?"

"She says she's an old friend in need. Shall I send her away?"

Huxford sighed and set down his fine brush. The worst part of being a manor lord was when his vassals demanded his attention. And he was sure this must be a vassal, as he had no friends, old or new. "No. I'll see her in the drawing room. Bring some fresh tea."

As Frida slipped away to do his bidding, Huxford carefully folded his letter to Juliana and placed it in the top drawer of his desk to finish later.

He stood, fastened the top button of his shirt, straightened his vest, and headed to the drawing room where his visitor awaited him.

The woman was standing with her back to him, warming her hands by the hastily-lit fire. From a brief glance, Huxford could tell that she wasn't a peasant but a noble. She wore a coat and gown of dark green velvet that hugged her figure and brushed the ground. Her dark hair was clasped loosely at the nape of her neck by a single jewel-encrusted clip, and cascaded down her back in gentle waves. The scent of rosewater perfume hung in the air.

"Can I help you, madam?" he asked.

She straightened and turned slowly, as if facing him were an imposition, and the pale light on her face made her appear amused. When she spoke, her voice was rich and melodious. "Prince Huxford, so lovely to see you again."

"Again?" He took a step toward her, intrigued by her boldness despite himself. Surely, he would not have forgotten meeting someone so striking.

"Of course, you were but a babe then."

"If I were a babe," he said, "you couldn't have been any older. How come you remember and I do not?"

"I'm older than I look."

For a moment, she was ancient, her hair gray and thin, her face carved with wrinkles, her back bent. The vision passed so quickly that Huxford wanted to believe he'd imagined it.

"How's that tea coming?" she asked, though he couldn't remember mentioning it.

Frida chose that exact moment to arrive, bearing a tray. Huxford stood tensely as she served them and bustled out again.

"You're a witch," Huxford mumbled through dry lips.

The woman perched on the edge of a stiff-backed chair and sipped at her tea. "Some call me that. Others say enchantress. More still call me the fairy godmother." Her appearance flashed again. This time she was short and plump, with silver hair styled neatly and glittering wings protruding from her back. "That was how your parents knew me when I gave you that gift of yours. And hasn't it done you well?"

Huxford took an involuntary step back. Every babe of royal blood was gifted with a tiny bit of magic, and he had to admit his head for business had served him well over the years. "What can I do for you, madam?" he asked again.

"I have a favor to ask in return for my beneficence."

"I will not be threatened."

The enchantress's eyebrows rose. "Oh, I do not need to threaten. I always get what I want."

"And what would that be?" Huxford wasn't opposed to negotiating.

"I have a *friend*, a delightful young lady who has found herself in a rather unfortunate predicament. She is unloved, unwanted, and would make a much better choice than your Juliana, I think."

"Is she of noble blood?" Huxford asked, though she would have to be great indeed to be a better bride than Juliana.

"Far from it."

"Does she have a sensible head on her shoulders?"

"Absolutely not."

Huxford forgot who he was speaking to and let out an exasperated breath. "Does she at least have the necessary skills to run my estates?"

"I can't imagine so."

"Then why would I consider marrying her?"

"Marry her? No. You misunderstand. She's but a child. I want you to take her in and give her the loving home she's never had."

Huxford glanced around. Although he couldn't see much from this one room, he knew how grand his manor now was. What the witch was asking didn't make any sense. "I've done all this work preparing for Juliana. Why would I risk that arrangement to take in some waif?"

The enchantress rose from her chair, her eyes narrowing as she stalked toward him, examining him like he was an insect pinned to a board. "I don't often make mistakes, and less often do I admit them, but I think I went too far with you. That gift I gave you has sucked all the love from your heart."

As if in response to the witch's words, Huxford's heart seemed to contract. "I don't see how that's relevant. And I think it's time you left."

"This is what I get for trying to be nice." Her voice hardened as she stepped closer to him, and though he was overcome with the urge to flee, his feet seemed rooted to the floor. "I can't undo my mistake, but I may be able to teach you a lesson." She reached her finger out and tapped him on the nose.

The air around Huxford sparkled, and his skin began to tingle. The hair on his arms darkened. Violent cramps twisted his fingers into claws and bent his body double until he collapsed to his knees on the hard floor. Something pulled at his face, and though he shook his head, he couldn't shake off the feeling. The colors of the drawing room grew muted, while the scents and sounds sharpened.

He opened his mouth to demand answers, but only a low growl came out.

The witch reached down to cup his chin, and her rosewater scent almost smothered him. "You will stay in this form until you learn to love and to be loved." She smirked. "I do hope it doesn't take you too long, or you might remain this way forever."

He let out another low growl, exposing his teeth.

She smacked his nose. "None of that nonsense. I am not above having you neutered."

Huxford whimpered and shrank away.

"Good luck." She let out a taunting laugh before clapping her hands together and disappearing in an acrid plume of smoke.

Huxford stared at the empty spot where she'd stood before turning toward a full-length mirror on the opposite wall. He took one step forward then crashed chin-first to the floor. He pushed himself up, struggled to get his four limbs into position, and took one careful step after another, alternating left and right, front and back. By the time he'd made it across the room, he had fallen into something of a natural gait. He peered into the polished surface, and a wolf stared back at him.

Huxford tried to scream, but again he only howled. He pawed at the glass, as if somehow that would change what he saw. But the mirror wasn't showing him an illusion, he could see his paws for himself.

The witch had turned him into a wolf.

Or something resembling one.

His shoulders were unnaturally large, and his shirt was too tight around his throat. He clawed at it and tore at his vest with his teeth until he managed to free himself and discard the shredded fabric. He'd lost his trousers in his journey across the room, and his tail curled up behind him like a furry standard marking his position. His underbelly fur was light gray and his back fur darker and highlighted by black. The coloring on his face gave him a rather pleasing visage. All in all, he was a handsome example of a wolf, but he would much rather have been human.

The door opened, and Frida rushed in. "My lord, I heard—by the stars." She fled from the room again and yanked the door shut behind her. "My lord?" she called from the hallway, her voice rising in panic. "Are you in there?"

Huxford padded across to the door. After two attempts, he managed to push up onto his back legs and lean his front paws against the wall. He batted the handle, but without thumbs, he couldn't grasp it to pull the door open toward him. He had to wait until Frida returned, and when she did, she had two groundskeepers with her, bearing garden tools.

"Out you go, you brute," the butler demanded, waving a silver tray in a threatening manner.

Huxford gaped. They were attempting to evict him from his own house. When he turned back into a human, there would be consequences.

One of the groundskeepers, a woman armed with a hoe, prodded his rump, and Huxford skittered to the left. The other groundskeeper, a man, blocked him with a rake.

"It's me, you fools!" Huxford attempted to cry. Nothing came out but a warbling wail.

"Ha!" Frida swung her tray side to side, taking up as much room as possible. "Go on! Out!"

Huxford had no choice. He never would have abided a wild animal in the house, and he doubted the servants would give up until he was gone.

Every door leading off the hallway was shut. He might have been able to jiggle the handles enough to push his way into the rooms, but not with the groundskeepers harrying him from behind. He bounded down the grand staircase and was confronted by servants clattering pots and pans and waving brooms to scare him off. Every crash and bang tortured his ears. Every sudden movement taxed his bleached vision. And the odor of a dozen unwashed servants tormented his sensitive nose. In the end, it was a relief to flee out the open front doors, which were quickly shut behind him.

But once he was outside, he had no idea what to do with himself. So he turned back to face the house, dropped his rear end to the ground, and waited for someone to make the connection between their manor liege disappearing and a strange wolf appearing in very same room.

The doors stayed shut for a very long time. Wolves in these parts were not known for being particularly aggressive. They mostly avoided people and kept to the woods. But to have one appear in the house had shaken the servants, even the generally unflappable butler and the stoic groundskeepers, and the fact he hadn't fled further than the front courtyard had probably made them worry he might be rabid. None of them had reason to suspect he was their lord transformed. In fact, from his absence they would draw only one conclusion: the wolf had killed him. He hoped the lack of remains would dissuade them from this assumption, but when the doors finally opened, the servants streamed out holding their makeshift weapons and flaming torches.

They chased him, hollering and wielding their tools, and Huxford retreated to the gardens surrounding the manor house and then into the woods beyond.

Over the next week, they began to abandon his employ. It wasn't so obvious at first, when the servants who went to their own homes in the nearby village of Riverlea at the end of the day simply did not return the following morning. It was more obvious when the live-in servants packed their meager belongings and left. It was startlingly obvious when Frida locked the doors for the final time, paused to drop her trousers and present her naked buttocks to the empty house, and left the manor for good. Huxford, who was watching from his hiding spot in the gardens, was appalled by the show of disrespect. He'd always found Frida to be an excellent employee, but apparently the feeling hadn't been returned.

After Frida left, Huxford tried the doors, but all they were firmly locked, and his paws were incapable of opening them.

Surely someone would come to investigate his supposed death. One of his cousins, probably. Maybe even the Grand Princess herself. Until they did, he had to keep himself alive. From his first shaky steps, he learned to run and jump and dodge. He had no choice but to hone his hunting skills if he wanted to eat. Hares and water dragons and dark blue swamp hens became his breakfast, lunch, and dinner. His enhanced hearing and sense of smell aided him enormously. His eyesight was sharp though the palate was muted, his night vision had vastly improved, and he soon forgot how vivid colors had once been.

He took to roaming further and further in his quest for food and shelter. He owned such vast tracts of land, knew so many people, that he believed he would eventually meet someone who would see through his appearance and recognize him for the man he truly was.

But people saw only a wolf.

Those he encountered on the road gave him a wide berth. In the villages, they took shelter.

A week became two then three then four. And still no one came, no one recognized him. And then one morning he woke up a man again. A naked man, shivering in the nest he had made for himself as a wolf the night before. He crowed with pleasure. Somehow, in the previous month, he must have completed the task the enchantress had set him.

After all, what did a witch know about love?

He missed his fur coat immensely, and he was grateful to find a cloak draped over a fence. He told himself it wasn't stealing. Since he owned this land, he would count it as part of the tithe.

The hard-packed road was agony on his bare feet, he had no money to buy food, and he'd lost the ability to hunt down his next meal. Relief washed over him when the familiar silhouette of his manor house came into view.

The servants hadn't returned, and the house was still locked up tight. With a twinge of regret, he broke a window to let himself in. He made his way through the silent house to his bed chamber and retrieved a fresh set of clothing from his wardrobe.

The day did not pass easily. There was no food in the house, only dry stores of ingredients. If Huxford had known how to cook, he might have been able to make them into something. As he did not, he settled for picking fruit from the trees in the orchard, which had grown wild in the groundskeepers' absence. He struggled through the laborious process of fetching wood and water so he could brew some tea, but had trouble lighting the fire and left the tea far too long.

A man such as he was not meant to live without servants.

At least the wood and water served another purpose: he was able to take a long, luxurious soak in the bathtub while he stewed on his situation.

You will stay in this form until you learn to love and to be loved.

Clearly it had been an idle threat. The witch had set about punishing him for some supposed indiscretion, made him suffer for a month, but now it was over.

He had no way of finding her to exact revenge, and considering how easily she'd transformed him, he had no desire to confront her.

Instead, he decided he would take the day to rest and again grow comfortable in his human form. Then he would set about finding his servants and convince them to return to his employ and set the house to rights.

But when the sun set that evening, as he was wandering through the house lighting candles and oil lamps, a strange tingle ran over his skin.

"No!" he cried, quickly snuffing out the candlelighter as the hair on his arms thickened. There was no pain this time, as if his body knew the form it needed to take and did so gladly. By the time the last glimpse of the sun had disappeared, he was a wolf once again.

He hadn't broken the curse at all.

HE SPENT THE NEXT month skulking around his home. No servants returned to chase him away, no poachers came to threaten him, no visitors arrived to investigate his disappearance.

When he next awoke as a man, he was more resigned than relieved. Unlike the first time, he didn't assume it would last.

You will stay in this form until you learn to love and be loved.

But how could he make someone fall in love with him when he spent only one day each month as a man? And how long would it take, considering he'd lived almost forty years without managing the task?

Clearly, it was a punishment, not a problem he was meant to solve.

As for why the witch had decided to punish him, well, she must've had some vendetta against him, because refusing to take in a young woman he'd never even met wasn't such a crime.

He wasn't a terrible person. He wasn't even the worst manor liege.

The gift of being business minded had served him well. His position and title may have given him a head start, but he'd earned every single coin of his fortune, every acre of his land. Sure, he may have done it on the backs of his vassals, by acquiring land and applying taxes, but that's why they were there. If the peasants didn't like it, it was on them to work hard, save their coins, and buy themselves a better life. It wasn't his job to help *them*.

And he certainly owed nothing to the witch's young friend.

As the afternoon wore on and his time as a human drew to a close, he considered writing a letter to the Grand Princess. She'd surely been alerted to his disappearance by now, and he was curious as to why no one had been sent to look for him. But even if he wrote a letter, he had no servants to deliver it, and he didn't want to leave it lying around as he would have no control over who found it. Asking his cousin (once removed) for assistance was one thing, having a rival lord discover his predicament was something else entirely.

No, it would be better to wait a month and present himself to her in person, though he was loath to reveal his misfortune lest his lands be confiscated. What good were land and vassals to a wolf? And what good was he without them?

ANOTHER MONTH LATER, HE made the journey to the city of Southport, which sat on the southern coast of Bretland overlooking the thrashing green ocean beyond the end of the continent. It was about as far away from his home near the northern border as one could get without leaving Bretland.

A great limestone palace stood on a hill in the center of the city. Huxford strode over the main bridge that crossed the surrounding moat, passed under the massive gateway in the outer wall, and followed the path that zigged and zagged up the hill, never once glancing up at the towering walls on either side, until he eventually presented himself at the inner gate of the palace.

One guard stood on each side of the gate, swords at their hips, pikes in their hands. Neither moved to open the gates and give him passage.

At any other time, their failure to recognize him would have landed them on latrine duty for a week. But although he'd cleaned himself up as well as he could and was wearing a set of his best clothes that had mostly survived the long journey unscathed, he knew his slightly disheveled appearance meant they wouldn't have looked at him too closely.

"No lollygaggers here," the guard on the left said.

Huxford drew himself up tall. "Prince Huxford to see the Grand Princess."

"Prince who?" she asked, sending a bored glance to her partner. "When was the last time you saw a prince turn up here on foot?"

This was a fair point. Normally he would have arrived on horseback or in a carriage, and surrounded by attendants.

"Got three this morning," the other guard replied with a snigger. "And we sent them on their way, too."

Huxford swallowed down his anger. "Tell the Grand Princess that Prince Huxford is here. I am her cousin. She will grant me an audience."

The woman let her gaze drift over him lazily. "Listen, *mate*," she said. "If you're going to pretend to be a prince, at least use the name of one who actually exists."

"But—"

The woman lowered her pike to point at his chest. "Move along, before we get annoyed and put you up in the cells for the night."

Huxford eased back, away from the point of her pike and her pointed threat. He couldn't spend a night locked up, because he had no idea how they would react when he turned into a wolf. If they didn't recognize his face or his name, what hope did he have they would see through his other guise?

He turned away, shame burning through him as the guard called, "And don't let us see you around here again."

As the sun started to sink below the horizon that evening, Huxford slipped out of his clothes, placed them carefully back into his satchel, and prepared himself for his transformation and the long trek home.

THREE MORE MONTHS PASSED before Huxford realized his human days coincided with the new moon's journey across the sky, hand in hand with the sun.

When the moon was at its fullest, he felt his wolfiest, as if his memories of his prior life were nothing more than dreams. On those days, he relished his solitary existence and avoided any humans he saw. On the days either side of his transformation, the solitude was a set of chains around his heart, dragging him close to the villages and the peasants who either threatened him with garden tools or slammed their doors against him.

He'd never suffered from loneliness before, and he didn't enjoy it now.

When he was human, he retreated to his manor house, comforted by its familiarity despite its saddened state. With no servants to light fires in the hearths, sweep dirt from the floors, or maintain the grounds, the estate quickly took on a unloved, run-down air.

He would head into the village of Riverlea for supplies, hoping someone—anyone—would recognize him, but no one did. Not even when he orchestrated a casual encounter with Frida, his one time butler. She looked at him blankly, traded pleasantries, and went about her day. He decided against confessing his story to her and asking for help, torn as he was between extricating himself from his predicament and risking something worse.

More time passed, and still no one came to investigate his disappearance. They didn't come to confiscate his lands, either. But as he watched his handsome home fall into disrepair, he wondered about the witch's warning. If he took too long, he would stay this way forever. And then what would happen to all he'd built?

But he could see no solution.

With his house falling into disrepair and his vassals no longer paying their tithes, he had nothing with which to attract a wife.

As the months turned into years, he roamed further afield. On his human days, he became adept at stealing clothes in the morning and returning them each evening. Though it aggrieved him, he learned how to perform menial tasks in exchange for a hot meal. No one ever recognized the grubby man with bedraggled hair as their missing lord. And for all the gossip he heard, no one wondered what had become of him. No one seemed to remember him at all.

The peasants, in general, were kinder than he expected. He always offered them something of value: a pile of firewood chopped in exchange for a meal, a garden of beans picked for a tub of warm water and a bar of soap, a hole in a roof repaired to have a wound on his hand tended. They didn't have to gift him a seat by their fire while he ate, a private room in which to wash, or a kit to trim his ragged nails, but they did. And he couldn't fathom why.

Despite the years he had spent accumulating land, he hadn't wasted much thought on the peasants he'd acquired with it, and now that he'd begun spending time with them, he rather wished he had.

After three years of repeated kindnesses, he'd almost forgotten how cruel people could be.

It was the middle of winter, and he'd spent his day as a human away from home, helping to harvest and pickle cabbage in the village that had grown on the Brettish side of one of his bridges. He waited for his transformation in the wood at the edge of the village, then made a nest for himself and curled into a ball, his tail covering his nose, to pass the long, cold hours.

Something woke him in the deepest part of the night. There was no moon, but the starlight filtered through the trees, and he surveyed the gray surroundings. Nothing seemed out of the ordinary.

He lifted his nose to sniff the air and was rewarded with the scents of owls and voles, mosses and ferns, decaying leaves and blooming night flowers.

The snap of a twig caused his ears to flick backward. Whatever had made the sound was downwind. He'd never met anything he feared in the woods, but that didn't mean he was eager to meet his first.

He rose to all fours and padded away. A crunch of dead leaves followed him. Then a whispered command. He broke into a run, dodging between the trees and flying over the uneven ground. Noise burst to life behind him, becoming a regular cadence. Grunts of exertion were interspersed with sharp words.

Someone was chasing him.

A brutal cry of "Ha!" came from his left, and he darted right.

An echoing cry of "Yo, yo, yo," came from his right, and he darted left.

The trees and scrub thickened, and there was only one clear path through. He dropped his pace and pricked his ears, wondering if he could hunker down and hide until they passed. But the yells and thunder of tools—weapons?—being banged against each other drove him on.

He ducked under a fallen tree and ran right into a snare. It snapped tight around his neck and yanked him to a halt. He lay panting from the shock before twisting to his feet and attacking the rope with his sharp teeth.

His pursuers crashed through the scrub, encircling him, bringing the stench of unnatural things: iron weapons, treated oilskins, and healthy doses of fear. Huxford dropped his head low, peeled back his lips to expose his teeth, and began to growl.

Their oilskins were large and bulky, their heads were covered by woolen hats, and their boots were sturdy, but as far as he could tell, there were two women and one man.

One of the women approached him warily. Keeping her gaze on him, she gestured to the other woman. "Rebekah, the net."

Rebekah crept forward, her arms loaded with a heavy bundle. Huxford backed away, to the limit of the rope, the edge of the scrub surrounding him. She threw the bundle with a practiced flick of her wrists, and it unfurled as it spun through the air, opening into a heavy rope net weighted with stones woven into the edges. Huxford flinched away but could do nothing to avoid the net descending upon him.

He shook himself in an attempt to throw it off, but it was even heavier than he'd expected. He tore at the cords with his teeth, but they'd been reinforced with thin threads of metal. The scent burned his nostrils, as if the net had been soaked in a herbal brew, most likely wolfsbane.

They moved in quickly after that, and no amount of growling and gnashing of his teeth dissuaded them. The man took hold of the rope, releasing the end from where it had been tied to a tree. Rebekah hauled on the net to pull the weighted opening closed around his feet. And the other woman used a long wooden pole to push him over. Then it was a fairly simple matter of binding him to the pole so they could hoist him onto their shoulders. He took a little pleasure from the fact that they grunted and groaned under his weight.

They bore him through the woods to the road, where a wagon waited. A cover concealed four crates, two of which were already occupied by other wolves.

With more grunts of effort, they lowered him into an empty crate. It was too small for his massive bulk, and Huxford lay awkwardly, his head jammed against one end, his paws in the air.

"Careful, Ardley," the first woman warned. "He's a big one."

The man—Ardley—nodded as he reached into the crate. He bound Huxford's legs before looping the snare rope around his muzzle. Huxford snapped at the man's fingers, but his quick reflexes saved him from injury and he drew the rope tight, clamping Huxford's jaws shut. Then Ardley hauled the net free and slammed the lid shut.

"Come on," the woman said. "We have time for one more."

"Yes, Ma," the other two chorused.

It was a couple of hours before the trappers returned with another wolf. Huxford peered between the wooden slats of his crate and watched as she went easily into the box beside him. Fear made her passive, and the bittersweet scent of it triggered a protective urge in

Huxford. But he was in no position to free himself, let alone any of the others. Ardley adjusted the cover so the crates were hidden, then the wagon rolled into motion. Huxford could see nothing, but he felt the change as they crossed the bridge, heard the rattle of the wheels on the stones, and smelled the fresh water flowing beneath them.

They had crossed into Caveline.

The darkness around them had started to lighten by the time the wagon came to a stop, and the watery light of dawn greeted him when the cover was finally drawn back. Judging by the buildings he could see, they had stopped in a town.

The older woman was standing in front of him, and he got his first good look at her. She had removed her hat, revealing thick, curly hair, dark skin, and a grim mouth. The man beside her was older and pale and stank of body odor.

"Wolves?" he sneered. "I don't want no wolves."

The words were Cavelian, a language Huxford hadn't heard spoken since he'd been cursed.

The woman stepped forward and thumped her fist on the top of Huxford's crate. He let out an involuntary growl through his bound muzzle. "This one's vicious. Put up a real fight."

"He's probably rabid."

"There's no sign of that. He's just a fighter."

The man stepped forward for a closer look. "He's a big one. But will he fight when it matters?"

"He tried to take off Ardley's fingers."

"How much do you want for him?"

They haggled over the price then Ardley and his mother heaved the crate off the back of the wagon and carried Huxford down an alleyway to a squat building. It stank inside of blood, excrement, and fear. A pit was set in the middle, fenced by a solid, chest-high wall. Mongrel dogs filled a row of cages built along one wall. Their fur was matted, their hides scarred.

It was a dogfighting ring.

Huxford recoiled in horror as he was dumped unceremoniously into one of the cages. With a deft flick, Ardley released the rope binding him, and the door was slammed shut. Huxford leapt to his feet, though they were still numb from being bound, and let out a series of growls and barks.

"Well, he's got attitude," the dogfighter said, tossing the woman a heavy purse. "We'll see how long he lasts in the pit."

CHAPTER THREE

THE DRAGON WAS A beautiful creature. Her name was Tomarriss, and she was larger than any horse Donella had ever seen. Midnight blue scales covered her back and faded to silver on her stomach. Massive wings lay tucked against her sides, and a long tail flicked behind her.

"Hold on tight," the old fishwife warned her, "she has a tendency to roll."

Donella straddled the dragon's back and clung to the sinuous neck as the creature launched itself into the air. She pressed her face against the scales, which were more velvety than she'd expected, and tried to shelter from the bitter wind that even her fine new clothes couldn't keep at bay.

The Seven Realms stretched out beneath them, but in the dark, Donella couldn't see much apart from the occasional spot of firelight. There was no moon, but stars speckled the sky like grains of salt. They flew through the night and into the next day, and as the sun poked its nose over the horizon, Donella loosed her frozen fingers from around the dragon's neck, wiped her streaming eyes, and took in the view.

It was more beautiful than she could have imagined. Tall, snow-capped mountains sat to her right, next to a deep blue inland sea. Green hills rolled away to her left, all the way to the east coast. The dark mass of a forest covered the land to the south. Hard-packed dirt roads criss-crossed the countryside, the brown lines like faded scars, and they linked everything from small clusters of buildings that could barely be called villages, to huge sprawling towns.

Leyton had always been her whole world, and the rest of the Seven Realms had seemed too vast, too far away. But now, from up here, the island didn't seem that large at all.

They covered in a day what would have taken over two weeks on foot. When they landed on the outskirts of a bustling town, Donella stroked the dragon's neck in gratitude.

"Take care not to be spotted on your way home," she told the dragon.

Tomarriss replied by giving Donella a slobbering swipe across the face with her rough tongue, before launching herself back into the air. Her absence left an ache in Donella's chest. She was truly alone now. No one in Leyton may have cared for her in any way that really mattered, but as least she had known them and what to expect.

She discreetly moved a few coins from her hidden purse into the inside pocket of her cloak so she wouldn't need to expose the extent of her wealth, and headed into the town to find a meal and a place to chase the chill from her bones. The streets teemed with people, and Donella shied away from the press of bodies. Every inn and tavern she found was crowded, and though the warmth of each called to her, she couldn't face entering.

Instead, she found a vendor selling pies and tarts from a street stall. She braced herself as she approached. This would be the first real test of her Brettish. A chalkboard menu listed the available pies, but as Donella glanced down the list, she found she couldn't decipher any of the words. Either Rory hadn't taught her well, or they weren't written in Brettish.

The woman behind the stall called out to her, but though her tone was friendly, the words skimmed past Donella's ears, leaving no sense of meaning behind.

Panic flooded through her, and she backed away, glancing around as if she expected an attack.

Where had the dragon deposited her?

"Traveler, are you?" the woman asked, this time speaking the common language.

Donella exhaled in relief, grateful for everyone who'd passed through Leyton from the other realms and kept her fluent in the shared tongue. She took a step closer. "Yes. Where am I?"

"Three Mile Bush." The woman's answer didn't help.

"Is that in Bretland?"

"Caveline." She gestured with a wave of her hand. "Bretland's about two hours' walk that-a-way. Over the river."

Oh. Donella had expected the dragon to take her all the way, but having to walk for two hours wasn't so bad, if she could find the way.

"What can I get you?" the woman asked. "We've got beef pies: plain beef, peppered beef, beef and vegetable, beef and cheese, beef and mushroom—"

"That's a lot of beef," Donella murmured.

The woman grinned. "It's cheap."

Donella selected plain beef. She worried for a moment that the woman wouldn't accept her coins, but she barely even glanced at the engravings on them before handing over the pie. The food warmed Donella's stomach, if not her bones.

"Excuse me," she said shyly, "but what do you know of the Dead Prince?"

The woman's expression softened. "Oh, he was a handsome lad. Been dead some five years now. More's the pity."

The woman's use of the word "lad" tripped Donella. She didn't know if it was a term of endearment for a favored prince or because he was still a child when he died.

"What happened to him?"

The woman leaned on the counter top and propped her chin on her hand. "He was all of fifteen summers old when he went hunting with his cousin, the princess Abigail. Had a fatal encounter with a boar, so they say."

Donella let out a murmur of sympathy. "His poor parents."

"Well, that's the thing. His mother was long gone by then, and his father, the king, died the self-same day, before anyone even knew about the prince."

"That's terrible." Donella wasn't exactly thrilled about the idea of robbing a grave to steal the heart of a long-dead child, but since she had no choice, she asked, "Where is the prince buried?"

"That's the other thing," the woman said, clearly enjoying passing gossip on to someone who was completely ignorant. "From what they say, he's got a nice spot in the royal cemetery, but it's empty. They never found his body."

Donella couldn't hold in her dismay. How was she meant to retrieve his heart when no one had retrieved his body?

After serving another customer, the woman leaned forward to catch Donella's attention. "I don't want to overstep, but I know travelers are often in need of coin, and you could get a pretty price for that hair."

"My hair?" Donella's hand drifted to her curls.

"It's too red, of course, but mix it in with some brown and you'd get a fair approximation."

Donella blinked. "Approximation of what?"

"The queen." When Donella showed no sign of comprehension, the woman gave a faint laugh and continued. "Esmeralda the First had red hair, so they say, and nobles still like to color their hair like hers. Wigs for those who can afford them, dyes for those who can't."

Donella had hated her hair as a child. Not so much the color but the way the curls tangled and frizzed. She'd never cut it short, though, as she had no choice but to do it herself in her gloomy room above the kitchens, and rather than risk an uneven mess, she'd stuck to merely trimming the ends.

The pie vendor took her hesitation for consideration, and said, "There's a barber two streets over who'll give you a fair price and leave you looking cute as a bunny."

Donella didn't currently need more coins, but she surely would in the future. And since she had a trim new outfit, it wouldn't hurt to have a trim new haircut to match. "Thank you."

The barber's shop was squeezed between two other buildings that looked equally grimy. Donella hesitated on the threshold, and again when she walked in and found the barber was a man. But the pie vendor had recommended him, so she stuck to her decision.

"I was told you would buy my hair."

The barber, a thin man with twitchy hands, regarded her with his brows knotted and mumbled something in an apologetic tone in what she assumed was Cavelian. She wished the pie vendor had warned her he didn't speak the common language.

She tried again, making a show of miming her actions. "You cut. Give me money."

He nodded his understanding along with another flurry of Cavelian before holding up a silver coin, flashing ten fingers, and pointing from him to her. "Yes?"

Ten silvers was a fortune for something that would grow back soon enough. "Yes."

She sat in a chair as the barber snipped her hair away and laid the strands on a small table beside him. There was no changing her mind now. As the pie vendor had promised, he did a good job. The remaining short strands curled around her face and accentuated her features. But she didn't look cute. She looked fierce.

When he had finished, the barber turned to inspect her hair. He hemmed and hawed as he rubbed a strand between his fingers, pulled it until it snapped, and scrutinized the ends. Then he fished some coins from his purse and handed them to Donella.

"Only five?" she gasped, holding up her fingers to show the numbers. "You said ten!"

He shrugged and gestured at the discarded pile of her hair, speaking rapidly in a conciliatory tone, as if he wasn't attempting to cheat her. Then he spoke the final blow. "Lice."

"I do not have lice!" Donella cried as she scratched at her scalp.

He showed her five fingers then shooed her, as if the decision was made and there was nothing he could do about it. The barber, though thin, towered over her, and Donella shrank back toward the door. As she moved to add the coins to her purse, her hand brushed the hilt of Rory's dagger, and she stopped.

Why was she running away from this man? He'd cheated her, treated her like she wouldn't fight for what was hers. Once, he would have been right, but now, as her fingers closed around the dagger, indignation made Donella set her shoulders and a red mist rolled across her vision, tainting everything around her.

"You said ten." Her voice didn't waver as she drew her weapon. The handle felt right in her hand, and she hoped the fishwife was true to her word. "I *get* ten."

"Whoa." The barber held up his hands defensively. "There's no need for that."

"So now you can speak the common language?"

Sweat beaded on the man's brow. "I don't want trouble. I can stretch to seven."

Donella raised her weapon, and the way the barber stumbled back gave her a boost of confidence. "I want fifteen."

"I suppose the ends aren't so bad," he stammered. "And maybe I was mistaken about the lice. Twelve?"

"Thirteen," she countered.

He dug out the extra coins, and she stashed them in the pocket of her cloak as she slid the dagger back into its sheath. He cursed her as she stalked out the door, and she turned back to glare at him. He quailed and lunged forward to lock the door behind her.

Donella stood on the street feeling equal parts amused and satisfied. If she'd known it felt this good to stand up to a bully, she would have done it years ago. And she hadn't even needed to use the dagger.

The peculiar red mist that clung to her vision hadn't faded, and she decided to return to the pie vendor to *thank* her for recommending the barber. But the high-pitched cry of an animal in pain stopped her before she'd taken two steps. People might be prone to abusing their power over others, but animals had never treated her cruelly, and she followed the sound down an alleyway between two buildings to an unassuming door.

Her heart pounded as she flung it open.

A tall, solid man blocked her way inside. His gaze tracked over her in a bored way, and he said, "Pay to play."

She had no idea what the game was, but if it involved hurting an animal, she certainly wanted to put a stop to it. She handed over one of her newly-acquired coins and squeezed past him.

Once inside, she pressed her hand to her nostrils to block the stench. The windows were boarded up, and the room was only dimly lit by lanterns hanging from the ceiling. A crowd of people were standing around a walled ring in the center of the room. She ignored them and discreetly made her way to where half a dozen mangy dogs were locked in a row of cages against the wall, lying in their own filth. The first dog was a small, solid beast with a square jaw and a missing ear. It backed away from her to huddle against the far wall.

A simple bolt would have been enough to keep the dog in, so the fact the door was padlocked must have been to stop someone from stealing—or rescuing—the animal. She checked the next cage, and the next. All the dogs were the same. Broken, beaten, bloodied. All were locked in.

Bile rose in her throat at their predicament, but she swallowed it down. There was no point wasting time feeling disgusted, not when she could do something about it.

In fact, she was rather looking forward to wreaking vengeance on their behalf.

Donella weaved her way through the crowd to stare into the ring, where two dogs circled each other in a pit dug into the ground. One was lean, its fur matted, its scars clearly marking it as a veteran of this cruel game. The other was larger and cleaner but bleeding from a series of bites and scratch marks. The smaller dog growled, its teeth exposed, and lunged for the larger dog's throat. The larger one skittered aside, suffering only another surface wound for his trouble, and didn't strike back.

Instead of fighting each other, they should have teamed up to attack the mob surrounding them, but the pit looked deep enough, and the wall surrounding it tall enough, to prevent the dogs from jumping out and doing exactly that.

"Not much of a fighter, is he?" a woman groused beside Donella in the common language.

"They told me he was fierce," a man replied. He was standing on the other side of the woman and leaning on the top of the pit wall, his hands dangling inside, as if taunting the animals to try to bite his fingers. "But if he doesn't show some mettle, at least his hide will earn back some of my money."

"Not if it's full of holes," Donella muttered.

The man sent her a sour look.

"Are these your dogs?" she asked.

"They're not for sale if that's what you're asking," he said, by way of confirmation. "But you're welcome to bet on the fights."

She held the dogfighter's gaze. "I'm not going to give you any of my money, but I *will* free these poor animals before I leave."

The woman standing between them gulped and slipped away, as if anticipating a fight.

The man rose to his full height and looked down on her. "And how do you intend to do that?"

Inside the pit, the larger dog still wasn't fighting back, but like the man, he too had puffed himself up and was dominating the smaller dog by sheer force of will. The smaller dog cowered then submitted, rolling over to expose his throat. The larger dog gave him a small nip then turned his back, the fight over, his dominance established.

"I'm going to ask you nicely to open their cages," Donella said, drawing both her daggers, "and when you don't, I'll carve you into a dozen pieces."

The man didn't quiver like the barber had. He didn't yield. He whistled sharply and two men—the one who'd been guarding the door and another just as large—swooped in. The rest of the crowd, as sensitive to a fight as the first woman, fled for the door.

Rather than wielding daggers themselves, one of the men was bearing a pair of hammers, and the other carried a heavy iron bar. Donella began a strategic retreat, attempting to keep the pit between herself and the men, giving herself room and time. She still wasn't exactly sure what skill with a dagger she'd magically acquired, but it didn't seem to extend to knowing the best tactics for a fight, let alone taking on two large men at once. But it looked like that was what she'd have to do, since they were circling the pit in opposite directions.

Before her hand was forced, the large dog sprinted across the pit and launched himself at the wall. Despite clearly being built to keep the dogs in, the pit couldn't contain one so large. The dog landed on the top of the wall and fired himself at the man with the hammers. Up close, the dog was even larger than he'd appeared, and he knocked his target to the ground easily. The man threw his arm up to defend himself, and the dog clamped his teeth around the limb. The man let out a howl of pain and rage and swung his other hammer, but the dog dodged easily and doubled back to tear a long gouge in that arm, too. The man cradled his arms to his chest, whimpering, his weapons abandoned, as the dog turned to growl at the dogfighter.

The man with the iron bar ran back around the pit, clearly seeing the dog as a bigger threat than Donella. She couldn't let the poor animal be hurt any more than he already was, but she'd never intercept the man in time.

With her heart racing, she threw her small dagger.

It sailed through the air and thudded into the man's shoulder blade with a wet *thwack* that sent a shiver down Donella's spine. Pressing her advantage, she ran after him, yanked the blade out as he reached back in an attempt to dislodge it, and made two quick strokes before darting away.

His one arm hung useless as he attempted to chase her, but she'd cut through his belt, and his trousers dropped. He tripped, fell to all fours, and dropped the iron bar, which skittered toward her. She kicked it away and stepped up beside the dog.

His fur was still puffed up, and his lips pulled back to reveal his sharp teeth.

Maybe she should have been scared of such a vicious beast, but his focus wasn't on her. It was locked on the dogfighter.

"Give me the key to the cages," she told the man.

The dog growled as if to reinforce her request.

The dogfighter had backed up so far he'd hit the wall. His gaze flicked from one hired hand to the other, both were lying injured on the floor, then he gave Donella a filthy look as he handed over the key. She ran to the cages, and her fingers shook as she fumbled the key into one padlock after another. But she wasn't scared, she was exhilarated, and as she released each dog, her chest swelled with satisfaction. She found a small gate in the pit wall through which to free the small dog still trapped inside, then yanked open the outside door so all the animals could flee.

They wouldn't be forced to fight ever again.

She returned to stand beside the large dog, who seemed to have no intention of leaving. He was still growling and showing his teeth to the dogfighter.

"We're going now," Donella said, "but you might want to think about a new career."

"You'd better not show your face in these parts again," he spat back.

"Why?" she asked, her confidence bordering on cockiness. "We defeated you easily enough."

The man lunged forward and loosed his belt from around his waist in one smooth movement. Only when he flicked it out did Donella realize it wasn't a belt but some sort of short whip. He walloped the dog's shoulder, sending the animal staggering sideways, before whipping it in Donella's direction, forcing her backward. She parried with her blades, the defensive moves coming without thought, but the dogfighter's reach was longer and she had no idea how to find an opening. Instead, she kept moving backward, drawing him forward, and positioning him unawares between her and the dog.

The dog regained his feet, launched himself at the dogfighter, and buried his teeth in the man's rear end. The dogfighter let out a scream before twisting around to lash repeatedly at the animal. Donella slashed his arm to make him drop the whip, and the dog tore out a chunk of his flesh.

Now that all three men were moaning on the floor, Donella ran for the door. She burst out into the fresh air, leaving the gloom of the dogfighting pit behind her. Back at the roadside, Donella paused. The red mist faded from her vision, along with her confidence and her desire to find the pie vendor. As much as she was certain the woman had known the barber would attempt to cheat her, all she wanted now was to get out of Caveline and into Bretland. The problem was, she wasn't sure which way to go.

The dog padded to a stop beside her, panting, his shoulder level with her hip.

There were dogs in her village—wild ones who roamed the streets and begged for scraps, and beloved pets who helped to pass the long dark nights and solitary early mornings of a fisher's life. Donella had never had much to do with any of them, but she couldn't remember ever seeing one so large. He licked at the blood that coated the fur around his mouth, and his lips curled in distaste, if a dog could express distaste. He didn't look threatening any longer—not to her, at least—but she *had* just watched him take down two men and didn't want to risk becoming another victim.

Yet, he could say the same about her.

He glanced up at her, and Donella was struck by the intelligence in his eyes. The arc of his eyebrows—sweeps of gray lighter than most of the fur on his face—seemed to suggest he was asking her a question.

As ridiculous as it was to speak to an animal who couldn't understand her, she said, "We made a pretty good team." Then she swallowed and offered him her hand, as she was fairly certain that was what one did with dogs. He dutifully sniffed her palm and licked her fingers.

"If you don't bite me," she murmured. "I won't stab you."

He nodded his head in a way that made it look like he was agreeing.

She tentatively stroked between his ears, and he pressed into her hand. "I don't suppose you know the way to Bretland?"

She didn't expect him to answer, but he let out a small yip and headed confidently down the street. When he paused and glanced back at her, she decided to follow.

It took two hours, with the dog leading the way, to reach a river spanned by a wide, stone bridge. Donella hoped it was the one the pie vendor had mentioned, because that meant the other side was Bretland. But she would have expected a border to have guards. Or someone charging a toll. This had neither.

On the far side, the road forked, and the dog headed left, but Donella paused. The right fork led to a small village, and she needed to be sure she was in the right place rather than aimlessly trusting a dog.

"Hey," she called, and the dog paused and looked back at her. She patted her thigh to beckon him. "Let's go this way."

The dog let out an unhappy whine and shifted on the spot.

"Come on," she said, keeping her tone light and encouraging. "It's just a village, no one's going to hurt you."

The dog hung his head, and after a moment, Donella realized he wasn't coming with her.

She supposed she couldn't blame him. After being trapped by the dogfighter, she shouldn't be surprised if he wanted to avoid human contact. She was lucky he'd let her tag along.

"Goodbye, then," she said, her words coming from a hollow place inside her chest. "And thank you."

She followed the road between the modest houses until she found a woman standing in her front yard, beating a carpet that hung on a wooden frame.

"Excuse me, madam," Donella said, finally trying out her Brettish, "but what village is this?"

The woman paused her beating to give Donella a wary look. "You're in Highbridge."

"In Bretland?"

The woman's expression softened as she laughed good-naturedly. "Yes, girl. Came over the bridge, did you?"

Donella nodded. "Do you, by any chance, know anything about the Dead Prince of Caveline?"

The woman spat to the side, as if clearing a bad taste from her mouth. "We don't care much for Cavelian royals around here."

Donella thanked the woman but silently cursed herself. She may be in Bretland, but she had no idea where to start looking for the Dead Prince. And worse, she didn't know who to trust with her quest. The pie vendor had steered her wrong, the barber had tried to cheat her, the dogfighter had been cruel, and it seemed like no one in Bretland would be of any help.

She suddenly regretted parting ways with the dog, since he, at least, seemed to have a destination in mind. There was nothing for it but to keep moving, and inquire at each village she came to, until someone could answer her query.

She followed the road back out of the village, and when she reached the crossroads, the dog was sitting in the middle of the road. He rose to his feet as she approached, and his tail began to wag.

She stroked his neck on instinct, burying her fingers in his thick fur, and felt him trembling. "I'm happy to see you too, boy," she said, continuing to speak Brettish, since she supposed neither language mattered to him. "If we're to be traveling companions, I can't keep calling you 'dog' or 'boy.' Would you like a proper name?"

The dog's brows twitched before he gave a sharp nod.

A shiver ran over her, and she withdrew her hand. That was the second time he'd seemed to comprehend her words, and twice was too many to dismiss. "Can you understand me?"

He glanced away before working his jaws and swiping his long tongue over his muzzle, which was now thankfully clean of blood. Finally he looked back and gave her another, definitive nod.

"Oh ..." She swallowed, unsure what to do with that information. She supposed he was no different to the dragon who'd also displayed a strange intelligence but couldn't speak to explain it. "I'd better pick a good name, then."

She tried to recall the names the people of her village had given their pets. Most of them were fishing related and didn't fit. Chum. Jig. Leader.

"Buddy?" she offered. "Cooper? Tucker?"

The dog gave her a flat look.

"No?" She pushed to her feet and set her hands on her hips. "Well, stick with me long enough and I'll find one. That's a given."

The dog flopped onto his rump and made a curious "Hrm-mm?" noise in the back of his throat.

"That's a given," she repeated. "Given? Is that your name?"

He huffed out a breath and pawed at his nose, as if frustrated. She was fairly sure dogs weren't meant to express frustration.

"It's *not* your name, but you like it well enough?"

He nodded.

"Given it is," she said, "and you can call me—"

What should he call her? With her new outfit, her new haircut, and her new attitude, she didn't feel much like poor little Donella anymore. And she certainly didn't need to be reminded of her father every time she heard her name—a man who'd never loved her and didn't want to claim her, and a name that had been chosen by a woman she'd never met, a woman who'd loved the sea more than her baby.

"Ella," she decided.

Given lifted his paw and Ella let out a delighted laugh as she shook it.

"Now, lead the way, Given."

The road hugged the river's edge, and there was nothing much to see apart from the slow-moving water and grassy fields dotted with skeletal bushes. The air was crisper than Ella was used to at home, making her glad of her cloak, and it was missing its usual salty tang. The people they passed on the road seem cordial enough—or, at least not openly hostile—though they tended to cast wary looks at Given. The dog, in turn, clung to Ella's side until they'd passed.

As the day wore on, it became clear that Given had no intention of stopping until they reached their destination, but Ella's stomach began to grumble, and when they came to an inn at a crossroads, she suggested they take a brief respite. Given shook his head.

"I know you want to avoid people, and I suppose they don't allow dogs anyway," she murmured. "But I need to eat."

They stood facing each other, at another stalemate, with Given unable to argue his perspective. Eventually, he pawed at the ground.

"You'll wait for me here?" Ella guessed.

Given nodded and loped off into the field beside the road, maybe to hunt rabbits or find a comfortable place to hunker down. Ella watched him go with the same hollow feeling in her chest. She had no guarantee he would meet her as he'd promised, but she sincerely hoped he would.

Lunch in her village often consisted of smoked fish soup or crab cakes or clams-and-eggs in the shell. The menu in this inn had ingredients she mostly recognized, but in combinations she'd never tried.

She asked the girl behind the counter for a recommendation, and in a bored voice she suggested the spiced noodles with vegetables.

As Ella sat at a table, twisting the noodles onto her fork and trying to shovel them into her mouth without splattering the spicy sauce on her vest, her mind drifted to the number of times she'd sat at a table with Rory, sharing a meal or an ale while he taught her Brettish. He'd never given her any lessons in the type of food they ate. He probably thought there was no point, as she would never leave North Lynnborough to taste any for herself. Well, she'd shown him. Or, she would show him, if she ever saw him again.

Not that she wanted to.

No, maybe the most important lesson he'd taught her was to ignore her foolish heart.

All the years she'd spent mooning over him were a blight on her memory. He'd clearly never felt the same, no matter how much she'd wished it.

Girls like her didn't get a happy ending like the queen in his book.

She'd have to be content with the one the fishwife had promised her.

A crash sounded across the dining room as the serving girl dropped a heavy tray of glasses. A man appeared from a back room—probably the innkeeper, maybe her father—and yelled obscenities at her. She babbled apologies as she dropped to her knees to clean up the mess, but that didn't stop the man from grabbing her arm in his meaty fist and backhanding her across the face. The girl burst into sobs as anger stirred in Ella's stomach.

How many times had she been that girl?

How many times had she wanted someone to step in and save her?

How many times had Rory sat there and ignored her predicament?

The red mist rolled across her vision, and her anger condensed into something dangerous. *She* would not ignore this girl's predicament. She would right this wrong, and she would have fun doing it.

She drew the short dagger from her belt and, trusting it would fly true, fired it in the innkeeper's direction. It flew through the air, flicked past his nose, and thudded into the wall behind him. His head snapped around to stare at her. Ella pushed up from her chair, drew her other dagger, and idly cleaned her nails with the tip.

"If you like bullying young girls," she said, "why don't you try me on for size?"

"This is nothing to do with you," the innkeeper snarled. "Move along."

Ella stroked her chin, as if considering it. "No, I don't think I will." Her gaze shifted to the girl. "Unless *you* want me to?"

The girl gave her a terrified look and a tight shake of her head.

The anticipation of giving this bully his just deserts filled the hollow inside Ella's chest until it overflowed. "The last man I met who treated a girl like that earned a dagger in the gut for his trouble." She let her gaze drift over him. "Do you have somewhere you'd like me to aim?"

The innkeeper finally released the girl—who winced and rubbed her arm where thick red bruises already marked her skin—and turned to face Ella. "Leave, now, before I teach you a lesson the last man didn't."

A wicked smile pulled at Ella's lips. "I do love to learn."

The innkeeper grabbed a weapon from under the bar—a short wooden club with nails protruding from one end. Ella let him come to her in the middle of the dining room where the tables and chairs could be used as obstacles.

He strode toward her with confidence in his expression, fully expecting to prevail in their encounter, swinging his club in long, sweeping strokes. Ella scrambled backward, out of his reach. She kept a tight hold on her dagger. She couldn't afford to throw it. If her aim was at all off, it would leave her defenseless.

The innkeeper swung his club in a high, overhead arc. Ella jumped back and crashed into a chair. She let out a hiss of pain and rubbed at her buttock. That was going to leave a bruise.

She kept backing up as he advanced, leading him around the dining room, which had cleared out, leaving only the serving girl to watch the fight play out. He shoved tables aside, kicked chairs out of his way, and growled threats. His attacks became more reckless and his breathing more ragged, and Ella realized she'd somehow chosen the perfect strategy.

She was used to being on her feet all day, running around after patrons. She could keep this up longer than he could, and when he tired, he would make a mistake, and she would take advantage of it.

She didn't have to wait long.

He swung the club and overreached, leaving his left side exposed. Ella lunged forward, struck quickly, and pulled back again. The dagger moved as if it were an extension of her hand. She didn't have to think about where to aim or how deep to make the cuts. The fishwife had indeed been true to her word.

A line of blood beaded through his shirt. She'd barely broken the skin, just enough to sting without doing any real damage. He cursed and countered, swinging wildly to the right, and she moved in again.

Soon, he was bleeding from a dozen shallow cuts, and frustration turned his face red and made him act carelessly.

They stood with a table between them, and the man grabbed it and sent it cartwheeling to the side. Before he had recovered from the motion, Ella leaped forward and made two quick slashes. His shirt fell open to expose a letter X written in blood on his chest. The blood flowed freely, his face paled, and he dropped his club to press his hands to the wound.

Ella's confidence momentarily abandoned her. It was a lot of blood. More than she'd expected. But they were only shallow cuts, she was sure of it. If he kept them clean he would recover well, with only a scar to remind him how to treat young women.

"Talia," he croaked. "A towel ..."

The serving girl—Talia—scrambled across the room, carrying a faded gray cloth. The innkeeper took it from her with shaking hands and pressed it to his wounds.

Ella shook her head to clear away her doubt. She'd done the right thing. She paused to clean her blade on the man's tattered shirt before relieving him of his purse—he was too focused on his injuries to even notice. She offered it to Talia.

"Is there another stash of coins somewhere?" Ella asked. "Anything else of value you can take?"

The girl nodded vaguely before her expression cleared. She headed behind the bar and came up with a lock box. Ella retrieved her dagger from the wall and used it to force the lock. Talia started to add the contents to the purse, but paused.

"You want half?" she asked.

Ella shook her head. "I have enough, and you're going to need every coin if you want to start a new life not ruled by men like him."

The girl's expression softened, and she pulled Ella into a hug. "Thank you," she whispered into Ella's neck.

Ella hugged her back, and the red mist faded.

GIVEN WAS A GOOD name for his wolf form. It rolled off the girl's tongue in her peculiar accent in a way that felt like an embrace. He'd never really liked Huxford. It was a traditional Brettish name but had always felt a bit stodgy to him. He would reclaim it when he became human again, of course, the same way he would reclaim his position and power, but while he was with Ella, Given would do.

And staying with her was the smart choice. She was clearly kind and brave, she'd been quick to realize he wasn't a normal wolf, and her ability to open doors and barter for supplies would be of great benefit to him. In return, he would offer her shelter in his manor house, equip her with any resources he had on hand, and do his best to aid her with whatever purpose had brought her to Bretland.

He hunted through the field beside the road and found a vole to sate his hunger then settled down to wait for Ella's return. It wasn't long before she stepped out of the inn, and more relief than he'd been expecting swept through him. Relief spread over her face, too, when he rose from the long grass to reveal himself. It would have been polite, if he'd been able to, to ask after her meal, but as she approached, the scent of adrenaline and blood assailed him, pushing all thoughts of courtesy aside. She seemed uninjured as she offered him her hand in greeting. He nudged it aside and nosed the dagger on her hip, where the metallic smell was strongest. Then he sat back and interrogated her with his gaze.

She glanced away and her jaw twitched as she pretended not to understand what he was asking. "This way?"

As he lacked the ability to question her further, he gave her a disappointed look and pushed to his feet.

His manor house was only about another hour's walk away, but Ella had been right to stop and eat. There would be no easy food at the manor for her, and she would need to make a supply run, but Given had no way to warn her of that in advance.

He was both grateful and anxious when the house finally came into view. Now that he looked at it with the eyes of a host rather than a solitary resident, the building seemed more rundown than he remembered, as if the weight of time and neglect sat heavily on it. Ivy grew unimpeded up the left-hand side. The auxiliary buildings were crumbling. And the gardens—the beautiful gardens he'd designed for a bride who'd never arrived—were a mixture of overgrown and barren.

"By the depths of the sea," Ella murmured. "Surely you don't mean for us to go there?"

Shame flooded Given until he felt drenched by it. It had been presumptuous of him to bring his new companion to such a derelict place. He gave his head a noncommittal shake.

She lifted her hand to shade her eyes from the watery winter sunlight. "I can't see any sign of people. Is it empty?"

He nodded.

"And it's safe for us to let ourselves in?"

He nodded again.

She let out an "Oh" that confused him with its layers of awe and anticipation. Then she dropped to a crouch, wrapped her arms around his neck, and buried her face in his fur. "It's the grandest house I've ever seen!"

Grand? Well, it may have been grand once. That was certainly the impression he'd wanted to make on Juliana. He relaxed into her embrace. At least someone was impressed.

As they approached the house, Ella insisted they tour the gardens. Her eyes lit up as they entered each one, despite their state of disrepair, and she chatted away happily to him or to herself. "What's this?" she would ask before answering her own question. "An orchard! A herb garden! A rockery!" She picked a sprig of rosemary, plucked a perfectly smooth stone from the path, and plaited a flax leaf into a long braid.

Half the manicured bushes in the rose garden had grown wild, and the other half had died, but Ella found one perfect bloom amongst the shriveled heads, carefully grasped the stem while avoiding the thorns, and snapped it off. She held it in front of Given's nose with a delighted grin on her face. He sniffed obligingly and sneezed dramatically.

When they finally reached the house, Given nosed open the unlatched door and endured another wave of shame at the dusty, cobweb-covered interior. But Ella either didn't see the dust or didn't care. She ran down the long corridors, bounded up the stairs, slid down the balustrades, and rolled around on the lush carpets. Her enthusiasm was infectious, and Given ran, bounded, and rolled along with her. His paws slid on the wooden floors, his fur charged with static on the carpets, and the house delighted him in ways it never had before.

Ella was maybe all of eighteen summers old, around the same age Juliana had been when Given had proposed marriage, and only now did he realize the mistake he'd made. For all that Ella was an adult, she was still graced with a childlike wonder that he'd lost long ago—or maybe never had. Juliana could have been the obliging bride and granted him the children he wanted to ensure his legacy, but what had he offered her except a fancy house, a comfortable fortune, and a stodgy husband twice her age?

Another wave of shame hit him, and he stopped his playful rolling. Ella snuggled up against his side and let out a contented sigh that made him shiver.

"Thank you for bringing me here, Given."

He turned to give her a gentle lick. He wasn't Huxford anymore, his mistakes were in the past, and he was determined to ensure Given didn't repeat them.

THEY SPENT A PLEASANT few weeks in the manor house, hibernating while they waited for warm weather to return. Ella set about cleaning the kitchens, cataloging the contents of the pantry, and replenishing the supply of firewood. Rejecting all of the splendid bed chambers upstairs, she settled herself in the cook's quarters. Whatever life she'd lived before, she was clearly accustomed to working hard and didn't have great expectations.

She made regular excursions to Riverlea while he waited on the outskirts, and she returned with ingredients that she turned into simple meals wholly unfamiliar to Given.

He couldn't offer much help, but he stayed by her side as she worked, opened drawers and cupboard doors when her hands were full, and trained himself to pick things up with a soft mouth so as not to bruise or pierce or tear the precious ingredients. In fact, he enjoyed the experience so much that he came to wonder why he'd never contemplated working in the kitchens until now. But then he remembered. That was what servants were for. It was much more efficient to pay someone to cook and clean than to do it himself.

Ella didn't eat in the formal dining room but at the work bench in the kitchens, near the oven for warmth, feeding him strips of hot chicken or beef or fish with her fingers. Hot food was a rare treat in his wolf form, and though he was quite content to hunt, he found that eating in Ella's company was worth the bother of juggling the food in his teeth so as not to burn his lips.

Ella spent most of the meals apologizing absently for having to substitute an ingredient she couldn't procure. "In my village," she would say, "we'd use fennel." Or, "In my village, the flavor of the fish is more subtle." And once, while stuffing her mouth with bread, "In my village, the spices aren't as hot."

It made him wonder why she'd left.

As the day of the next new moon approached, Given's anxiety returned. This last month had been the best of the past three years, maybe of his entire life. Ella didn't place any expectations on him, she didn't judge him on his wealth, she didn't yearn for more than this simple life.

If she awoke to find a man sleeping on the foot of her cot instead of a wolf, he imagined she would feel at first horrified and then betrayed. And if she agreed to talk to him, she would want an explanation, and he would have to tell her about how he'd ended up in this predicament. And when he turned back, she wouldn't look at him the same.

No.

It was better if she didn't find out what—who—he truly was.

When she fell into bed on the night before the new moon, and patted the covers next to her, inviting him up, he didn't join her as was his habit. Instead, he lifted only his front paws onto the cot and nuzzled her face before dropping down again and glancing at the door.

She pushed up onto one elbow. "You're going?"

He nodded.

"For how long?"

He tapped his paw once.

"One day?" Her brow furrowed, but she forced a smile and scratched him under his chin. "Well, don't let me keep you from your important canine business. I'll see you when you get back."

He huffed out an agreement, a promise to return, and slipped out through the kitchen door carrying his satchel. He spent the night on the edge of Riverlea, and in the morning dressed in the clothes he'd brought with him. They weren't his clothes. He couldn't turn up in the village in his finery. Instead he wore the rugged working clothes of a groundskeeper.

It was the day of the village market, and he spent the morning hauling baskets for a local farmer in exchange for a couple of coins.

After weeks of Ella's unusual meals, Given had a hankering for good Brettish food, and he found a stall selling savory egg pancakes. He took the warm pancake, wrapped in a dry banyan leaf, and found a spot on the village green where he could sit and rest his back against a tree.

He was licking the last of the grease off his fingers when a familiar figure walked across the green. Ella hadn't told him she would be making a supply run today, but then, he hadn't been able to ask.

A warm, contented feeling filled his chest as he watched her stroll around the market, adding produce to the bag dangling from her shoulder. Her hair wasn't the muted yellow-gray he was used to seeing as a wolf, but a stunning red. Her outfit wasn't dark gray but burgundy. Now he had seen her true colors, he wouldn't forget.

He wondered if he could orchestrate a casual encounter, bump into her at a stall. He didn't have to reveal who he was, but to speak to his friend would sustain him for another month. He bounced to his feet.

Before he could move, a ruckus broke out to his right.

A hulk of a man with broad farmer's shoulders had hold of a young girl's arm. Given thought he recognized the man, but couldn't recall his name. The girl he didn't know at all. She was clasping a basket filled with bunches of wildflowers, and judging by the number of young couples in the crowd who were holding flowers or had them tucked behind their ears, the girl had been doing a good trade. The man shook her roughly, and she dropped her basket, sending flowers and coins scattering over the grass. She reached for them, but the man threw her to the ground and gathered up the coins himself.

Then Ella was there, planting herself between the prone girl and the man. Her voice rang across the green, her tone cold. "I don't believe those are yours."

Given took a step forward. Ella looked like she was about to bring trouble down upon herself.

"Those flowers are," the man said, waving his arm to encompass the entire green.

Ella glanced down at the girl. "Did you steal his flowers?"

"They grow along the roadside." The girl had rolled to her knees and was regathering the bunches that had bounced out of the basket. "No one owns them."

"Is that true?" Ella turned back to the man. She was running this conversation like a manor liege running a trial.

"Well ..." The man's olive complexion flushed pink. "They grow in front of my field."

"Not *in* your field?" Ella's voice dripped with feigned innocence.

The man's flush deepened. "Everyone knows they're mine. My wife picks them to sell at the market, but this morning, they'd been stripped."

Ella scratched her head, as if she were confused. "Let me get this straight. This girl took something that *doesn't* belong to you, and you took something that *does* belong to her in revenge?"

The man looked like he was on the verge of seeing the error of his ways. Ella had called him out in front of a crowd of his peers, and they would remember his unjust attitude the next time he and his wife set up their flower stall. "Maybe I overreacted."

But Ella wasn't done, and her voice frosted over. "So you laid your hands on her as if she was your property? You threw her to the ground as if she was a piece of rubbish? Even now you stand there holding her coins as if you have some claim to them."

Her hand flashed forward, bearing a dagger which delicately sliced the back of the man's hand. He hissed in pain and grasped his hand to his chest. The coins tumbled to the grass.

Given had moved a few paces closer, but he froze again.

As far as he could see, the man had no weapon. He'd certainly behaved in way that required an apology and possible reparation, but there was no need for Ella to take it out of his flesh. He wasn't like the dogfighter.

"Next time, don't claim what isn't yours." Ella punctuated her words with more quick strikes. The man threw his arms up in an attempt to protect himself, but it seemed as if Ella's aim was carefully placed. His trousers dropped, revealing a pair of threadbare under-shorts.

"Next time, don't lay your hands on someone smaller than you." She sliced again, and the man's shirt peeled away like petals dropping from a flower.

"Next time, don't assume no one is waiting to take revenge on *you*!" She slashed wildly—a move designed to intimidate rather than make contact—and the man threw himself backward. The pooled fabric of his trousers tangled his feet and he stumbled to the ground.

Ella turned her back on him, bent over, and started plucking the coins from the grass.

A ripple of laughter ran through the crowd, and with it, the man's expression turned from scared to embarrassed to furious.

Given shouted a warning, but his words were lost in the babble of the crowd.

The man let out a growl and launched himself off the ground at Ella. She snapped upright and spun around, her dagger hand swinging.

Given's eyes slammed shut, unwilling to show him the imminent collision, and by the time he'd forced them open again, the man was lying on the ground and Ella was sitting on top of him.

The man screamed as Ella carved something into his cheek.

Given stared in horror.

When he'd fought for his freedom from the dogfighter's den, he'd known what future lay ahead of him. He hadn't wanted to fight the other dogs, but if he hadn't, he would have had no worth and his life would have been short. Even if he *had* fought and survived, the moment the new moon had risen and they'd seen he was a man, they probably would have killed him to conceal their foul deeds. Even then, he'd taken no pleasure in biting the men. He'd done what he had to when his life was at stake.

The flower girl's life wasn't at stake. Nor was Ella's.

"There," Ella said as she pushed to her feet. "A small souvenir that might help you remember how to treat other people." She glanced around, her fierce grin slowly fading, as if she only now realized she had an audience to her cruelty. She threw a handful of coins into the girl's basket, picked up the bag containing her purchases, and fled from the green.

CHAPTER FOUR

ELLA HEADED DIRECTLY OUT of the village, practically tripping over her feet in her desperation to return to the crumbling manor house, her bag of goods heavy on her shoulder. The strange red mist that had marred her vision when she'd seen the girl being mistreated had long since lifted, leaving her horrified.

She knew she'd done the right thing defending the girl, but the actions that had seemed so right at the time now disgusted her. She'd taunted the man, humiliated him in front of the other villagers, and let her anger turn her cruel. He may have been a bully, but she shouldn't have taken pleasure in being a bigger bully. She never used to be like this.

She could still see the fear in his eyes as she'd carved a flower into his cheek.

Bile rose in her throat, and she rushed to the side of the road to purge the contents of her stomach.

She was so lost in the maelstrom of her thoughts that she didn't notice the sky darkening as she walked. It wasn't until the wind picked up and raindrops pelted her that she took any notice of her surroundings. When she searched for a tree to shelter under, she was surprised to spot a building that looked identical to the fishwife's ramshackle hut, sitting at the side of the road. Ella rubbed her eyes and blinked against the rain, but the vision didn't change. The door banged open, and the fishwife leaned out and beckoned to her. "Come out of the rain, child."

Ella's feet carried her forward.

The interior of the hut was exactly the same as it had always been, as if a giant had plucked the entire hut from its spot on the shore and transplanted it here.

"Grandmother," Ella murmured. "How are you here?"

"I'm neither here nor there, child," the fishwife said from where she was hunched over her cooking fire. "Tea?"

"Please," she said numbly, feeling as if the past month had been a dream and she'd never actually left Leyton.

The fishwife handed over a steaming mug then stood tall and regarded Ella shrewdly. "A month has passed and you have not yet brought me the Dead Prince's heart."

Ella swallowed sharply and the hot liquid scorched her throat. She coughed and said, "I didn't know—"

"Hold your excuses. I know I did not set a deadline, but my patience will not last forever. Are you not satisfied with my part of the bargain?"

Ella swallowed. "I can't deny my skill with a blade. My aim is always true."

"And yet you are unhappy?"

The hair on the back of Ella's neck prickled. She'd seen a glimpse of the fishwife's power and didn't wish to vex her. "Not unhappy, no, but I don't exactly feel like myself when I wield the blades."

"Feel a bit of fury, do you?" the fishwife asked, the words rolling off her tongue as if they tasted delicious. "I did warn you there was no point in being too meek to use your power."

"It's not the fury that worries me," Ella said, and an expression which might have been doubt flashed across the fishwife's features. "The fury comes from a place of justice, of righting a wrong. What worries me is how things get out of hand, how much I ..." She paused and sipped at her tea, feeling its warmth flow through her, allowing her to face the worst of herself. "I enjoyed it."

And she *had* enjoyed putting that man in his place, but she'd gone too far, let cruelty be her guide. She didn't want to be that person.

The fishwife waved her hand dismissively. "However your righteous indignation manifests, use it. That feeling gives you your skills, it aims your blades, there's no point wasting time feeling guilty about it."

Ella gasped. "So I have to lose control of myself to control my daggers?"

"Don't you want all I promised you?" the fishwife said, her expression darkening. "I was right about your rogue abandoning you, wasn't I? Do you doubt my other predictions will come true? You've had a taste of a grand manor, don't you want to claim it? Don't you wish to win the heart of a prince? Don't you wish for your happy ending?"

"I don't wish to become someone else in the process. I don't wish to hurt people."

"Isn't this better than the simpering victim you once were, too afraid to even raise a hand to defend herself?"

Ella dropped her gaze. She wished she hadn't murdered her father. Her life would've been miserable—subjected to Dyson Doon's lascivious demands—but at least she wouldn't have guilt piercing her like the spines of a stingray. But it was too late for wishes.

Or was it?

"I wish you'd take it back," she said, her voice trembling.

The fishwife stared at her for a long moment while Ella attempted to tamp down her hope. Finally, in a matter-of-fact voice, the fishwife said, "I could take back that mug of tea, if I so pleased, but you have already partaken of it. Would you have me reach down your gullet and retrieve what is mine?"

Ella's hope flickered and went out. "I—"

"Do you think the heart of the Dead Prince is too much to ask? I would've desecrated his grave already, had I sworn to."

Ella couldn't undo what she'd done, but maybe she could stop herself doing worse. She could sequester herself away in the manor house, only going to the village when absolutely necessary, and avoiding people as best she could. But before she could do that, she needed to complete her part of the bargain. "I don't know where to find the Dead Prince. You told me to come to Bretland, but I can't knock on every door and ask if they're hiding his body."

The fishwife let out an exasperated breath. "Honestly! Must I do everything myself? You don't have to ask everyone, just the one who knows where to find him. And out of all the people in this wretched realm, who would know more than the Grand Prince himself?"

The ground seemed to shift under Ella's feet at the fishwife's words. The Grand Prince? Was he the prince whose heart she was meant to win? Not that it was likely to happen if she locked herself away. And how was she even meant to get an audience with him to ask about the Dead Prince? Just walk up to his castle and ask?

"But be warned," the fishwife continued, and her expression darkened. "Do not think you can renege on our deal without paying a high price. Hunting down the Dead Prince is an insignificant task compared to the tortures I can dream up."

Ella fled from the fishwife's threats but spent the rest of the walk back to the manor house chewing over her words. She had to find the Dead Prince. In that she had no choice. But she would have to be careful not to lose too much of herself along the way. That was a price she wasn't willing to pay, even if it meant she wouldn't achieve the happy ending the fishwife had promised.

She was so fixated on her destination and her doubts that she didn't notice the figure in black trailing discreetly behind her.

GIVEN RETURNED TO THE manor in time for sunset. He disrobed, tucked his neatly folded clothes into his satchel, and rubbed the goosebumps from his arms while he waited.

The incident with Ella played over in his mind. He'd known she could be brave—she'd shown that with the dogfighter—but the man in Riverlea was no dogfighter. The way she'd played with him, taunted him, teased him, reminded Given of a cat playing with a cricket.

He would be eternally grateful that she had intervened with the dogfighter, and he was sure that the girl she'd defended on the village green would feel the same, but he'd noted the expression on Ella's face as she'd fled the village. All the playfulness was gone, as if she'd come back to her senses a moment too late, leaving her aghast at what she'd done.

He wondered again at where she'd come from, who she'd been, what she'd endured that made her insert herself into situations that didn't concern her.

Shaking off his thoughts, he glanced up. The sun—and with it, the invisible moon—had almost disappeared, but he was still a man. The witch's words came back to him.

You will stay in this form until you learn to love and to be loved.

Had he broken the curse? The only thing that had changed between this month and the last was Ella. Did he love her? Surely the fact he had to ask himself that question meant the answer was no.

It seemed ridiculous to even consider it. Such frivolous emotions hadn't factored into his assessment of either Alyssia or Juliana as a suitable bride, and he certainly didn't have any such intentions toward Ella.

Thinking of his young friend brought a smile to his lips.

She was brave, kind, hardworking. He enjoyed spending time with her, and he wanted to protect her from whatever trouble was hounding her.

Maybe he *should* present himself to her now, as a man. It would give them time to talk over what had happened, an opportunity for her to explain her past.

But would she let *him* explain? Or would she carve him up like a swamp hen destined for the stew pot before he had a chance to convince her of his identity? Even if she did, she was sure to feel betrayed. Abandoned, even. Her faithful pet replaced by a man who'd never been that great.

And what if she decided she didn't need him any longer? What if she left the manor house and never looked back?

If Ella left, no amount of servants or guests would fill the hole she'd leave in his heart.

He buried his hands in his hair and stared at the horizon.

Why? Why now? Was this another trick of the witch's? Another way to torment him, like the first time he'd changed with the new moon and thought himself free of it? Why break the curse now, when he'd finally found true happiness?

No.

He was having none of that.

He had to be the wolf. He *had* to be Given, not Huxford. Ella wouldn't abandon Given, and he wouldn't abandon her.

He glared at the last sliver of sun and willed the change to come.

His fingertips began to tingle.

He dropped to all fours, closed his eyes, and dug his fingers into the dirt.

The tingle spread up his arms.

Given might be a wolf, but he was a better person than Huxford had ever been. He enjoyed the company of the peasants who'd spent their whole lives working his land. He listened more than he spoke. He gave more than he took. He cared for someone other than himself.

And Ella needed him, he was sure of it.

The tingle covered his entire body, and with a sob of relief, he transformed.

He gathered the satchel in his mouth, but as he was about to head for the house, movement caught his eye. He surveyed the gray landscape, and spotted one shadow darker than the others. Given lifted his muzzle and sniffed, but the shadow was downwind. He let out a low growl around the bag in his mouth and puffed up the fur on his shoulders. If any trappers were here, they wouldn't get him again without a fight.

The shadow didn't move or make any indication it was anything other than a trick of the fading light. Given gave one last warning growl and slipped through the encroaching darkness to the house. He nosed his way through the kitchen door, made sure it latched behind him, left his bundle on the floor, and turned to face the waiting Ella. She dropped to her knees and wrapped her arms around his neck. Her breath made his fur tremble like trees in a storm, and he relaxed into her embrace.

When she pulled back, her face was tight with emotion that she couldn't completely conceal. Then something in her expression softened, and she smooched his cheeks and kissed his nose before bouncing to her feet and saying, "Let's make some dinner." And he knew he'd made the right decision.

It wasn't until the morning, when Given once again lay on the foot of her cot, that she tentatively asked, "Do you know the way to the royal city?"

He lifted his head from the soft covers, twitched his ears, and nodded.

"Will you show me?"

He couldn't ask her why she wanted to go, or when, or if she was no longer happy here with him, but as long as she let him tag along, he wouldn't deny her, so he nodded once again.

She reached over to stroke his head and rub his velvety ears between her fingers. "Thank you, Given."

THEIR THREE-DAY JOURNEY TO Southport wasn't entirely uneventful. Ella seemed drawn to trouble, and it always came in the shape of a grown man abusing a young girl. A horrible suspicion began to grow in Given's mind, about what Ella's life had been before he'd met her.

The blanket, and flint and steel he'd made her pack, proved their worth when she had to flee from an inn and they both spent the night camped beside the road.

Every now and then as they walked, Given's hackles would rise, and he would scan the road behind them. He caught no scents other than those of the people they passed on the road, the animals in the fields, and the plants that grew along the way, but Given suspected they were being followed, regardless of any evidence. He stuck close to Ella's side.

When the city came into view on the third day, Ella slowed to a halt and let out a murmur of awe. Given hadn't been back since his one failed attempt to see the Grand Princess, and the city had grown from what he remembered.

"Is that where the Grand Prince lives?" she asked, pointing to the limestone palace that rose from the center of the city. Even with his muted wolf's vision, it glittered in the late afternoon sun.

Given nodded. He hadn't been aware there'd been a change in ruler. He was so removed from politics that he hadn't heard whether the Grand Princess had retired or died, or if her son—his cousin

Rickett—had taken over as expected. But no matter who currently ruled, the palace was where they would reside.

"All right," Ella said, stroking his head. "Let's go pay him a visit."

Before she could move away, Given caught her cloak in his teeth and let out a low growl. One did not simply walk up to the palace and request an audience. If the Grand Prince stuck to tradition, he would hold an open day once a month, when anyone from the lowliest peasant to the richest noble could approach and make an appeal. But Given's days were ruled by the moon, not by labels people had made, and he had no way to find out when the next open day was or to inform Ella of the protocol.

"I have to, Given." Ella carefully freed the fabric from his mouth. "I have no choice."

A wolf would be no more welcome in the city than in any small village, but Given knew he couldn't leave her side. He only hoped he would be able to prevent her from making a misstep from which she wouldn't recover.

The city provided an entirely new range of scents for Given to investigate. He picked up the trails of animals that scavenged the streets for food, was confronted by the lingering odor of rotting food, and assailed by the stench of human waste.

The smells lessened as they approached the palace, but the crowds intensified. Luckily, a path always opened before them. People spotted him and scattered, even though Ella kept her hand on his shoulder, gently worrying his fur while he did his best to look like a harmless—if large—dog.

They crossed the bridge and followed the zig-zag path up, and this time Given was acutely aware of the towering walls on either side of them, which provided plenty of places for defenders to rain arrows down on an attacking horde. Not that he was attacking. Or a horde. But he remembered how lacking the welcome had been on his last visit.

The path ended at a wide open lawn, artfully arranged with flower gardens, but there were no large trees or even medium-sized bushes to offer shelter to any attackers who made it this far. But it was a place that offered plenty of spots for picnicking, and many groups of people were taking advantage of the pleasant evening to do exactly that.

Again remembering the shame of his last visit, Given wanted nothing more than to avoid the scrutiny of the two guards by the inner gate, but that was the only way in.

"Move along," the guard on the left said with a dismissive wave of his arm, which was exactly what Given expected him to say.

Ella didn't move along. She kept her eyes downcast and fidgeted with the cuff off her blouse. "I want to see the Grand Prince."

The one on the right snorted as he leaned heavily on his pike. "And I want a nice, comfy chair to sit in, but I guess we're both out of luck."

Ella lifted her gaze, her brow furrowed. "I need to see him. Please."

"Open days are the third Monday of every month," the left one said in a bored voice. "Come back then."

Ella still didn't move. "I can't wait that long. I have to see him now." Her voice rose with every word, and the guards' postures stiffened. They no longer saw her as a nuisance but as a problem. Given, who up until now had been half-hiding behind her, stepped forward and pressed his head against her hip, as if he could move her backward. The guards' eyes bulged upon seeing him, and Ella shoved him roughly with her knee.

He let out a little yip of displeasure, and the guard on the left eased his sword from its scabbard.

"Last warning, girl," he said. "Move along and take that monster with you."

Ella's posture shifted, her timidness replaced by a predatory look, and her voice carried a warning as she drew both her blades. "Take me to the Grand Price, or—"

Before she could finish her threat, the guard on the right moved, bringing his pike to bear. Given darted forward to put himself between them and bared his teeth, but the guard didn't flinch. He simply adjusted his grip on his pike, and altered his swing, in one smooth motion. Given scrambled backward, his paws skidding on the cobblestone path. He crashed into Ella, who let out a cry of "Stupid dog!" Her words cut more sharply than the guard's blade ever could.

He dodged another swing, backing away from Ella. He couldn't duck inside the man's reach to tear at him with his teeth, and in all honesty, he didn't want to. This guard wasn't a cruel dogfighter. He was merely doing his job and didn't deserve to be bitten for it. He wasn't even trying that hard to hit Given; his swings were defensive, to drive him back. But if Given kept him busy, that might give Ella time to run.

Only, she didn't run.

The other guard was advancing on her, making short, precise strokes with his sword. But Ella was fending off every blow. Her hands moved quickly, as if she knew where he was going to aim before he did. Then she caught his blade between both of hers, forcing his weapon down as she slid hers up toward the hilt, and for a moment, Given thought she might have the advantage.

But instead of resisting, the guard dropped his weapon, grabbed both her wrists, and cracked his head into her cheekbone.

Ella didn't even make a sound before sagging to the ground, dazed.

"A night in the dungeon will sort this one out," the guard said, relieving her of her daggers.

"Unless His Highness gets wind of it," the other one muttered. "Now help me with this wolf."

The guard yelled up to another guard on the wall behind him, who dropped a flaming torch down.

"Ha!" he cried, thrusting the torch in Given's direction, while the other guard kept swinging his pike in lazy strokes. "Get out of here, you mongrel."

Given growled, his hackles rising, but the flickering light, the heat, and the blade's sharp edge all forced him back. He cast a last desperate look at Ella, but with no voice, no hands, and no prestige, he couldn't help her.

He turned tail and fled across the lawn, zig-zagged down the path, retreated across the bridge, and came to a skidding stop under the wooden porch of a tailor's shop. He pressed his belly to the ground and let out a pathetic whimper as he gazed at the castle. So much for his desire to be her friend, to stay by her side. The wolf had proved to be no use at all.

Hours passed and no rescue plan came to Given. He would have to hope the guard had spoken true—that Ella would be released in the morning, none the worse for wear—and that the worrisome comment about His Highness was unfounded.

A muted whistle drew Given's attention. The streets had emptied as the sun had set, though there was plenty of warm light and noise spilling from the buildings around him. Inns hosting guests, taverns plying ale, merchants retiring to their upstairs apartments. And just to his left, a shadow darker than the others shifted slightly.

Given, still on edge from his encounter with the guards, launched himself out from under the porch as the shadow coalesced into the shape of a man.

The man cursed and threw himself sideways, rolling neatly to settle into a crouch, but Given pivoted with ease, knocked the man over, landed on top of him, and let out a series of ferocious barks. The man raised his arm, bringing a dagger to bear, and Given's jaws snapped shut around his wrist.

His teeth didn't pierce the man's flesh. They bit into something leathery, and stuck.

The silence of potential violence spread out around them.

"Well," the man said in a casual tone. "This is rather a predicament."

Given made a low growl.

"You cannot bite through my bracer," the man continued, "and if you loose your jaws to choose a better spot, I'll stab you in the neck." He lifted his free hand to show another small dagger held casually between his thumb and forefinger. "On the other hand, if I stab you first, I have the distinct impression you'll attempt to rip my arm from its socket, which is an experience I'm not keen to repeat."

He paused, as if giving Given time to comprehend the significance of his words. He'd offered up a weakness.

Given let out a quick, curious growl around the man's arm, his saliva oozing over the leather bracer to fall and splatter on the man's cheek, before shifting his gaze back to the casual threat of the dagger. There was enough light to let him pick out the startlingly familiar scorched pattern on the handle. Ella had one that was identical.

"I'm a friend." The man flicked his wrist, tucking his dagger away in his bracer, before taking the other one from his trapped hand and slotting it away too. "I want to help. But you'll need to trust me."

THE RED MIST FADED at the same time as the dungeon door slammed shut behind Ella. Her head throbbed, and regret draped over her like a cloak as she lay on the cold, hard ground.

The guard laughed as he walked away, as if he saw her as merely an annoyance and not a threat. And he was right. Her magical skill with a dagger didn't mean she was guaranteed to win a fight against a trained soldier.

She pushed herself up and tentatively touched her cheek. It felt swollen and tender under her fingers, but not broken. That was probably more luck than she deserved for giving in to her indignation so soon after promising to hold herself in check.

Her cell was small, with a wooden shelf attached to the wall that she assumed was a bed. She sat upon it, propped her elbows on her knees, and rested her chin in her hands.

What a fool she'd been to think she could simply present herself to the Grand Prince and ask if he had possession of a certain heart. But she couldn't fathom why the old fishwife had sent her here if the Grand Prince wouldn't see her, let alone give her answers.

If she hadn't been caught up by her righteous indignation, she might have thought to ask the guards if there was any other way to get an audience. Now, even if she returned on the next third Monday, she doubted they would let her in. She'd made too much of a fuss, and they had no reason to be generous.

She leaned back against the wall.

Choosing to attack the guards wasn't the only mistake she'd made. She'd treated Given poorly. He'd been a loyal companion for the past month, he'd attempted to dissuade her from confronting the guards, and he'd fought beside her. Even before she'd lost what little sense she had left, she'd discounted his advice. She'd shoved him, she'd cursed him, and she'd left him at the mercy of the guards.

She'd behaved just like the bullies she hated.

Her skin crawled with guilt, like she was coated with so much of it that even if she bathed in an ocean's worth of water, she would never be clean.

If he abandoned her, she would deserve it.

If he abandoned her, she would lose the only friend she had.

A shiver ran through her as loneliness settled into her bones, and she pulled her feet up onto the hard bed and hugged her knees.

She had to figure something out, some way to speak to the Grand Prince and find out where the heart was. That was the only way to end this.

Then she would happily spend the rest of her days with Given in their rundown manor house.

Assuming he still wanted to spend his days with her.

Dawn had barely broken after a bad night's sleep when a guard came to release her. She wore the same uniform as the men from last night, and she eyed Ella with pity.

"Am I to be freed?" Ella asked carefully.

The guard didn't meet her gaze. "Soon enough."

Ella didn't resist as the guard clamped manacles around her wrists and led her from the dungeon. When they came into the light, she was surprised to find they weren't underground as she'd assumed, but instead in a low, stone building built against the inner wall. The beautiful palace rose above her, but she didn't have time to admire it as more guards surrounded her and escorted her through the gate, across the lawn, down the zig-zag path, and over the bridge into the city.

A crowd had gathered in front of the bridge, as if the citizens had paused their morning tasks to watch some sort of spectacle.

The guard led her to a tall wooden post standing to the side of the bridge, and connected her manacles to an iron ring set at head height. Ella's heart burst into a sprint as she realized *she* was to be the spectacle.

"What is to happen to me?" she choked out.

The guard gave her a tight look. "It'll be over soon, and then I suggest you flee the city for good."

A murmur ran through the gathered crowd, and Ella fought to control her panicked breathing as she followed their gazes to the bridge. Two men rode across on horseback. They wore the finest clothing she'd ever seen. Even their horses—one white, one gray—were bedecked with saddlecloths and headgear embroidered with golden thread. The man on the white horse wore a thin gold band atop his dark hair, and dread solidified in Ella's gut as she realized he must be the Grand Prince.

He was younger than she'd expected for a ruler, maybe in his mid-twenties. His shoulders were slim, his long hair was pinned back, his cheekbones were prominent against his olive skin, and his brows were set in a frown. When he spoke, the crowd fell silent, and his every word carried.

"My people, it has come to my attention that last night, someone attempted to force their way into the palace ..."

The lump in Ella's gut hardened.

"Though the people of Bretland are welcome in the palace grounds at any time, this does not mean I will bow down to the demands of a foreigner."

Boos and hisses ran through the crowd in support of his words.

Ella wondered how they'd known she wasn't Brettish.

"She attacked my guards, which I consider an attack on my person."

Ella yanked on her manacles, squeezed her fingers together as she attempted to pull her hand free, but nothing worked. She was trapped.

"Should I let this foreigner go free without punishment?"

A jeered "No!" was the answer.

"Should I show our neighbors that Bretland will not tolerate this disrespect?"

"Yes!"

The Grand Prince turned to the guard who had brought Ella out. "Give this girl ten lashes and send her back to her masters."

"I don't have a master!" Ella cried. Her voice cracked and her knees trembled. "Please, sir ..." She had no idea how to address a Grand Prince. "I'm sorry."

"Oh, you're sorry?" The Grand Prince turned his withering gaze on her before surveying the gathered citizens. "In that case, is there anyone here willing to take this girl's punishment?"

Silence fell over the crowd, as if no one dared breathe too heavily lest they were mistaken for a volunteer.

Then a familiar voice rang out. "I will."

Ella's heart leapt then crashed as Rory shouldered his way between two rough-looking merchants, Given following on his heels. He wore the same black outfit as always, and when he pushed his hood back, the sun kissed the same red tones in his warm brown hair. The only difference was the month's worth of growth on his jaw.

How had he found her? Although, *found* implied he'd been looking. And why would he do *that* when he'd missed their meeting? And why now? Why would he turn up at the exact moment she needed rescuing when he'd missed so many other opportunities?

"I'll take her punishment, Your Highness." He strolled toward Ella as if he'd merely offered to untie her from the whipping post, Given shadowing him still. "Though I have one request, if you'll indulge me."

The Grand Prince's eyes narrowed, but he nodded.

"I would have the Prince Consort deliver the blows."

The Grand Prince turned to the man on the gray horse. "Do you know this rogue?"

The Prince Consort eased his horse forward. He was maybe a year or two younger than his husband; his shoulders were broader, and his dark hair was cut short and neatly styled. In a voice that was muted but still carried, he said, "That is the rogue who kidnapped me three years ago."

Ella knew that Rory must have sold his services to whomever was willing to pay, but she couldn't imagine him kidnapping anyone.

The Grand Prince's attention shifted back to Rory, his gaze vicious. "Are you the one who left my love bruised and battered?"

Rory's jaw twitched. "I am."

Ella gasped. There had to be more to that story, as she couldn't imagine him giving anyone a beating, either.

"In that case, I will deliver your punishment myself." The Grand Prince swung down from his horse and barked commands to the guards around him.

As the same guard stepped forward to release Ella from the manacles, Rory didn't change his mind and flee; he merely focused on unbuttoning his vest.

"What are you doing here?" Ella demanded, her voice sharper than she intended. She shot Given a look, but he provided no answers.

Rory didn't pause his undressing as he regarded her. His expression was tight, but his words were soft. "You didn't wait."

"I waited," she snapped. "You didn't come."

"I admit I was late," he said, not rising to her tone. "I apologize."

He finished the last of his buttons, slipped out of his vest, and offered it to her. Her gaze snagged on his chest. He wore a leather cord around his neck, and from the end dangled a silver ring. But that wasn't what made her breath catch.

She thought she knew all his scars. The one in his eyebrow, the one to the side of his chin, the mess of flesh on his shoulder, and the puncture wounds on his biceps. But she'd never seen him shirtless. She'd never seen the scar on his stomach. It cut through his flesh like a bolt of lightning, from his breastbone to his trousers.

She couldn't fathom how he'd survived such a wound.

He winced as her gaze settled upon him, but he didn't offer an explanation. He merely gave the vest a shake, and she reached to take it automatically.

He turned to the guard and offered his hands to be bound.

"Wait," the Grand Prince said, and his brows dipped as his gaze shifted between Rory's face and chest. "Bring them both." He spun on his heel and stalked back to his horse, clearly knowing his orders would be carried out without question.

A grumble ran through the crowd, as if disappointed they wouldn't witness a spectacle that day, but Ella almost crumpled with relief at the Grand Prince's apparent change of heart.

"And my dog, Your Highness?" Rory called.

"Yes, fine." The Grand Prince swung up into his saddle. "Bring the dog, too."

The guards stripped Rory of his weapons—the dagger strung around his waist and one from each of his bracers—and escorted them all up the path to the palace's inner grounds. With every zig,

Ella's stomach flipped with joy at seeing Rory again, and with every zag it flopped with fear of what would happen when they reached the top. She threaded her fingers into Given's fur to steady herself.

They weren't returned to the dungeon as Ella expected. Instead, the guards escorted them into the palace itself and up a spiral staircase to a rather pleasant suite. Rich draperies framed the windows, a lush quilt covered the large bed, thick carpets softened the floor, two easy chairs sat beside an empty fireplace, and a private washroom and privy provided for their immediate needs.

But most worryingly, it had only one exit, and Ella was certain that at least one of the guards would be positioned outside. There would be no escape.

Rory—his vest firmly back in place—opened each window in turn, as if checking for alternative exits, then took up a position leaning against the fireplace, where he had an unimpeded view of the door.

Given sniffed every corner of the room before leaping onto the bed and settling down—though not relaxing. He, too, stared at the door.

Ella couldn't stand still and followed Rory's lead by peering out the windows, but she found nothing but a sheer drop. She sat briefly on the bed to stroke Given's back, but, for once, the motion didn't soothe either of them. The tension in his muscles didn't ease, and the roiling in her stomach didn't cease. She strolled over to where a row of books stood on top of a writing desk, ran her finger along the spines, and read the titles. Finally, she could take the silence no longer and turned to face Rory.

"You didn't need to do that," she said, "but thank you."

Rory's jaw twitched, but his gaze didn't leave the door. "Considering it's my fault you're in this situation, I thought it only right I intervene."

"Your fault?" She supposed that was true. If he'd turned up on time, she wouldn't be here.

"Donella, I never fully—"

"Ella."

His eyebrows arched as his gaze finally flicked to her.

"It's Ella now," she continued, her confidence failing her and her cheeks heating.

"Rory isn't my real name, either, *Ella.*" The tiniest of smiles pulled at his lips. "Your hair suits you like that."

Ella lifted her hand to tug awkwardly on the strands at the nape of her neck. "Oh. Thanks. I sold it."

"You sold your hair?"

Now she was the one who couldn't meet his gaze as she shrugged. "Apparently some old queen had red hair and all the nobles like to copy it."

Rory laughed gently. "The new queen will hate it if everyone starts copying her like that."

"I saved all the coins you gave me," she said, silently cursing herself. It was as if she no longer knew how to talk to him and had reverted to her awkward, younger self. She tried to regather the anger she'd felt on the night he hadn't shown up, but in the month since it had become as ephemeral as the red mist that sometimes coated her vision. "But I thought it would be good to have more."

"Wise," he murmured, "but coins won't do you much good stuck in here."

"But we won't be stuck for long, will we? Once you tell him why you volunteered to take my punishment, won't he let us go?"

Rory winced and gave her a look that suggested there was more to it than she knew. "I met him once. He was just a prince then, and I was just a child, but I think he recognized me."

"And that's a bad thing?"

He gave a non-committal nod.

She couldn't imagine what would bring a prince in contact with a young rogue, unless … "Were you trying to kidnap him?"

He let out a surprised, "No."

"But you really did kidnap his husband?"

"They weren't married then, but yes."

"And you mistreated him?"

Rory pushed off from the fireplace and took three steps toward her before pulling up short. "No. Yes, we fought but by mutual consent. Things got out of hand, but he wasn't the only one hurt."

Rory wasn't overly tall or broad. The Prince Consort had a clear advantage in both. That Rory had managed to inflict any damage at all said something about his fighting skill.

"Why did you kidnap him in the first place?"

Before he could answer, the door swung open and the Grand Prince and Prince Consort strode in. The guards—once again showing Ella she had no idea what to expect—remained outside when the door closed.

Up close, the Grand Prince was coldly handsome. He wore stiff gray trousers and a burgundy jacket with the collar buttoned high to keep his chin up. The Prince Consort hovered one step behind him. He was no less elegantly dressed, and his posture was no less rigid, but there was a hint of concern in his expression as his gaze lingered on Rory.

The Grand Prince also focused on Rory, as if Ella and Given were merely pieces of furniture. "You have one chance to answer my questions, and if I suspect you're being untruthful, we will finish what we started at the whipping post."

Rory straightened, the only sign he was at all affected by the Grand Prince's threat. "I understand."

"Show me that ring you wear around your neck."

Rory hesitated before drawing it out from under his vest.

The Grand Prince stepped closer to inspect it. "Finest Cavelian silver."

"So they tell me," Rory murmured as he tucked the ring away again.

"Where did you get it?"

Again Rory hesitated, as if assessing his options, deciding whether to tell the truth or lie. "It was a gift from my father."

"And how did you get that scar?"

"I have a lot of scars, Your Highness. You'll need to be more specific."

The Prince Consort winced and muttered Rory's name. His exasperated tone suggested a familiarity that Ella wouldn't have expected between a kidnapper and their victim.

Luckily, the Grand Prince didn't seem to take offense. "The one on your chest."

Rory licked his lips. "Would you like the accepted story or the truth? Everyone knows the first one, and nobody knows the second, so neither will give you the confirmation you seek."

"Tell me both."

Rory let out a long breath. "I was gored by a boar while out hunting with my cousin Abigail."

Ella bit down on a murmur of surprise. The tale sat oddly at the back of her mind, as if she'd heard it before. But she knew he'd never mentioned it. She would have remembered.

The Grand Prince nodded, as if this was the answer he'd expected. "The other version?"

"In truth," Rory continued, "she stabbed me."

Ella couldn't contain her gasp this time. "Your cousin stabbed you?" she echoed, but when the three gazes swung her way, her cheeks flared again, and to hide her concern and discomfort, she muttered, "Were you late to meet her, too?"

Ignoring her, the Grand Prince spoke to Rory in a language Ella didn't understand, but it had the same rhythm as the words spoken by the pie vendor in Caveline, so Ella assumed it was Cavelian.

"Forgive me," Rory said, "but it's impolite to speak in a language that some in the room cannot understand."

The Grand Prince spoke again, his tone more demanding, and Rory begrudgingly replied in the same language. Whatever he said made the Grand Prince's eyes pop.

"What is this about, my love?" the Prince Consort asked.

The Grand Prince turned to him. As he gazed upon his husband, his expression finally softened. "It appears you had the honor of being kidnapped by Gregory, the Dead Prince of Caveline."

CHAPTER FIVE

RORY WAS THE DEAD Prince of Caveline.

Ice bled through Ella's veins, and darkness crept around the edges of her vision. She sank to the floor like a spoonful of batter plopped onto the hotplate.

None of the men seemed to notice her slow collapse, intent as they were on eyeballing each other, but Given hopped off the bed and nosed his way under her arm. She clung tightly to his neck.

She had doomed Rory with her foolishness, her fear, and her desire to flee Leyton. And what a fool she'd been. Why had she assumed the fishwife would offer her a fair deal? Why hadn't she asked if the Dead Prince was actually dead?

Her grasp on Given tightened. He let out a small yip, but she couldn't make herself release him; his reassuring presence was the only thing keeping her despair contained.

"A prince?" the Prince Consort gasped.

"Prince Gregory," the Grand Prince confirmed. "The Queen's supposedly dead brother."

"Rory is fine," Rory muttered. He crossed his arms. "If you intend to use me against my sister, I have to warn you, I will not allow it."

Ella remembered the pretty woman whom Rory had brought to the tavern, the woman who'd saved her from Dyson Doon's wandering hands. She certainly had the confidence and poise to be a queen.

The Grand Prince took another step closer to Rory, who eased back. "Let me be very clear, I will use you in whatever way I see fit to neutralize the scourge that is Caveline's new queen."

Rory let out a strangled laugh. "I assume you haven't met Esme? She's only been in charge for a month, and she certainly isn't a scourge."

The Grand Prince's expression darkened. "I don't know where you've been since your supposed death, but for the past three years Caveline has repeatedly harried our borders. We have lost leagues of land along the river. My mother was unable to convince the ministers to stage a campaign to reclaim our territory, but I will do everything in my power to succeed where she failed. Even if that means starting a war with Caveline."

"The Queen won't want a war," Rory said. "My uncle may have attempted to move the border by stealth, but Queen Esmeralda wouldn't keep what isn't rightfully hers. If you would but talk to her—"

"I *will* talk to her," the Grand Prince said, "now I have a bargaining chip." He inclined his head. "I hope the room is to your liking, Your Highness. I will arrange another for your companion." His gaze drifted to Ella, and his expression curdled as he saw she was seated on the floor, hugging Given.

She stared back at him. She could barely comprehend the enormity of her mistake; she certainly had no capacity to deal with any assumptions he might have about her. But there was some judgment in his expression that she felt she deserved.

"She stays with me," Rory said, his voice tight.

"So be it." The Grand Prince strode to the door and yanked it open, and the guards on the other side snapped to attention.

The Prince Consort's gaze lingered on Rory before he followed his husband.

After the door closed behind them, Rory scrubbed at his face, as if he were waking from a bad dream.

"You're a prince," Ella said weakly. She felt like she was on her knees in a storm, fruitlessly piling sand into a sea wall while larger and larger waves washed her efforts away.

"I *was* a prince," he said. "Now everyone thinks I'm dead, and I'm merely the rogue you know and—" He cut the last word off, clicking his teeth together, and shot her a sideways look. "I have to apologize. I lied when I told you I was from Bretland, but my life depended on keeping my true identity a secret."

And now his life depended on her finding some way to get out of her deal. A lump formed in Ella's throat, and she couldn't push any words past it.

"And I'm truly sorry I didn't come when I said I would. I—"

She swallowed hard, but her words still came out thin and reedy. "You've already apologized for that."

He looked slightly shocked that she'd interrupted, but she couldn't bear to hear him apologizing. Not after what she'd done. He rubbed at the back of his neck. "In my defense, I was locked in a dungeon at the time."

"What did you do?"

"I had the audacity to be born closer to the throne than my cousin." He gave her a self-deprecating smile.

"Prince Gregory?"

"Just Rory, Ella."

She couldn't ask him what she really wanted to ask him, which was whether there were any other dead Cavelian princes that the fishwife could have meant, so instead, she said, "I made it to Bretland. All on my own."

Given let out a disgruntled growl.

"Yes," she murmured, nuzzling his ears. "You helped."

"When Prince Rickett is done with me, assuming I'm still in one piece, we could always try one of the other realms." Rory took a few hesitant steps across the room. "That is, if you're still amenable to the idea. Of going somewhere. With me."

Ella wanted nothing more than to tell him she would go wherever he wanted, but how could she? Once he learned the truth, he would want nothing to do with her. And if she didn't come up with a way to save his heart, he wouldn't be going anywhere at all.

Her eyes burned with unshed tears. "How did you know the Grand Prince wouldn't whip you once he recognized you?"

Rory blinked. "Oh, I didn't."

"But then—" The words caught on the lump in Ella's throat again, and the storm surged and overflowed her inadequate sea wall, sending hot tears cascading over her cheeks. He'd been willing to take a beating for her, and she hadn't even been willing to wait a single day for him.

She screwed her eyes shut in an attempt to stop the tears and covered her mouth to hold in her sobs.

"Ella?" Rory murmured.

Her eyes flew open. He'd closed the distance between them to kneel in front of her, close enough to touch, his expression horrified, his hand hovering beside her arm.

"It's my fault you're in this situation," he continued. "I'll get you out of it, and then"—his gaze dropped—"I'll leave you in peace. I swear it this time."

Ella lunged forward, keeping one arm wrapped around Given while she grasped Rory with the other, and burst into a new round of sobbing.

ELLA'S ARM WAS CLENCHED so tightly around him that Given had started to lose feeling, but he didn't move. He would sit here as long as she needed him. Rory, who was crouched on the floor beside him, eventually pried Ella's fingers from Given's fur, scooped her into his arms, and carried her to the bed. She looked like a squeezed dishrag as he laid her on the covers. Her grip tightened around his neck, and after standing bent over for a long moment, he somewhat awkwardly lay down with her and began to murmur reassurances.

And that was quite enough of that.

Given leaped up onto the bed and nosed his way in between them. Ella's arms shifted to encircle him instead of Rory, and she snuggled into his fur.

"Really?" Rory whispered, pulling back. "I may be a rogue, but I'm still a gentleman."

Given wasn't sure what to make of this rogue, this prince.

It was clear he cared for Ella, and the realization sent a spasm of bittersweet pain through Given's chest. If she had a sweetheart who was willing to sacrifice himself for her, she didn't need him. Certainly not as a human. No, it was yet more evidence that he only had worth as a wolf.

He'd felt a grudging respect for Rory last night. Someone who could talk their way out of a fight deserved at least that much. Plus, he somehow knew that Given wasn't a normal wolf. Whether Rory had been the shadow lurking in the manor garden when Given had transformed wasn't entirely clear. He'd been unable to ask.

Respect had given way to appreciation this morning when he'd offered to take Ella's punishment. That hadn't been part of their plan.

Rory had suggested rescuing Ella from the dungeon, but that would have necessitated them fleeing the city. Given still didn't know exactly why Ella had wanted to come here, but he doubted she had accomplished it. He'd managed to dissuade Rory, thanks to the young man asking if it sounded like a good plan and Given shaking his head in a resounding 'no.'

Forming an alliance had been a wise move. He was more than grateful that Rory could speak and had used his words so carefully. A voice box would have been incredibly useful when Prince Rickett had been talking. Given didn't know why the Grand Prince was under the impression that the border was under threat. No one had taken his land, and apart from people like the trappers, no one had invaded. But a sinking sensation had settled in his gut when the Grand Prince had spoken of the timeline. The trouble had started three years ago, around the same time the enchantress had cursed him.

Maybe there was a reason no one had ever noticed his disappearance or come to investigate, a reason tied up with the fact no one seemed to recognize him. If the enchantress had made everyone forget him, that might explain why Rickett didn't know who owned the land, and that lack of knowledge had led to an unfortunate assumption.

Given didn't know how to resolve that problem. It was nearly a month until his next transformation, and by then Rickett might have already done something foolish, such as start a war with Caveline.

Rory whispered reassurances until Ella cried herself to sleep. Then a look of grim determination settled on his features, and he rolled smoothly off the bed. Far less gracefully, Given eased out of Ella's grip to follow him. Rory threw open one of the windows and peered out. He'd already done this when they'd first entered the room, and Given wondered if anything would have changed in that time. He hopped up to rest his front paws on the ledge and tried to see what Rory was looking at.

"Here's the thing," Rory whispered. "There's a decent chance I could climb down there." He flicked his wrist, and a dagger sprang from his bracer into his hand. He reversed the motion and it disappeared again. Given had no idea how he'd concealed it from the guards when they'd searched him, but he was suitably impressed. "But I cannot do it carrying Ella and certainly not both of you. And I won't leave either of you behind."

He padded to the empty fireplace and reached inside to check the back, but there were no secret passageways to be found. Then, as confident as the prince he'd once been, he yanked open the door, somehow knowing it wouldn't be locked. Two guards were positioned outside. Their hands went to their weapons, but Rory made no move to attack them. He merely said, "My companion is rather overcome by today's events. Could I trouble someone to light the fire and bring some warm water?"

The guards exchanged a look. It wasn't clear whether they knew exactly who their prisoner was, but either way, he had to be someone important to be held up here instead of in the cells with the common folk.

"Someone will see to that soon," one of them finally said.

Rory nodded sharply before closing the door. His mouth settled into a thin line. "This is the nicest prison I've ever had the misfortune to occupy, but it's still a prison, and I don't think we'll be able to effect an escape."

Rory was right. This might not be a dungeon, but it was a chamber designed to house royal prisoners and had been used regularly when wars had raged between the realms and hostages had been taken and traded. But as far as anyone knew, Given wasn't a royal. He wasn't even human. He padded to the door and pawed at the handle, whining gently.

Rory, proving the worth of opposable thumbs, opened it, and the guards eyed him once again.

"Uh ..." Rory gestured to Given. "My dog wants to go out."

The guards exchanged another look.

"He's very well trained," Rory added.

Given hung his head and whined pitifully.

"Fine," the same guard said. "But if he makes a mess, you're cleaning it up."

Given slipped past them before they could change their minds. As he thumped down the steps, he heard Rory say, "I believe that's what servants are for."

The stairs led to a corridor that opened into the palace proper. He hadn't spent much time here in the last twenty years, even before he was a wolf, but it was familiar enough for him to find his way around. Servants skittered out of his way, and two High Councilors who were standing outside the council chambers in their formal robes gaped as he approached.

He let his tongue loll out and wagged his tail as he jogged past them before pausing to sniff at nothing on the ground.

One of the councilors was his cousin, Oxden. The years since Given had last seen him had taken their toll. His dark hair, swept back into a smooth ponytail, was gray at the temples, and his once-trim figure had developed a middle-aged paunch. Given felt only the faintest trace of curiosity regarding whether he was still happily married to Alyssia.

"I fear we're headed toward war," Oxden said. His words were so quiet they barely carried to Given's sensitive ears, and his expression was forcefully plain, as if he were discussing the weather.

"If the Grand Prince won't take our counsel, I'm afraid there's little we can do," the other councilor replied in the same mild tone. She was an older woman of his parents' generation, named Saxa Tarr, and she'd been a councilor for as long as Given could remember. Her hair was silvery gray and hung loose to her waist, and her robe and trousers draped gracefully to the floor. The Grand Prince could ask for no one better to guide him.

"We cannot *afford* a war," Oxden said.

Saxa's eyebrows rose. "Is that your concern? The royal coffers?"

Oxden shook his head as he rubbed at his temples. "You know it isn't. I don't want to pay for this war with our people's lives, but we'll lose far more if we cannot provide them with weapons and boots and food."

Saxa grasped his arm. "Then we must convince His Highness to make peace."

They headed inside the council chambers, and Given raced forward to catch the door before it closed, and nosed his head inside. It was a stately room with a large table in the center, and Bretland's six High Councilors stood to the side, exchanging pleasantries.

When he was certain no one was watching, Given slipped inside and settled down under the table to listen.

The Grand Prince arrived a moment later.

Rickett was a good ten years younger than Given, but he'd already lost some of his youthful vigor, as if his short time ruling the principality had drained him. Dark circles shadowed his eyes, and his mouth was turned perpetually down at the corners.

The Councilors sat while Rickett stood at the head of table. "For three years, this council has refused to take action against the encroaching scourge of Caveline. I have made the point before that we have little enough land to lose and an attack by stealth is still an attack. We had some hope that things would change when the new queen took control, but a month has passed since that bloody coup, and she hasn't withdrawn or made a diplomatic approach. We may assume that Queen Esmeralda plans to continue King Wybert's occupation of our land."

Given rubbed his paw over his eyes. He couldn't believe his cousin was being so foolish.

"Have you considered," Oxden said, "that her lack of approach has something to do with our refusal to acknowledge her coronation? She may have *assumed* our silence was due to the questions around her legitimacy to rule. I warned you we may have turned a potential ally against us—"

Rickett thumped his fist on the table. "If she wanted allies, she should have sought us out. But I know why she didn't. Nessah?"

The name wasn't familiar, but a councilor to Given's right shifted in her seat and addressed the table. "His Highness asked me to look into the records of the disputed land. There is a history of occupation going back twenty years."

Given's ears pricked up.

"It began with one estate and spread along the river, like pestilence in the water. They acquired land and fishing rights by stealth. They used the bridges to charge passage and prevent goods from passing deeper into the Seven Realms. All those stolen taxes are filling Caveline's coffers instead of our own."

A shiver ran down Given's spine, setting his fur on edge. The previous kings of Caveline hadn't done any of those things. *He* had. *He* was the reason they were verging on war. Him. His actions. *And* the curse that somehow made everyone forget he existed.

"How many years will this new Queen spend accumulating *our* coins before she decides to annex us completely?" the Grand Prince demanded.

"We cannot start a war based on an assumption," Saxa said, and Given had to fight the urge to nuzzle her legs in appreciation of her common sense.

"We may be able to avoid a war all together." Rickett's voice filled with the smugness of victory. He thought he was about to deliver a winning blow. "We finally have a weapon we can use against Caveline, but what I am about to tell you cannot go beyond these four walls."

Around Given, all the councilors stilled as they waited for the Grand Prince's pronouncement.

"The guest in the east tower is the Queen's brother."

"The Queen has a brother?" Oxden asked.

"The Dead Prince."

Silence blanketed the table before Oxden finally murmured, "Your Highness ..."

"Don't tell me I'm mistaken. He carries a ring with the family crest. He has the scar. He speaks with the Prince's rhythm. I can see the face of the boy I once met in the man he is now."

"The scar could be a coincidence," Saxa said, though her voice lacked confidence. "The speech disorder can be faked."

"Plus there is the fact he's meant to be dead," Oxden added.

"If he is the Dead Prince," another councilor to Given's left said, "how do you propose to leverage that fact?"

"I intend to threaten his life, and if that doesn't persuade the Queen to withdraw from our land, I'll stir up the rumors of her illegitimacy and offer him as an alternative to weaken her grasp on the throne."

"Do you believe that he'll be able to take it?" Oxden asked.

"Or that Caveline will be a better friend to Bretland with him in charge?" Saxa added. "After you used him as a pawn?"

"I don't care about Cavelian politics or who is in charge." Rickett's careful control cracked. "I want Caveline to retreat beyond our borders and leave us in peace."

Debate raged around the table, and Given despaired over what would happen to both Bretland and Rory.

Finally, Saxa said, "We won't achieve lasting peace by threatening war. Assuming he is the Dead Prince, who can say whether the Queen knows he is alive or would want to keep him that way? We need to attempt a diplomatic solution before we make any threats we cannot carry out."

Rickett, who had thumped down into his seat during the debate, stretched out his legs. "Thank you for your counsel. I admit we shouldn't move with too much haste. Let's reconvene tomorrow. I'll invite the Dead Prince to join us. Once I've convinced you of his identity, we can grill him on his relationship with the queen."

The councilors rose, groaning as if they'd been sitting too long, and agreed to return at the same time the next day. They all filed from the room except for Nessah, who lingered with the Grand Prince.

"What will you do now, Your Highness?"

Prince Rickett drummed his heel against the floor, and his voice came out bitter. "I've waited three years to be able to take action. I won't let these cowardly councilors hold me back any longer. I will ride into Caveline with the Dead Prince in tow and demand the Queen withdraw from our border lands."

"A wise decision, my lord."

Given slipped out the door after the councilor and the Grand Prince, and watched them stride away. He'd learned a lot, but he wasn't sure what he could do with that information. He had no idea how the Queen of Caveline would react when Rickett accused her of invading land she hadn't invaded. And he had no way to warn Rory of the Grand Prince's plans.

It seemed like he needed to break the curse not only for his own benefit, but in order to prevent a war.

When Ella awoke, she buried her puffy face in the pillow. She didn't want to face Rory. She *couldn't*. Not only had she been a fool to agree to the fishwife's deal, but she'd made a bigger fool of herself by weeping uncontrollably. She'd never been one for tears. There wasn't much point. As a child, an emotional display was more likely to irritate her father than elicit any sympathy. He didn't like her making a scene in front of the customers, and she made sure that any tears were shed in private. The horror of her mistake still filled her, like flood waters that hadn't yet started to recede, but she wouldn't let herself give in to the despair again. That wouldn't help her save Rory.

"There's water, if you'd like to wash," Rory murmured.

Ella steeled herself before giving up the pretense of sleeping and rolling over to face him. Flames licked around a small stack of wood on the hearth, warming the room. He was sprawled in a chair beside the fireplace, twisted sideways, one leg draped over the arm, a book in his lap. While she'd slept, he'd shaved and changed his usual black vest for a soft fawn-colored shirt with the sleeves rolled up. It was the first time she recalled ever seeing him in anything other than black, and she took a moment just to stare.

She couldn't believe he'd picked her up, carried her to the bed, and lain with her until she'd fallen asleep. How often had she dreamed of that exact scenario? And why had it played out so wrong?

He gave her a concerned look. "I apologize for earlier. Am I to understand that you *don't* want me to leave you in peace?"

She sighed his name and pushed herself into a sitting position. She couldn't believe he was apologizing—again—when she was the one who'd made such a fuss, when it was *her* fault he was here, when *she* had promised his heart to the fishwife.

"I ..." Her gaze drifted around the room, pointedly avoiding his. Something was missing. "Where's Given?"

"Is that his name? He went exploring, I think."

"Is he coming back? Will he be safe?" Worrying and talking about Given was much easier than the other conversation that she didn't want to have.

"I'm certain he will. On both counts. We'll all be safe as long as I do what the Grand Prince wants."

"And what is that?"

"I'm sure I'll find out eventually, but in the meantime ..." He set his book aside and straightened in his chair. "The last time we spoke in Leyton, I told you I hadn't been free to do as I pleased. I need to tell you the whole story. If you'll hear it."

Ella hesitated. If he was willing to spill his secrets, how would she be able to keep hers from him? She wished Given was here, but she also knew that if he was, he would give her a look that said she needed to tell Rory the truth.

"There's something I need to tell you, too."

Rory nodded and began.

He'd grown up as the Crown Prince of Caveline. As the woman with the pie stall had told Ella, his mother had died when he was too young to remember, and when he was fifteen, his uncle and cousin had hatched a plot to take the throne. His uncle had killed his father with poison, and Rory had gone hunting with his cousin Abigail. He hadn't, as Abigail had told everyone, been killed by a boar. She'd stabbed him and left him for dead.

"What about your sister?" Ella asked.

"Oh, Esme was safe. She was in hiding with her mother."

The surprise must've shown on Ella's face, because Rory smiled faintly.

"But that's a story for another time. As I lay dying, my father's ghost appeared and demanded I avenge him. I wasn't keen to oblige. He kept haranguing me, and I eventually wished he would go away." His eyes filled with regret and shame. "That was when Godmother appeared. She promised to banish my father's ghost after I'd complete ten simple tasks. It took me five years."

A weight dropped in Ella's stomach. His story sounded so familiar. "Godmother?"

"The fairy godmother. She ..." He hesitated then gave a helpless shrug. "She's the most powerful being in the Seven Realms. She wields more magic than everyone else combined, possesses more knowledge than a library, and manipulates people like we're her playthings. She grants wishes for a price, casts curses for fun, and gives gifts with a sting in the tail. And, for all the time you've known me, I've been working for her, kidnapping people and holding them prisoner until they get rescued by a passing royal."

Ella shivered. She felt as if she'd gone for a quick dip in the ocean, only to have swum directly into the open mouth of a giant shark. "And the Prince Consort was one of your tasks?"

Rory nodded. "He was."

"What about your companion? The older rogue?"

"Bernard. He worked for her, too."

Dread made her words come out wispy. "What does she look like?"

"Indeterminate age. Tall. Long, dark hair. Coldly beautiful. But sometimes she's short and plump with wings. Other times she's old."

Ella closed her eyes, struggling to control a second wave of despair as the shark's jaws closed.

The mattress shifted as Rory sat down on the foot of the bed. "What did you wish for, Ella?"

"You didn't come," she groaned. "My father sold the tavern to Dyson Doon. He sold *me*. I killed him. I had to leave."

"Wait. Who did you kill?" Rory asked, his voice sharp.

Her eyes flew open. "My father. He found my stash of coins. We fought. I ... I murdered him."

"Your father isn't dead."

Ella wouldn't have been more shocked if Rory had taken her face in his hands and kissed her. "What?"

"I saw him a few days after the night we were meant to meet. He was wounded, yes, but recovering. And definitely not dead."

"But, I thought ..."

"This is what she does," Rory said gently. "She finds you when you're vulnerable and takes advantage of you. I didn't think my ten tasks would take five years. And even now, I don't think she wants to let me go. This may sound conceited, but I believe she targeted you because of me."

"But she's lived in my village for years. I took her a meal every few days. She was kind if a little befuddled."

Rory gave his head a shake. "It was an act. She manipulated you."

The fishwife's predictions rang in Ella's mind. "She knew you wouldn't come."

"Of course she did. She orchestrated my stay in the dungeon." He paused before repeating his question, "What did you wish for, Ella?"

The words fell through her numb lips. "I wished I knew how to use your dagger, so I could protect myself, so I wouldn't have to worry about men like Dyson Doon ever again."

"And did she grant it already?"

Ella managed to nod.

Rory closed his eyes briefly. "And what did she demand in return?"

Ella screwed her eyes shut. An emptiness filled her chest and left no room for her to take a breath. She knew she had to tell him, but she couldn't do it. She couldn't admit his life was forfeit.

The mattress shifted again as he moved closer. "Forgive me. I certainly kept my secrets long enough; you're entitled to keep yours."

She kept her eyes closed, struggling to control her breathing, fighting to build up enough courage to force the words out. *I promised her your heart.*

"My lady?" Rory said, and the ridiculousness of being addressed in such a way made her open her eyes and look at him. "Would you care to give me a demonstration?"

"A demonstration?"

His gaze was tender, his brow ruched with concern. "I've heard you've recently acquired talent with a blade, and I would feel a lot more confident in our situation if I was assured you could defend yourself."

"Now?"

"Unless you'd rather talk."

"No," she said quickly. "I'd give you a demonstration, but I don't have—"

Rory flicked his wrists and a dagger appeared in each of his hands. He offered them to her, hilts first.

"I thought the guards took your weapons," she said as she grasped the familiar handles. Both were identical to the first one he'd given her.

"They did. I have more."

"How many more?"

"As many as I need." He repeated the flicking motion to show her that he had at least two more, before tucking them away again. "The bracers are magic."

Ella laid her daggers on the bed beside her and took hold of his hand to poke at his bracer, peering inside the cleverly designed pocket where the dagger should be. It was empty. "Magic," she murmured. Then, realizing she was still holding his hand, she dropped it and glanced around. "What should I aim at?" The room was beautifully appointed, and she didn't think the Grand Prince would approve of her leaving dagger holes in his furniture.

Rory crossed the room to where a tray of food had been laid on the small dining table. He picked up a plump orange fruit that Ella didn't recognize and set it on the mantelpiece. "Can you hit that?"

Ella stared doubtfully at the fruit as she recalled her conversation with the old fishwife. She wasn't sure she would be able to use her skills when she wasn't feeling particularly indignant, but she dutifully climbed off the bed and positioned herself some way from the fireplace. Taking aim, she threw the dagger with her left hand, but it spun wildly off course, hit the wall, and clattered to the floor.

Rory's eyebrows rose. "I believe you may be entitled to a refund."

Though his tone was gently teasing, heat flooded Ella's cheeks. "She tricked me. It doesn't always work."

Rory crossed his arms as he contemplated her words. "Godmother does enjoy tricks, but she wouldn't give you a power then take it away, not if she wants you to uphold your end of the bargain. So there's probably a caveat, perhaps something that triggers it. Does your life have to be in mortal danger, for instance?"

Ella was startled by how quickly he'd guessed the truth. "She said righteous indignation fueled my ability."

Rory scratched absently at his jaw. "I suppose a persimmon doesn't stir those feelings?"

"Persimmon?" she asked, echoing the unfamiliar word.

He pointed to the fruit, a slight frown on his face. "I have no word for them in Lynnbrovian."

"I suppose," she said somewhat self-consciously, "it only worked when I was fighting some*one*, not some*thing*."

"Well, surely I can help with that." Rory shifted into a fighting stance. "You must feel somewhat aggrieved that I failed to make our meeting."

Ella shook her head, though that was exactly how she *had* felt.

"Not even a little?" he pressed. "You have every right to be vexed."

"Maybe a little," Ella said, feeling her cheeks heat, "but you were locked in a dungeon. I should've known you'd have a good reason. You always came eventually."

Rory winced. "That's the thing. You were right not to wait for me. I wasn't going to come."

A spark of indignation flared in Ella's chest. "What?"

Rory's posture sagged, and he retreated three steps to collapse into one of the easy chairs. "When I was in the dungeon, God-mother came to me. She offered to help me escape in exchange for ten more tasks." He swiped a hand across his face. "I agreed. I couldn't bear telling you I had to renege on my offer, so I made the decision *not* to come." He let out a small, self-deprecating laugh. "Despite everything, I'm still a coward."

Rage spread through Ella's body, and she rejoiced when red bled across her vision. Her grip tightened on her remaining dagger, but the person she wanted to stab wasn't here. Rory might have triggered her feelings, but he wasn't their target.

"Then why are you here?" she asked, her voice as sharp as her blade.

Rory blinked. "I beg your pardon?"

"You're such a coward that you weren't going to come, but you obviously did come. So what changed?"

He shifted awkwardly. "Esme outwitted Godmother to free me from my bargain, and when she realized she'd lost, Godmother threatened you. I was worried. And not without cause, it turns out."

He'd come to save her.

Anger burned hot under Ella's skin. There was none of the joy she'd felt toying with the bullies. The fishwife—Godmother—fueled pure rage. Not only had she kept Rory in servitude for five years, she'd tried to trap him again, and when that had failed, she'd set Ella up to hurt him.

How dare she. How. Dare. She.

Ella fired the other dagger at the mantelpiece and it *thunked* squarely into the fruit, which rolled off the mantelpiece and hit the floor with a splat.

Rory's jaw dropped. "That is some talent with a blade."

Ella strode across the room to plant herself in front of him. New tears pricked at her eyes for an entirely different reason. "You are *not* a coward," she growled, and his eyebrows rose in surprise. "The fact you lived under that witch's power for five years and still came out as kind and gentle as you are points to a strength you don't even realize you possess. You followed me across the Seven Realms despite knowing it could put you in Godmother's path, you offered to take a lashing for me, and you stood up to the Grand Prince while locked in his fancy prison. If that's not bravery, I don't know what is."

Rory frowned. "But—"

If not for the fishwife's enchantment, Ella would never have dared be so bold, but she cut off his protest by clasping his face in her hands and pressing her lips to his.

When she pulled back, his eyes were wide. He swallowed hard and said, "You cannot imagine how often I wanted to take you away from that tavern."

"I think I can." She stroked her thumb over his jaw, wanting to make up for the five years she'd spent carefully *not* touching him before her indignation wore off and she became too shy. "When I next see Godmother, I'm going to have words with her. But for now, I just have one thing to say, and I want you to *really* listen."

He nodded.

"I wasn't some princess, locked in a tower. And you weren't some passing royal. It wasn't your job to rescue me."

THEY SPENT THE REST of the morning sparring. Maybe they should have used the time more intimately, but, as bold as Ella felt, her secret built a barricade between them that she couldn't easily breach.

Rory was as patient and careful a teacher as ever. There wasn't time for more than an introduction to the basics of hand-to-hand combat, but he showed her moves she could use to give herself distance from an opponent, and with some distance, she could hit any target he gave her. She even surprised herself by achieving things that would have been impossible without magic, such as curving a dagger through the air to hit a target behind him. When they were close, Ella found her concentration wavering, and she had to focus on Godmother's cruelty to stop the red mist dissolving into clouds shaped like lovehearts. Soon enough, with Rory holding her wrists, she could drop a dagger, bounce the handle off her knee or foot, and deflect it into a target of her choosing.

By the time a maid arrived with their lunch, the daggers were safely concealed back in Rory's bracers, and they were both seated in the easy chairs, reading.

The maid wasn't alone.

Given loped in behind her, and Ella gasped in relief and dropped to the floor to hug him and smooch his cheeks.

And behind *him*, came the Prince Consort.

Rory lurched out of his chair then everyone froze and stayed silent until the maid had laid out their lunch and left, closing the door behind her.

"Rory," the Prince Consort said.

"Is there something you need, Your Highness?"

The Prince smiled tightly. "I apologize for the intrusion, but I hoped we could talk."

Ella wasn't so naive that she couldn't read the tension in Rory's posture. Whatever else had happened during the kidnapping, it seemed that Rory had been enamored with the Prince Consort. Suddenly his comment that the Prince hadn't been the only one hurt had a deeper meaning. She bristled on his behalf, and the faintest pink tinged her vision.

"I would give you some privacy," she said, her voice waspish, "but I don't think the guards will let me pop outside."

The Prince's smile tightened further. "I don't believe we've been introduced. I'm Prince Paxton, but you can call me Your Highness."

"Really? Well, you can call me—"

"Ella," Rory blurted out, giving her a stern look, as if he knew she'd been about to say something inappropriate, before turning back to the Prince. "What do you need, my lord?"

"You don't have to serve me any more, Rory."

"Then you're here for a rematch?"

The Prince's gaze flicked briefly to Ella before he sighed. "You were a prince all this time?"

"A dead one," Rory said, "but yes."

"Why didn't you tell me?"

"If I recall, we didn't discuss our pasts."

"Whose fault was that?"

Rory's jaw twitched. "I see you're as vexing as ever, my lord."

"You don't need to 'my lord' me. You were content to call me Paxton once."

"That's what a friend would call you, my lord." A frosty layer of civility coated Rory's words.

"And we're not friends?" When Rory didn't reply, the Prince Consort continued, "What have you been doing these past three years?"

"Same as I was doing when we met."

"Kidnapping people?"

"Teaching pompous fools not to eat poison berries."

Paxton snorted. "I might take you up on that offer of another fight. I believe I won the last time."

"I never yielded." They glared at each other for a moment longer before Rory huffed out a breath and flopped back into his chair, as if their verbal sparring had already drained his energy and he had none left for a physical fight. His voice softened. "Tell me, at least, that you're happy. Your prince seems rather ... highly strung."

The Prince retrieved a chair from the small dining table and positioned himself in front of them, his gaze taking them both in. "I assume *you* can keep a secret, but what about your ... Ella?"

"We're both rather skilled in that regard," Rory muttered.

The Prince shot a worried glance toward the door and lowered his voice. "The loss of the border lands has always troubled His Highness, but since he became ruler, reclaiming them has become his obsession. He's changed. I fear for him and all of Bretland."

Rory sat up straighter, his expression marred by concern. "Don't tell me he truly wants war?"

"Could you act as a go-between? Curry Queen Esmeralda's favor?" Paxton leaned forward, his hands reaching absently in Rory's direction.

"Of course I'll speak to Esme." Rory waved vaguely at the door. "But diplomacy was never my strong suit."

A smirk pulled at Paxton's lips. "I remember."

Something very close to indignation pounced on Ella's shoulders. If Paxton had been the one to hurt Rory, how dare he come here asking for favors and acting so familiar? She took a deep breath and let it out slowly. Then another. The Prince wasn't someone she could attack.

As if sensing her distress, Given stood up, gave himself a shake, and sat down again in front of the Prince, eying him like a juicy steak.

Paxton watched him warily as he spoke. "What's up with your dog?"

"He's not mine," Rory said. "He and I only came to a fairly tentative truce last night in order to help Ella. And he's not a dog. And I believe he finds you as vexing as I do, my lord."

"What do you mean he's not a dog?" Ella asked, glad of the distraction.

Given turned his head to give her a flat look.

"He's a demi-wolf," Rory said, which didn't explain anything. "Surely you knew?"

"Of course," Ella murmured. It had been clear from the start that Given wasn't an ordinary dog, but that didn't mean she knew what he actually was. "What's a demi-wolf?"

"He's half—"

Given let out a loud ro-ro-ro that drowned out what Rory was trying to say.

"Half what?" Ella pressed.

Rory shot Given a look, winced, and said, "Half wolf?" in a way that sounded like a question.

Half wolf and half dog wouldn't really explain Given's size or his intelligence, but it seemed like she and Rory weren't the only ones with secrets they wanted to keep.

"I wish—" Rory clamped his free hand over his mouth then carefully said, "I regret my father is no longer here to advise me. If I could warn Esme, I'm certain she would relinquish any claim on the disputed land. I doubt she's even aware of the situation."

"She wouldn't fear it would make her appear weak?" Paxton asked. "After all, she's only held the crown for a month."

"She's not like that," Ella said. Although she didn't truly know this, she couldn't imagine the nice young woman from the tavern being a tyrant.

"Ella's right, she's not. And I'll do my best to help both our realms."

"Thank you." The Prince Consort pushed to his feet. "As enchanting as this reunion has been, I must be on my way before my husband suspects you've murdered me and returns in a fury."

He reached the door before Rory chased after him. "Pax, wait."

Paxton turned around, his fingers grazing the door handle.

"Is there anything else I can do to help remedy *your* situation?"

Paxton reached out, as if to lay his hand on Rory's shoulder, but Given let out a low growl, and the Prince's hand stopped short. "If you can help resolve this mess with the border lands, I think it will put His Highness in a much better frame of mind."

When the door closed behind the Prince, Rory leaned against it, and his gaze took a long time to find Ella.

"Should I be jealous?" she asked, making her voice light, as if his answer mattered not a jot.

"Paxton was waiting for a prince, but that prince wasn't me." Rory wandered back across the room. "It stung then, and I admit that seeing him stings a little now ..." He sat down beside her, took her hand, and gently stroked her fingers. "But I think he made the right decision."

He started to drift in toward her, and Ella's heart beat faster with anticipation of another kiss, but also apprehension of how he would feel when he found out the truth. But before he got too close, Given made another low growl, and Rory's head snapped sideways.

"Right," he said, his expression slightly abashed as his gaze swung back to her, "we'll continue this later, but for now, shall we have some lunch?"

Chapter
Six

As nicely appointed as the noble prison quarters were, Ella had never been so bored. Never, in all her life, had she been left with so much time to *sit*.

If she'd been a noble lady who spent her time embroidering handkerchiefs, she would have been well-served. If she'd been as full of nervous energy as Rory, she could have joined him as he ran through a series of calisthenics. If she hadn't already partaken of a tear-stained nap, she could have curled up with Given, who lay on the foot of the bed, dozing the afternoon away, his ears twitching whenever Ella and Rory came too close to each other.

But she was a waitress, used to rushing around after customers. The only time she'd ever sat still was when Rory had been teaching her to read, so she returned to the book she'd chosen earlier—a collection of poetry—and worked her way through the curious, curly sentences.

Over a lavish dinner they shared their stories. Rory told her of how he'd met his long-lost sister Esme, how she'd defeated their cousin Abigail to become queen, and how she'd freed him from his deal with the fairy godmother. In return, Ella told him of how she'd fled Leyton on the back of a dragon and saved Given from the dogfighter.

"You rode Tomarriss?" he asked, his face blanching. When she nodded, he shook his head and rubbed absently at his shoulder. "I tried that once. It didn't end well."

It was when the sun sank and darkness encroached on the room that Ella's feet really started to itch. She was used to spending her entire day inside the tavern, but she'd always been free to roam at night. The only thing she could do was fling a window open, lean out, and breathe deeply as the sun painted the sky orange then purple, and lights started to appear in windows across the city.

Eventually, when the air had cooled so much that goosebumps broke out on her skin and her cheeks started to sting, she turned to face the next, immediate problem.

There was a chest at the end of the bed which contained a selection of clothing in various sizes. It was where Rory had found his fawn shirt, and where Ella looked to find something suitable for sleeping in. She came up with a nightshirt and pair of leggings that would fit well enough, and retired to the washroom to freshen up. The basin of water had long gone cold, but she rubbed a damp cloth over herself anyway, ran wet fingers through her hair, and changed her clothes.

When she came back out, Given was curled up in front of the fire, but Rory was sitting cross-legged on the floor with his back against the door.

Ella hesitated. She was almost overcome with awkwardness, worried about what he would think, as she asked, "Do you plan to sleep there?"

"Yes."

"But there are guards outside the door."

He gave her a half smile. "The guards are there to keep us in. I'm here to keep everyone else out."

"Are you expecting an attack?"

"This used to be easier," he said. "My father didn't need sleep as a ghost, and he would alert me to any danger. I haven't slept as soundly since he left."

Given let out a low whine and padded across the room to lay his chin on Rory's knee. Rory hesitated, then stroked him between the ears.

Ella chewed on her lip then said, "A piece of furniture could perform that task."

Given let out something that sounded a lot like a snigger, scrambled back to his feet, and ran over to stand beside one of the heavy easy chairs before looking back at Rory expectantly.

"I can see I'm outnumbered."

Once the chair was in place, Rory glanced at the bed before taking a step toward the fireplace. He was either aiming for the other chair or the carpet, neither of which would be very comfortable.

Ella settled herself in the bed and patted the covers. "Come on. There's plenty of room."

Given yipped and bounded up onto the foot of the bed.

She let her gaze slide to Rory. "You too."

He stood undecided for a moment, eying Given, who didn't make as much as a single growl. "This is beyond the realm of my experience."

"Mine, too."

Rory hesitated a moment longer before circling to the far side of the bed. He left his shirt on but stripped down to his undershorts, and lay down an arm's reach away.

Given ratted around before flopping full-length between them.

"He's very protective of your propriety," Rory said, amusement pulling at his lips.

Ella shuffled forward to wrap her arm over Given, laying her hand on the covers as an offering. "Or yours."

Pink tinged Rory's cheeks, but he slipped his hand into hers.

"I know this isn't an ideal situation," he said. "But I will protect you, I swear."

Ella squeezed his hand. "That's not your responsibility."

As his eyes slid shut, Ella glanced away. She needed to keep her feelings in check. He wouldn't look at her with such tenderness if he knew the truth.

She didn't know how, but tomorrow she would start searching for a way to save him.

ELLA SLEPT POORLY, PLAGUED by bad dreams. Dreams where they were left to rot in the prison. Dreams where the old fishwife plucked Rory's heart from his chest while he stared at Ella and forlornly asked why. Dreams where she was chasing Given through the maze-like rooms of the palace, but only ever got close enough to see his tail disappear around the next corner.

She woke in the morning, relieved to find they hadn't been disturbed during the night, but even more relieved to have escaped her dreams. Given still lay in the middle of the bed, sprawled on his back, snoring heartily, paws twitching as if he were dreaming of running. She peered over his furry belly and found Rory staring back at her. He smiled softly, and she forced herself to return it, though a heavy ache filled her chest.

Rory had barely moved the easy chair away from the door and back to its spot beside the fireplace when two servants arrived to stoke the fire, provide warm water, and supply breakfast.

Ella took great pleasure in freshening up, but she wasn't yet ready to swap her day clothes for those of a stranger.

Breakfast consisted of soup that was thin but tasty, steamed fish, and boiled eggs. Given got a freshly gutted rabbit. They were still eating when the Grand Prince burst in, flanked by two guards.

Rory rose from his seat and moved to the center of the room. Though it might have been an act of respect, Ella suspected it was to put himself in a better defensive position if it came to a fight, which she hoped it wouldn't, because the guards were both armed and armored. "Your Highness."

The Grand Prince inclined his head. "I hate to interrupt your meal," he said, in a way that made it clear the opposite was true, "but we're to leave immediately."

"Leave for where?"

"Alderness. We're going to pay Caveline's new queen a visit."

Ella knew that the Grand Prince was giving a command. They had no choice but to obey.

Rory glanced at her. "Are you ready, my lady?"

"The girl stays."

Rory's head whipped around. "I will not leave her."

The guards shifted, their hands going to the swords at their waists as if the movement had been choreographed in advance.

"Rory ..." Ella's voice caught, and nobody heard her.

"Let me make this very clear," the Grand Prince said. "You can leave the girl here in this comfortable room and walk out the door under your own power, or I can move the girl back to the dungeon and drag you out of here in chains."

Rory drew himself up tall, and his voice took on a tone of command that Ella had never heard from him. "You will not hurt her."

"Rory ..." Ella tried again, louder.

"That is entirely up to you."

Rory's jaw twitched. "She's not important. Let her go and I'll come willingly."

The Grand Prince's eyes narrowed. "Perhaps, during your absence, you forgot how this works. Or did you never learn? You have no power to negotiate. This girl may mean nothing to me, but I believe she means something to you. And I believe you will be much more cooperative if she remains our guest."

The twitch in Rory's jaw turned into a clench so tight that Ella feared for his teeth. And worse, she feared he would reach his limit, whip out a dagger, and attack the Grand Prince.

"Rory ..."

He still didn't hear her, or chose not to listen.

"If anyone lays a hand on her," he said, forcing the words out, "there will be no threat great enough to prevent me from—"

"Rory!" Ella shoved up from her chair as she stoked a tiny flicker of indignation in her stomach. It wasn't difficult. Having two men debating her worth and deciding her fate while completely ignoring her was suitably infuriating. She snatched her butter knife from where it was resting on her plate of fish and fired it at the floor between Rory's feet, where it hit with a clatter then bounced away harmlessly. "Stop!"

He finally looked at her.

So did Prince Rickett.

And his guards.

She smothered her anger before it grew out of control, and held up her hands to show she wasn't a threat. "He'll go with you," she said. "Just let us say goodbye. Please, Your Highness."

The Grand Prince gave her another distasteful look but nodded.

Ella crossed the room to stand before Rory and took his hands in hers. "I appreciate what you're trying to do, but you don't need to protect me any more than you needed to rescue me from the tavern." And he certainly didn't need to start a battle of wills that he would surely lose. "I'm sorry if I ever made you feel like it was up to you."

He started to speak, but she rushed on before he could.

"You have to go." She squeezed his hands. "And I'm quite capable of biding my time in this splendid chamber until you return."

His brows dipped. "I may not *have* to protect you, but I want to."

His words were what she'd always wanted to hear, but now they brought a pang of guilt. "I want to protect you too, so go."

Some of the tension eased out of his posture, and he let out a self-deprecating laugh. "I guess I am a self-absorbed prince with a hero complex after all."

She reached up to cup his jaw and farewelled him with a kiss. She hated to let him go, not knowing when she would see him again, but knowing she would need every moment he was gone to figure out how to save him.

"Here, take this." Rory eased back, unbuckled the bracer from his left wrist, and strapped it around hers. It was comfortably tight and warm from the contact with his skin. He gave her a meaningful look. "Remember, if anybody gives you any trouble, keep your distance."

His words were carefully neutral, but she understood his meaning. If she had to get in a fight, it was better to avoid close combat, and instead use her daggers as projectiles. And with Rory's magical bracer, she would have as many as she needed.

Given sat at Ella's side while she finished eating. The room felt too quiet, too empty, without Rory. Ella looked at Rory's abandoned breakfast then set his plate of fish on the floor. Not wanting to waste it, Given scarfed it down, but the food sat heavily in his stomach.

He was worried for Rory. He'd known the young man for less than two days, but he liked him, and he didn't entirely trust that Rickett was in his right mind.

He also worried for Ella. No one would enjoy being confined to this room for an indefinite amount of time. Even Given could feel the weight of the four walls after spending years roaming free. Add in the fear she was sure to feel for Rory, and it would feel like the prison it truly was.

After a servant had come to remove the tray, Ella wandered over to the easy chairs and picked up a book. She flicked through the pages and set it down again. Then she wandered to one of the windows, threw it open, and gazed out over the city. Then she turned and glanced forlornly around the room.

"What do I do now?"

Given padded over to her, bunted her hand, and pawed at the bracer on her wrist.

"I suppose so," she said, with so little enthusiasm it was as if he had suggested she clean the privy.

She spent the next hour practicing with the bracer, learning how to flick her wrist the way Rory did to eject a dagger, learning how to catch it, learning how to slot it away again. Then she set a pillow on the mantelpiece and fired dagger after dagger into it.

"Where do they all come from?" she asked, fascination in her voice and fervor finally in her eyes. "And where do they go?"

She switched the bracer to her right wrist and repeated her practice until she was equally good with both hands.

At midmorning, Given scratched at the door. Ella knocked before carefully opening it, her free hand held before her to show the guards she meant no harm. They let Given pass without a fuss.

He made his way back past the council chamber, and his curiosity was piqued when he saw Oxden head into the room. Given snuck in after him, wondering why a meeting would go ahead when Prince Rickett had already left. He hid himself under the table again as the other councilors trickled in. They chatted idly until Nessah, who was the last, arrived.

She settled herself into the same seat as the day before. "The Grand Prince won't be joining us."

Oxden snorted. "Is he sulking, because he didn't get his way?"

"No. He's taken the Dead Prince and ridden for Alderness."

"What? We must send a messenger after him, call him back."

"Do you think he would return on your command?" Nessah asked coolly.

"If he didn't listen to our counsel before," Saxa said, "he certainly won't listen now."

"I presume you knew of his plan," Oxden snapped.

"Of course I did," Nessah shot back. "I'm the only one he still confides in."

"Not the only one," Saxa said. "Summon the Prince Consort. We'll find out what he knows of this situation."

When Prince Paxton arrived, he admitted he knew of the Grand Prince's desire to take Rory north to confront the Queen of Caveline, but he'd been unaware of the council's opposition to the plan.

"Prince Gregory doesn't want a war any more than we do," he assured them. "He could be a great ally."

"How much of an ally can he be if everyone thinks he's dead?" Nessah asked.

"Aren't we talking about the same rogue who kidnapped you?" Oxden said at the same time.

"That may be to our advantage. Rory—Prince Gregory—spent five years in hiding from his own family. He's about as far removed from King Wybert as it's possible to get. If he says the queen is a different kind of ruler, I would take him at his word. He can approach her as her brother and as an outsider. This doesn't have to be a diplomatic nightmare."

"Assuming the Grand Prince doesn't storm into her castle carrying the Dead Prince's head on a pike."

"Yes," Prince Paxton said tightly. "Assuming that."

It was clear to Given that Paxton cared for Rory. He crawled forward to where the Prince was seated at the foot of the long table, carefully caught the Prince's trousers in his teeth, and tugged. The Prince's leg jerked then stilled.

The debate raged on, but in the end, the High Council was helpless. The Grand Prince had already left, and they couldn't control how he approached the Queen of Caveline. All they could do was prepare for the worst-case scenario: war.

When the councilors left the room, Paxton lingered behind. He closed the door, dropped to his knees, and peered under the table.

"Well," he said with a shrewd smile. "I guess this means Rory was right and you're not merely a dog."

Given scrambled out from under the table, headed for the door, and looked back at the Prince.

"Am I to follow you then?"

Given let out a small yip as he pawed at the handle.

"Well, certainly. Lead the way."

The Prince's personal guard, a short, stocky woman, was waiting patiently outside the door. Her eyebrows rose when she saw Given, and there was amusement in her voice as she said, "I thought you might've fallen asleep, Your Highness, but were you merely distracted by your new friend?"

"He requested I follow him."

She blinked. "He did what?"

Together, the three of them headed back through the palace to the east tower, and upon reaching the stairs met a scullery maid bringing lunch for the prisoners. Paxton relieved the wide-eyed girl of her tray and carried it the remainder of the way himself.

The guard on the left reached for the door handle, and Paxton stopped her with a pointed cough.

"It's polite to knock."

The guard's mouth twisted, as if showing common courtesy was too much effort. "Of course, Your Highness."

She rapped on the door like she was attempting to break it down, and there was a pause before Ella called from inside, "Um, yes, hello?"

Paxton nodded, the guard pushed the door open, and Given led the Prince inside while his personal guard remained with the others.

"Oh, Your Highness, sir." Ella had been sitting in one of the easy chairs, reading, but she rose and bobbed an awkward curtsy. "Rory's not here."

Given padded over to her, and she threaded her fingers through his fur.

Paxton shut the door behind him with his foot and set the tray of food on the table before saying, "So I heard."

"Oh, you're here for me, then." She glanced around, as if looking for an escape route, but none had magically appeared.

"Not like that," the Prince said. "Your demi-wolf brought me."

Not like that. It took a moment for Given to realize what the Prince meant. The last time he'd been here, their conversation had been full of barbs, and Ella probably thought the Prince was here to exact some sort of revenge. She was, after all, at the mercy of anyone who entered the room.

Before her fear made her whip out a dagger and threaten the Prince, Given jogged over to him, wagged his tail, and let out two happy barks.

Ella let out a steadying breath. "Is there something I can do for you, Your Highness?"

"Would you mind if I joined you for lunch? I wouldn't impose, but I believe your demi-wolf invited me for a reason."

"Then I suppose I shouldn't send you away." She gestured vaguely at the table, inviting the Prince to sit.

Paxton pulled a chair out for Ella before seating himself. Then he set a bowl of red meat on the floor, which Given wolfed down gratefully.

Ella perched on the edge of her chair, her voice still wary. "Did Given tell you why he wanted you to come?"

The Prince let out a faint snort. "I was hoping you could enlighten me."

"Sadly, he keeps his own counsel."

Given grumbled under his breath and temporarily abandoned his lunch to nose at the bracer on Ella's arm.

"Something about Rory's bracer?"

"Or something about Rory in general?" the Prince mused.

Given yipped in the affirmative. Finally, someone was thinking.

Still, they sat in silence, as if unsure where to start. Ella took her napkin from the tray, laid it on her lap, but didn't eat.

"Were you really friends?" she finally asked, fidgeting with the hem of her napkin.

"I'd like to think so," Paxton said softly.

"He thinks—"

"I can imagine what he thinks. Things ended rather abruptly; I didn't get a chance to explain, and we haven't seen each other since. I imagine he doesn't think very highly of me any longer."

"You do still care for him, though?" Ella's voice trembled, which Given hoped was due to nerves and not a jealousy-fueled rage.

"Of course. Regardless of the circumstances, yesterday was an unexpected gift."

Ella let out a low moan and pressed her napkin to her face like a handkerchief.

Given laid his muzzle on her lap.

"Miss Ella?" the Prince murmured. "My lady, I didn't mean to upset you. If you'd rather—"

"I'm not a lady," she groaned. "I'm a stupid fool of a girl. I promised his heart to the fishwife."

The Prince frowned. "I don't think I heard you correctly. Or did you perhaps misspeak?"

Paxton may have doubted his hearing, but Given's was excellent, and his heart shriveled in sympathy. What had Ella done?

Ella dropped her hands. Unshed tears pooled in her eyes, and Given hoped she wasn't about to succumb once again to the sorrow that had plagued her earlier.

"The old fishwife in my village was a witch, the fairy godmother. We made a bargain. She gave me skills with a blade in exchange for bringing her the Dead Prince of Caveline's heart. Only, I didn't know the Dead Prince was still alive. I didn't know it was Rory. And now—" Her voice broke, and her face flared red, and it took her a long moment to get her emotions under control to be able to speak. "I don't know what to do. She won't let me out of our deal without paying a higher price. But how can I hold up my end of the bargain? How can I give her his heart without killing him? And how can I figure it out when I'm stuck in here?"

The Prince stared at her, his mouth hanging open.

Given watched him silently, unable to add to the conversation. When he'd brought the Prince up here, he'd hoped he could offer Ella some reprieve from the solitude and maybe share stories of the one person they had in common. He'd had no idea what Ella would dump on him. It would be a true test of his character.

"I'm sorry," Ella said. "I shouldn't have—"

"I poisoned him," the Prince croaked.

"What?" Ella wiped at her cheeks, but as far as Given could see, no tears had fallen.

"'Prince Consort' is an honorary title. I wasn't born a prince. I was born the third son of a baron who'd frittered away his fortune. My sister's hand had been offered in marriage to some pompous prince twice her age—"

Given's head whipped around. That story sounded horrifyingly familiar.

"—because my parents thought it was the only way out of our financial situation. I wished I could marry a prince in her place. The fairy godmother appeared and offered to grant my wish in exchange for one small task. I had to poison a rogue." He threw his hands up. "I didn't even know any rogues. I thought sacrificing a stranger to save poor Juliana was worth it. I didn't think I'd fall for the impertinent little ruffian when I finally met him."

Juliana! Given studied the Prince. Could he really be one of the baron's sons that Given had met at that wedding all those years ago? Nausea twisted his stomach. His proposal had been accepted willingly by the baron and baroness, but he'd never asked Juliana directly. Had she been so horrified about facing a future as his wife that her brother had made a deal with the fairy godmother to get out of it? And had that led directly to the beautiful enchantress—the fairy godmother in one of her guises—turning up on his doorstep asking for aid?

A shiver shook his whole body.

And if he'd only taken up her offer instead of insisting on having Juliana as his bride, would he have avoided this accursed fate?

"You fell for him?" Ella asked.

Paxton sighed. "He has a certain charm that grows on you over time, don't you agree?"

Ella twisted her napkin like she was wringing the neck of a swamp hen. "Then why did you poison him?"

"I had to." The Prince's face fell. "To save Juliana, I had to sacrifice Rory. The fairy godmother was *very* clear about that. And although it hasn't been the happily-ever-after I'd hoped for, I do love my husband. And if I were faced with the decision a second time, I would make the same choice."

"You didn't kill him, though." Ella's voice was hollow, and Given returned his head to her lap, so she could stroke his fur instead of murdering her napkin.

"No, I didn't." The Prince glanced down at Given. "I think this is why your demi-wolf wanted me to come. I don't want Rory to die any more than you do. Together, we can come up with a solution."

Given didn't feel right taking credit for that, but he had no way to explain that the Prince was wrong.

"After all," Paxton continued, "Rory offered to aid my love. It's only fair I do the same for his."

"Thank you, Your Highness."

"You're welcome to call me Paxton. In private, at least."

Ella shook her head. "I'm not sure I'll still be his love when he finds out what I've done. If he still resents you for a non-fatal poisoning, he certainly won't forgive me. But I have to save him, and the only help I've gotten so far is from the fishwife, who only makes things worse."

The Prince gave her a confident smile, and Given felt a wave of hope and gratitude. "Then we need to turn to someone else for help."

'PRINCE CONSORT' MAY HAVE been an honorary title, but it came with some perks. When Paxton dragged the door open and told the guards, "I will be taking Miss Ella to my estate for the duration of the Grand Prince's absence," they didn't laugh, lock the door, and throw away the key. They simply nodded, murmured, "Yes, Your Highness," and escorted the party down the stairs. He swept through the palace, issuing orders, and Ella trailed in his wake.

Within an hour, they were on their way.

They were a smaller party than Ella expected. Only two guards on horseback accompanied them, while she and Paxton rode in an elegant carriage driven by a coachman who offered Ella his hand as she climbed in. She'd never ridden in a carriage before, nor anything resembling one. She found the way it shook and rattled beneath her rather worrisome, but Paxton didn't seem at all perturbed, so she assumed it was normal.

She would have felt more reassured had Given been sitting at her feet, but he relished the chance to run after two days stuck inside, and she couldn't deny him that pleasure simply for her own peace of mind.

It took two days of solid travel to reach Paxton's estate.

They spent the first night at an inn where the innkeeper fussed and fawned over them. Ella kept her head down. She hoped he wouldn't lay his hands on one of the waitresses, because she wasn't sure she would be able to contain her reaction, and she didn't want to make a scene in front of the Prince. But the innkeeper seemed jovial enough, and Ella made it through the night without incident.

The next day was just as bruising and boring. Paxton was pleasant enough company, but his life as a noble and now a royal was so far removed from Ella's life as a peasant that she struggled to think of anything that wouldn't bore him, and she certainly didn't want to relive those days.

The only thing they had in common was Rory, and he didn't seem like a wise topic of conversation. Despite Paxton's reassurance that nothing had happened between them, and that he was happy with his husband, Ella couldn't deny the twin flares of jealousy and umbrage she'd felt, both for herself and on Rory's behalf.

She was afraid those flares would catch and grow into righteous indignation and she would do something foolish.

So they spent some time speaking of idle things—the weather, the countryside, the cuisine—but then they fell silent, and Ella was grateful she'd brought a book with her.

They arrived at Paxton's estate on the afternoon of the third day. The grounds were expansive, reminding Ella of the manor where she and Given had spent so much time, but this one didn't have the carefully-crafted gardens. When the carriage drew to a stop in front of the grand front doors, there was a moment of silence, as if this house were as abandoned as the other one. Then the doors flew open and dozens of people descended upon them. Stable hands to handle the horses, porters to port their baggage, and attendants to attend them.

Even though she was perfectly capable of opening the door, Paxton indicated that she should let the coachman do so, though it seemed ridiculous to sit inside waiting while there was such a flurry of activity going on outside. Finally, they were allowed out, and were greeted by a woman in a prim blazer and trousers. While Paxton exchanged pleasantries with the woman, Ella glanced around.

"Given?"

A small whine came from behind her, and the dog—wolf—crept out from under the carriage. She scratched between his ears, which were down, and he pressed himself against her leg. Even his fur was flat, as if he were attempting to make himself as small as possible.

A startled squawk came from the attendant, and Paxton rushed to reassure her that Given was a pet and posed no danger.

"We can house him with the hounds, my lord," she said.

"I believe Miss Ella would prefer that he remain with her," Paxton said. "He is house trained."

As they headed toward the house, a second wave of people flooded out, but these weren't servants. They were dressed in finery and walked with a speed that suggested they would rather be running. In fact, one young woman, not much older than Ella, did break into a run. She had long, dark hair clipped in loose loops behind her head and wore a flowing silk suit in pale pink. She let out a shriek of joy as she threw herself into Paxton's arms.

He hugged her and spun her in a circle. When he set her down again, she smacked his arm and playfully scolded him. "You didn't tell us you were coming."

"I do apologize, it's an impromptu visit."

The young woman turned her beneficent gaze on Ella. Her smile hitched briefly as she took in Ella's outfit. When the fishwife had gifted the clothes to Ella, she'd thought them the most magnificent things in the world. They made her feel brave and safe, but here, they were no better than the peasant's clothes she'd worn waiting tables. They marked her as other, lesser.

"And who is your guest?"

"Lady Juliana, let me introduce Miss Ella. She's a guest of His Highness, but I thought she would be more comfortable spending her time at our estate. Ella, my sister, Juliana."

"Delighted to meet you," Juliana said, extending her hand.

Ella shook firmly. "It's nice to meet you too."

"Well ..." Juliana reinforced her smile as she extricated her hand from Ella's grasp. "Your accent is delightful, where are you from?"

"Leyton. In North Lynnborough." Now that Juliana had mentioned it, Ella felt her accent thicken, so it came out like, "Norflyn-bro."

"You're far from home. And who is this?" Juliana crouched down and offered her hand to Given, who whined and retreated behind Ella, over-playing the role of tame pet. "He's gorgeous."

"He's my wolf, Given."

"Well," Juliana said again. "You're both welcome. Come along."

She took Paxton's hand and practically dragged him up the steps. His parents were waiting patiently by the door, and he greeted them with a short bow and a crisp, "Mother, Father." The formality lasted only a moment before they broke into smiles and each embraced him in turn.

They too were surprised at his arrival, and he repeated his polite apology and introductions. Ella didn't know how to address a baron and baroness, so she defaulted to calling them 'sir' and 'madam' as she would the customers in the tavern. To her relief, they didn't seem to take offense, and she hoped they'd put her lack of manners down to foreign customs.

Paxton showed her down a series of corridors and up a flight of stairs to a guest room that was nearly as grand as the one in the palace. She was no more likely to escape out the window, and one of the guards lingered outside the door. Ella wondered what his family would think of that, or if they would assume that the guard was there as her protector rather than her custodian.

After Ella had freshened up, a maid escorted her to dinner. In the center of the dining room was a long table made of polished wood, with beautifully carved legs and a dozen matching chairs.

The baron and baroness were already present, standing beside the tall patio doors at the side of the room. Paxton wasn't there, and Ella, abandoned by the maid now she'd been delivered, stood awkwardly by the door, Given pressed against her side.

The baroness took pity on her and swept across the room. "Welcome, dear. Can I offer you a glass of wine?" She gestured to a servant who scurried over carrying a delicate glass with a long, thin stem. It was half filled with a pale red liquid that resembled the red mist far too much for Ella's liking. "And can I get anything for your wolf?"

Ella was surprised by how smoothly the baroness offered, as if hosting wolves was an every day occurrence. "Some water, if you don't mind."

The same servant fetched a large crystal bowl full of water and placed it on the floor. Given lapped at it dutifully.

Ella had no more idea how to talk to the baroness than she had with Paxton, and she sipped at her drink to cover the silence. There wasn't much call for wine in the tavern, and she'd never got the taste for ale, but this had a pleasantly fruity tang.

"You simply must tell us all about North Lynnborough," the baroness said. "We've never been."

It was a generous question, neatly avoiding topics Ella didn't feel comfortable discussing, such as why she was here in Bretland or why she was a 'guest' of the Grand Prince, and one that gave plenty of room for Ella to waffle on despite the fact she'd barely seen more of North Lynnborough than the baroness had. So waffle on Ella did, between sips from her glass, which was refilled by a servant the moment she drained it. First Juliana arrived, then two older brothers—one with a wife on one arm and a baby in the other—and finally a younger sister. Serafina was maybe all of thirteen summers old, and her eyes widened with delight as she spotted Given.

"May I pet your dog?" she asked, the words tumbling over one another in her excitement.

Ella thought it probably wasn't a good idea to let on that Given wasn't a dog but a wolf, and a special one at that, so instead of asking his permission, she simply said, "Hold your hand out, and if he comes to you, you may pet him."

The girl dutifully dropped to her knees in the middle of the floor—eliciting a groan of disapproval from the eldest brother, Dexter—and offered her hand. Ella nudged Given with her knee. He let out something very close to a sigh but padded forward to snuffle at Serafina's palm. She cooed in delight and proceeded to smooch his cheeks, scratch behind his ears, and scrub at his sides.

"His fur is so soft," Serafina gushed, "and he's so beautiful."

Given must've come to enjoy the attention—he flopped onto his back so Serafina could rub his belly, and let out a self-satisfied rumble.

"I wish I was allowed a dog." She sent her parents a disparaging look, and Ella wished she'd had the girl's confidence at her age. "Where did you get him?"

Before Ella could answer, the door opened, and a servant declared, "The lord of the manor has arrived."

Ella wondered how Paxton had become the manor lord when his parents were still alive and he had older brothers. She assumed titles such as that passed from parent to eldest child, like they did in North Lynnborough. Not that anyone she knew had a title or a fancy estate to pass on.

Paxton stepped into the room and shot the servant an irritated look.

"Thank the stars," Dexter said with casual mockery. "I believe poor Margita was about to succumb to exhaustion."

Margita, who was Dexter's wife, lifted her hand to her forehead, as if she were about to faint.

Ella pressed back against the wall, her heart pounding. If she'd mocked her father like that, his retaliation would have been swift and brutal. Though Paxton wasn't Margita's father, he was the lord here, and if he responded that way, Ella wouldn't be able to contain her indignation.

"Yes, the manor lord has arrived," Paxton said. "Everyone genuflect three or four times before you take your seats."

Nobody bowed. In fact, they all laughed. Even Paxton. Ella drained her glass and it seemed to steady her nerves. She felt herself relaxing, warming to him a little. All the family seemed enormously pleased that he was home. Ella might not have a big family like theirs, but she couldn't imagine ever receiving such a welcome from her father or offering him one in kind.

"Can Ella sit by me?" Serafina asked, slipping into a chair at one end of the table.

"If it pleases her." Paxton pulled out the chair next to the girl and invited Ella to sit.

She had no reason to reject the offered seat, though she suspected Serafina was less interested in her company than Given's. The wolf positioned himself under the table at Ella's feet and Serafina quickly reached down to continue stroking his head.

Paxton took the seat at the head of the table. "What scintillating conversation did I miss?"

"Miss Ella was regaling us with tales of her homeland," the baroness said.

"And she was about to tell us where she got her dog," Serafina added.

Paxton smirked. "Actually, he's a wolf."

Serafina let out a yelp and snatched her hand back. The other siblings snorted with laughter at her horror, like they were all still children. The injustice scratched at Ella like a cheap blanket. In an effort to tamp it down, she ignored the others and turned to Serafina.

"He's only half wolf," Ella assured her. "And he's tame."

Serafina gave Ella a worried look, but she couldn't resist the pull of Given's soft fur, and quickly returned to petting him. Ignoring her siblings as Ella had, she asked, "Where *did* you get him?"

"Well, it's a bit of a sad story."

"But it ends happily?"

"I suppose."

Serafina stuck out her bottom lip. "Please tell me ..."

Ella glanced around the table. They all watched her curiously as the servants slipped around, placing bowls of soup in front of everyone. She'd never told a story before, certainly not to such a captive audience, but she'd heard Dyson Doon regaling his friends with tales of his exploits so many times that she felt she could do no worse.

She reached for her drink, which had been refilled, and began, "I was coming through Caveline when I stopped to find something to eat, and I heard a cry, like an animal in pain. I followed the sound and found myself in a dogfighter's pit, where half a dozen dogs were caged, including Given."

"What did you do?" Serafina asked in awe.

"I told the dogfighter to free them, or I would." The more wine Ella drank, the easier her words flowed as she recounted the fight for the dogs' freedom. Finally, she finished with, "And he hasn't left my side since."

She was rather pleased with her first attempt at storytelling until the baron asked, "You came across the border?" with such a crease between his thick brows that she worried she'd said something wrong.

"Yes, sir."

"What was it like?"

"Well, I've never crossed a border before, but we had no trouble."

"You've never crossed a border?" Dexter asked. "How did you get *into* Caveline?"

Ella's head started to spin. The curiosity in their faces suddenly seemed hostile. "I rode?"

"Horses don't have a magical ability to skip borders."

"No, but dragons do." Ella set her glass on the table, but it hit the edge of her plate and tipped. She tried to catch it but missed, and the liquid stained the tablecloth red. She didn't know why she was so clumsy. After all, she could carry four heavy flagons of ale without spilling a drop. How had a simple wine glass defeated her?

"A dragon!" Serafina gasped. "I want to ride a dragon."

"Where did you find a dragon?" the baron asked.

Maybe Ella should have stopped speaking, but she had lost all sense of self-control and the words poured from her like a king tide. "It was the old fishwife. She told me I had to come to Bretland and that the dragon would take me, but the creature stopped short for some reason known only to herself. And it was the fishwife who told me to visit the Grand Prince because he would know where Rory was. And it was the fishwife who sent me on the quest for Rory's heart in the first place, but I didn't know it was his heart I was hunting or I never would have agreed."

The flood of words finally stopped, and Ella gripped tightly to the table. Like vomiting after eating bad mussels, she felt shaken, but it was a relief, really, to have it all out.

The baroness cleared her throat. "Perhaps you should start at the beginning," she said, turning her gaze on Paxton.

He sighed and said, "I was planning to wait until breakfast, when we're rested."

"I'm rested," Dexter said, turning to their other brother, Maxwell. "Are you rested?"

"Fine." Paxton gestured for the servants to leave, and once the room was clear, he recounted a version of Ella's story. He didn't tell them Rory was the Dead Prince of Caveline or that he'd been the one to kidnap Paxton or that she was the Grand Prince's prisoner, but he did tell them that Ella had been tricked into promising to give her true love's heart to a witch.

Ella cringed at the oversimplification—and at Paxton's offhanded comment that Rory was her true love—but didn't contradict him. In fact, she was careful not to open her mouth at all. Not to speak, and certainly not to drink any more wine. She'd seen the detrimental effect that alcohol had on the customers in the tavern, but she'd never experienced it herself, until now.

When the story was told, silence hung over the table like a death shroud. Finally, the baron set down the soup spoon that he'd held poised over his bowl for the duration of the story, and said, "You need to take her to the goblin king."

CHAPTER SEVEN

GIVEN SQUEEZED OUT FROM under the table at the mention of a goblin king. He couldn't believe that the Grand Prince—or Princess before him—would allow someone who called himself a king to remain within the borders of the principality.

"Well, yes," Paxton said with a dramatic roll of his eyes. "That is why I brought her here."

"Who's the goblin king?" Ella asked.

"I trust that what I am about to tell you will stay between us," the baron said. When Ella nodded, he continued, "We used to have an estate not far from here, and on the border of our land was the strangest place. Most people didn't acknowledge it, as if it wasn't there at all, but we could see the massive stone walls and the castle rising above them. And occasionally the strangest creatures would appear on our land, and we would have to chase them back inside."

Ella's hands twisted in her lap. "Was it, by any chance, surrounded by a barberry hedge?"

"Yes. How did you know?"

"The dragon. We didn't talk about it in front of strangers, but everyone in my village knew of her. She lived in a cave in the side of a cliff, but the top was ringed with a barberry hedge."

"The goblin king keeps to himself. He isn't interested in the politics of Bretland nor the lives of people like us, but he has power of his own, magic, and if you need a way out of your bargain, he may be able to suggest one." Pity filled the baron's gaze. "But there will be a price. You may find yourself deeper in debt or facing a more difficult choice."

Ella nodded, her face set. "How do we get an audience with this goblin king?"

"There's only one way I know of," Paxton said. "We have to find our way through the labyrinth that surrounds his castle, and ask."

"Labyrinth?" Ella asked. "I'm not familiar with that word."

"It's a giant maze."

Ella let out a disheartened sigh. Given pushed his head into her lap and she worried his ear between her fingers. "When do we start?"

Given lay on the foot of Ella's bed as she spent the night twisting the sheets. He gave her as much comfort as he could, crawling up beside her so she could rest against him before finally slipping into an exhausted slumber.

They left for the labyrinth and the goblin king's castle after breakfast, only waiting as long as it took to pack some supplies. As Ella couldn't ride a horse, they took Paxton's carriage, the two guards flanking them on horseback again.

Given trotted alongside them, sometimes running ahead, other times darting into the scrub beside the road following whatever intriguing scents caught his nose. He was enjoying the growing wildness inside him as the moon waxed day by day, and he hoped he wouldn't be locked back in that tower in the Grand Prince's palace by the full moon.

An eerie stillness descended as they reached their destination. The birds fell silent, the wind dropped, and Given, running ahead at the time, went straight past it, and even when the carriage stopped behind him and he returned to it, he almost kept going, as there were far more interesting things to sniff than whatever was behind the barberry hedge. But at Paxton's insistence, they left the carriage and horses under the care of the coachman, shouldered their packs, and followed him through a rickety wooden gate.

A stone wall towered ahead of them. It stretched left and right as far as Given could see and was about twice the height of the people around him. A cobblestone path led from the gate to an open archway in the wall.

"When you said 'giant maze,'" Ella murmured, "I didn't imagine it would be *this* big."

"Each side is over a mile long," Paxton replied.

One of the guards—the same woman who'd been guarding the Prince the day before and who Given had ascertained was named Leandra—stepped in front of Paxton and stared at the entryway. "Are we going in there, Your Highness?"

"Indeed."

She exchanged a look with the other guard, a quiet, grizzled veteran named Kerr. Neither of them looked particularly happy. "What should we expect inside?"

"I can't say for certain. Rory went in there once and came out with a vicious bite on his shoulder."

Ella winced. "That scarred quite badly."

"I did my best to treat it," Paxton said absently.

"Wild animals?" Leandra asked.

"Possibly."

"Does anyone know what a goblin looks like? Are they large or small?"

"We'll find out when we meet one."

Leandra drew her sword as Kerr did the same. "I'll take the front, you bring up the rear, and you"—she gave the Prince stern look—"stay in the middle." She turned to Ella. "I assume your wolf will protect you if it comes to that?"

Ella flicked her wrist and a dagger appeared in her hand. "I'll protect myself."

Both guards pivoted to aim their blades at her, and Ella paled slightly, tucking the blade away again.

Paxton waved them off. "Leave her. If she didn't stab me when we were alone in the carriage, I doubt she'll do so now."

Leandra gave Ella a hard stare. "Once this is over, I'm relieving you of that."

They stepped through the archway one after another. A wooden sign hung on the opposite wall.

Leandra strode forward then read it aloud. "Welcome humble traveler. To reach the center of the labyrinth you must pass three tests: one of strength, one of stamina, and one of strategy. Only then can you achieve what you desire."

She gave Paxton a questioning look.

"So be it," he murmured.

The walls of the labyrinth stretched as far left and right as Given could see, and a peculiar scent clung to the ground like fog. It smelled like tea that had been brewed too long: sharp and bitter with a base of rotten vegetation.

The passageway formed by the walls was wide enough for three people to walk abreast; the ground was packed dirt occasionally broken by tree roots, though there were no trees to be seen; and the walls themselves were built of stone, slightly sloped rather than perfectly vertical, covered in moss and lichen, and possibly climbable for someone who had hands rather than paws.

"Which way, Your Highness?" Leandra asked.

"I suppose one's as good as another."

"You don't know the way?" Ella gasped.

Given glanced up, glad she'd voiced his concern.

"Unfortunately, no. All we can do is start and see what the first turn offers us. Let's try the right."

Leandra took the lead, setting a steady pace. The Prince followed, Given padded along beside Ella, and Kerr came at the back, sending regular glances over his shoulder.

The walled pathway continued on and on with no breaks or turns. One minute turned into two, then five.

Leandra held her hand up for them to stop. "Are we expecting a turn, Your Highness?"

"I assume one will come eventually."

Given stared into the distance. If there were gaps in the walls, he couldn't see them, but the passageway did seem to end eventually.

"Unless it's some sort of trick," Ella said quietly. "Shouldn't there be twists and turns to get us lost?"

"That depends if it's a labyrinth or a maze," Kerr said in a deep rumble. When everyone turned to look at him, he cleared his throat.

"You see, Your Highness, a maze has twists and turns like the lady thinks. It's designed to get you lost and keep you trapped. Whereas a labyrinth is a winding path that leads to the center and then out again. No false turns. No dead ends. And if that's the case, Your Highness is right. We'll come to a turn eventually."

"When did you become an expert in labyrinths?" Leandra quipped.

"Some of us have better ways to spend our down time than losing all our coins playing tiles."

Paxton held up his hand to stop their playful bickering. "I've always heard it called a labyrinth. Let's hope it lives up to its name."

"But if it isn't designed to get us lost," Ella said, "where's the challenge?"

A loud caw answered her, like a bird's cry but deeper pitched.

Paxton scanned the skies. "I assume the challenge comes from making it to the center alive."

THEY WALKED FOR ANOTHER five minutes before finally reaching a sharp left-hand turn.

Ella gasped in horror then let out a shuddering breath. "Oh, I thought ..."

Given knew exactly what she'd thought. Statues were half-buried in both walls. Some short and squat, others tall and lean, all with monstrous visages and realistic enough that at first glance they looked like real people—creatures—who were trapped.

Given trotted up to the closest one, which was the same height as him. Its expression was frozen, its gaze blank.

"They're statues," Paxton murmured. "Such intricate detail."

Given glanced at the Prince, who was running his fingertips over another statue's cheek.

The tiniest sound, a scrape of stone, made Given look back. His statue's lips were pursed, its tongue poking out, as if it was blowing a raspberry. He was sure it hadn't been that way before.

"Who would do this?" Ella asked, stepping up beside Given. "What purpose can statues serve *here*?"

"Turn back!" the statue said, stretching out the vowels.

Given flinch back, his heart racing.

The other statues took up the call, echoing the words. "Save yourselves! Go no further!"

"Get back, Your Highness," Leandra commanded.

But Paxton didn't move. "They're some sort of automatons."

"Who are you calling an automaton?" the statue in front of him asked.

"What's that?" another one asked.

"He thinks we're not real."

"Who's not real?" a third asked.

The statue by Paxton rolled its stone eyes. "This hoity-toity meat suit thinks we're not real."

A ripple of annoyance ran down the wall before they returned to their dire warnings with renewed enthusiasm.

"Ignore them," Paxton said. "They cannot hurt us."

"You're alive?" Ella asked the short statue in front of them.

"As alive as you are."

"And you're trapped?"

This statue was more buried than some of the others. It looked as if it had been standing with its hands raised and had been pushed back *into* the wall, so only its face, rotund little belly, fingers and toes were protruding. "Decidedly."

"We have to help them," Ella cried. She scraped around the statue's face, as if it were buried in sand, not stone, and she could dig it out.

"Ella ..." Paxton laid his hand on her shoulder, saying what Given couldn't. "We can't. They're trapped."

"But ..." Her mouth drew into a thin line, her brow furrowed. "It's not fair."

"No," he said. "It's not."

"You can't help us, but we can help you," the statue said.

The next statue, its face slightly higher on the wall, picked up the message. "If it gets too hard ..."

"If you think you can't make it ..." another chimed in.

"Then all you have to do ..."

"Is say 'I quit,' and an exit will appear."

"We're not quitting," Ella snapped, though her anger didn't seem to be aimed at the statues but at whoever had trapped them.

Given felt her pain. It seemed wrong to leave these poor creatures, but there was nothing they could do.

"That's what they all say," the statue said, making an attempt to shake its head but doing little more than wiggling its jaw.

"Don't say we didn't warn you," another added.

"Ella ..." Paxton said softly. "We need to keep moving if we're going to reach the center."

"It's not fair!"

"I know."

Ella shot one last look at the statues. "I'm sorry," she murmured before stalking away.

As bad as he felt for them, Given was glad to leave the statues behind.

After a minute in this new direction, they turned left again, and the next section was curved instead of straight. A series of straight and curved stretches followed, and every turn took them to the right. The curves were disorientating, but Given was certain they were making their way around in a square. They saw nothing of interest. No people, no animals, no plants. Just tall, stone walls, hard-packed dirt, and a gray sky above.

Finally, after an hour of walking, Given picked up a noise that wasn't from his companions. Leandra clearly heard it too, as her steps slowed. A clank, a bang, an outraged cry. Then more of the same until it sounded as if a group of amateur musicians were tuning their instruments.

"Stay behind me, Your Highness," Leandra said.

A low growl grew in Given's throat that he couldn't hold in. Ella's fingers dug into the fur of his neck.

They were currently walking a curved section, with no way to see what was ahead. Leandra crept forward, leaning to peer around the bend. They only followed when they were in danger of losing sight of her.

The cacophony ahead stopped as if a shroud had fallen.

The path ended in a narrow archway, and when they caught up, Leandra led them through. On the other side was a large square that resembled a hodge-podge village. Squat huts sat in uneven rows.

Makeshift fences penned in goats and pigs. Mud hovels clung to the walls like giant swallows' nests. But there were no people.

The fur on the back of Given's neck stood up, and he glanced around, certain someone was watching him, but seeing no one.

A stone slab crashed to the ground behind them, blocking the archway. They couldn't go back. Another archway stood across the square, but it was blocked as well. They were trapped.

Something yanked on Given's tail. He spun around and growled, but the only thing behind him was a stack of firewood and a stout wicker basket.

"What is it, boy?" Ella asked.

"How do we get out of here?" Kerr grumbled. "The passage is blocked in both directions."

"Is this the first test?" Leandra asked.

Ignoring them, Given crept forward and sniffed around the basket. There was something inside it. Pungent and earthy. He lifted his paw and batted at the basket. It was solid and barely wobbled. Whatever was inside it was heavy.

"There's no point going back," Paxton said.

"Look, here," Kerr said.

"It must lift," Leandra said. "But how?"

Given nosed at the lid of the basket. It started to slide, and a wave of the pungent odor assailed his nostrils. The groan of stone scraping against stone sounded behind him, and Given glanced around. The slab blocking the archway across the square was slowly rising. Kerr stood barely six feet from it, hauling on a rope that hung out of the wall above him. His expression was tense, the muscles in his arms bulging.

Something tugged on Given's whiskers. He turned back to the basket and found himself face to face with a small, rotund goblin. Her skin was gray, her eyes coal-black, her hair bright green. Her wide mouth pulled into a grin as she hefted a short cane and cracked him over the head.

Given let out a yip of pain and surprise. The goblin swung the cane a second time, and he skittered backward in an attempt to get out of reach. He crashed into Ella who let out a surprised yelp of her own. "What's wrong?"

But when Given looked back at the basket, the lid was back in place and the goblin was nowhere to be seen.

Ella took a step closer. Given whined and tried to block her, but she merely gave his shoulder a reassuring pat and reached for the basket. As her fingers brushed the lid, the goblin burst out again.

Ella's shriek was drowned out by the ruckus of a dozen more goblins who sprang from inside the hovels, pounced from behind the huts, and burst out of carefully camouflaged holes in the ground. They swarmed toward the group, bearing canes and staffs and howling war cries.

Leandra ordered them to form a semicircle around Kerr, and they were all quick to comply. She and Paxton defended with their swords, Ella blocked desperately with her daggers, and Given snarled and snapped his teeth.

He wouldn't have thought that a bunch of feverish goblins with wooden sticks would have been a match for bladed weapons, but there were so many of them that Given and his companions were in danger of being overwhelmed. He suffered from not having a long range, and the same goblin who'd surprised him in the basket kept running in to bop him on the head with her cane before darting away again, while still others struck at his shoulders. Finally he caught the goblin's cane in his teeth, wrenched it from her grasp, and shook his head frantically to send the others scrambling.

"We need to retreat, Your Highness," Leandra growled.

"We have to move forward."

"I've got the door." Kerr grunted as he hauled on the rope once more. "I'll hold it till you're through."

"What about you?" Leandra demanded.

"I'll be right behind you."

When Kerr had heaved the door high enough for a person to duck under, revealing an empty passageway beyond, Leandra let out a curse and pushed forward to clear a path through the goblins.

"Go, Ella," Paxton urged.

She shot Kerr a guilty look but did as she was told.

Given, knowing he could run faster than any of the others, lingered, snapping wildly at the goblins so Paxton could follow next. Ella called his name and slapped her thigh to summon him, as if he were a dog who needed to be summoned. He turned tail on the goblins, flew over the ground, and darted past Leandra to skid under the archway.

"Come on, Kerr," Leandra growled as she backed through the gap. "You can make it."

He gave her a tight look. With no other targets, the goblins had started to attack his legs. He released the rope, but instead of bolting for the door, he drew his sword and turned to fight.

"No!" Leandra darted toward the gap as the slab dropped, but Paxton grabbed her arm and hauled her to a stop. The heavy stone hit the ground with a clap like thunder, dulling the sounds of fighting. She yanked free of the Prince's grasp and pounded her fist on the stone. "Kerr!" When the stone didn't give, Leandra spun around and gave the Prince a vicious glare. "Why did you stop me?"

"You would've been crushed!"

"Kerr's back there. We need to help him."

"We can't."

A roar went up from the other side, as if the goblins were urging each other on, renewing their attack. Leandra beat at the stone again, digging her fingers underneath as if she had a hope of lifting it.

"I'm sorry," Ella said, wrapping her arms around herself. "This is my fault."

Leandra turned on her, but Paxton spoke before she could. "None of us knew what we were getting in to." He swallowed hard. "Let's not waste Kerr's sacrifice."

"Sacrifice?" Ella gasped. "But, he's not—"

"Of course he's not dead." Leandra's voice was thick with emotion, and Given wasn't sure she believed her own words. "He's one of the best guards we've got. If anyone could escape those gnarly little bog rocks, he could."

Ella shivered, her expression crumbling. Given pressed up against her side.

Leandra took one final glance back at the blocked archway, as a victorious cheer rang out. Then she steadied her breathing, set her shoulders, and strode past them to take the lead again.

WHEREAS BEFORE THE TURNS had mostly been to the right, now they were to the left, as if the path was unwinding. The mix of long curved sections and short straight ones seemed to go on without end. Around each corner was always another identical, empty passageway. But the only alternative was to go back, so they trudged on until they eventually found a passageway almost as long and straight as the first.

The entire party was subdued, the silence that hovered over them somber now that their number was one fewer. They paused to rest their feet, chew on their rations, and drink from their waterskins. Ella fished a wooden bowl from her pack, set it on the ground, and filled it with water. Given lapped at it gratefully before gnawing on the pieces of dried meat she shared.

"I'm sorry about Kerr," Ella said into the silence. "I didn't think anyone would get hurt."

"Stop talking about him like he's dead," Leandra bit out.

"Of course," Ella said, worrying at Given's fur. "I'm sorry."

Not for the first time, Given regretted being unable to offer any words of support.

"I assume that the test of strength is complete," Paxton said. "Do you suppose the test of stamina is merely walking the length of the labyrinth?"

Ella scuffed her boot on the ground. "My luck has never been that good."

As they resumed trudging down the long straight path, a strange clacking pricked Given's ears.

He darted forward and pushed in front of Leandra, letting out a warning growl.

"I hear it," she murmured.

There was something ahead, in the distance, but Given couldn't make out what it was. As they slowly approached, a horrifying sight confronted them. A skeleton hung from a rock bridge that spanned the two walls. That was where the clacking was coming from. Its bones were shifting in the breeze, knocking against each other.

Given paused, a shiver running over him.

There was no breeze.

"Do you think *that* is an automaton?" Paxton asked, stopping beneath it.

Leandra fingered the hilt of her sword. "Stay close, all of you."

Before they could move forward, the skeleton came to life, plucked off its foot, and began firing phalanges down upon them.

Ella let out a disgusted, "Ew!" as she plucked a toe bone from her hair.

Then a skeletal hand burst from the ground and clamped around her ankle. She screamed, yanked her foot from its grasp, and stomped down hard.

All around them, the hard packed dirt erupted and skeletons clawed their way out. Without skin and muscle, they shouldn't have been able to make any sounds, but an eerie call went up from them as they reached for the group. "Bones ... bones ..."

Leandra hacked and slashed as the skeletons closed in, using the flat of her blade rather than the sharp edge, so it didn't get stuck. She decapitated one but it merely plucked the head from its neighbor, set it on its own neck, and continued its advance. Another, having lost an arm, grabbed another's humerus and attached it to its own body. A third stole a ribcage after its own went sailing away.

"They won't die!" Leandra cried.

"I think they're already dead," Paxton said between grunts.

A skeleton grabbed Ella's hand but she buried her dagger in the shoulder joint and levered its entire arm off.

Given didn't have any weapons, so he launched himself at the closest skeleton instead. His massive bulk exploded the collection of bones on impact and they dropped to the ground. But Leandra was right. The skeleton wouldn't die. The disjointed, twitching mass began to pull itself back together, all the while emitting the sorrowful cry for bones.

"Anyone know how kill them?" Leandra yelled.

"We don't! Look!" Ella waved the skeletal arm she was holding, but Given didn't see anything enlightening about it. "Hey!" she yelled up at the hanging skeleton. "Could I have your right index finger, please?"

The skeleton paused as if considering her request. Then it plucked off its finger and tossed it down. Ella caught it, attached it to the arm she was holding, then offered it back to the skeleton she'd taken it from.

The skeleton stopped pawing at her with its one remaining arm, took the offered arm, and slotted it back into place. Then it dropped to the ground and started to dig itself back into the dirt.

"They're all missing a piece," Ella explained, fending off another skeleton that was attempting to grab her. "If you make them whole, they'll stop coming after *our* bones."

There was a stunned moment of silence before Paxton yelled, "I need a little toe, left foot!"

That had been one of the first bones the hanging skeleton had thrown. Given dropped his nose to the dirt and sniffed around, but there were too many clustered bodies to pick out individual scents. Luckily, his eyes were also close to the ground.

He let out a sharp yip when he found the correct toe, wiggling on the ground like a maggot.

Slowly, while Leandra kept the skeletons at bay, the others worked to collect the pieces and identify which skeleton was missing each part. The one above kept tossing its own bones down, sometimes on request, other times at its own discretion, until it had been completely dismantled and the others repaired.

When the last skeleton was busily reburying itself, Leandra pulled a face. "That was ..."

"Horrifying?" Paxton offered.

"The worst puzzle ever." Leandra let out a short laugh, and Given was tempted to join in as the adrenaline from the frantic searching subsided.

"Those poor things," Ella said. "Do you think they're pulled apart every time someone comes through?"

"I suppose so."

Ella's fists clenched. "It's all so unfair."

Given pressed up against her, wanting to tell her to take a breath, that it wouldn't be wise to give in to rage. She slowly uncurled her fingers to stroke his head.

There was a sense of relief when they turned the next corner, finally putting the bone yard out of sight. They moved again from a straight path to a curved one, and Given wished he could see the labyrinth from above, as he was fairly certain the shape of the walls would form an intricate design.

They passed through a settlement where giant chicken-like creatures were nesting on roosts built into the walls. When one laid an egg, a goblin appeared from underneath and snatched it from the nest. The giant chicken let out a loud squawk and struck out with its sharp beak, but the goblin was too fast. Ella wanted to stop and help, but Paxton urged her to keep going while the creatures were distracted.

Everything they encountered seemed perfectly set up to stoke feelings of injustice until Ella was simmering in it, and there was nothing Given could do to help her.

In another section, the hard-packed ground gave way to a swamp, with trees reaching overhead and long, mossy vines dangling to the water. Hidden in the branches were furry creatures with long arms and sharp talons, feasting on the yellow, star-shaped fruit that grew there. They had to climb way out on the branches, secure the fruit, then retreat to a safer spot before they could eat. Given saw more than one struggle to stay perched on the thin ends and splash down into the swamp. He never saw any come out again. But even those who managed to hold on weren't safe. Long tentacles would burst out of the swamp, shoot into the trees, and snatch the fruit from their grasp. And if one of the creatures hadn't managed to grab a fruit in time, the tentacle would grab *it* instead.

The only path across the swamp was a series of wobbly stepping stones. Leandra, Paxton, and Ella picked their way across, holding their arms out for balance and grabbing a branch or vine if one was within reach. Given followed along behind, more stable on his four paws.

He was halfway across when a tentacle broke the surface of the water, wrapped around his leg, and pulled. He hit the water with barely time to take a breath before he went under. It stung his sensitive nose, scratched his eyes, and scoured his skin. The murky water smothered his vision with shadows, but he kicked frantically at the vague shape holding him. Its grip on his leg tightened, another tentacle caught his foreleg, and a third slipped around his hips to pull him closer.

He kicked and clawed and clamped his jaws around something that was as tough as overcooked swamp hen. When his teeth finally penetrated its hide, a foul-tasting liquid flowed over his tongue.

More tentacles battered his head, his ribs, his rump. He thrashed his head side-to-side, tearing at the creature. His lungs were screaming for air before it finally released him. He loosed his jaws, kicked for the surface, and coughed out a mouthful of black goo before he inhaled the sweet air.

He paddled frantically to the edge of the swamp and scrambled out to stand dripping and shivering on solid ground.

His companions were nowhere in sight.

ELLA STALKED DOWN THE labyrinth's walled pathway, trying to tamp the fire in her belly. She needed to keep her indignation stoked just enough to enable her talent with the blade, but it was threatening to blaze out of control.

Losing Kerr had been bad, but he wasn't her friend.

Losing Given felt like the cotton threads holding her tattered, often-mended heart together were snapping one by one.

She refused to believe he was dead.

He'd simply been delayed or distracted by another weird creature. She wasn't even entirely sure when he'd disappeared. One moment he'd been trotting along behind her, the next he was gone.

She'd wanted to search for him, but Paxton had pointed out that turning back might be taken as a sign they were quitting. Considering the whole labyrinth was built on injustices, it was highly likely that he was right.

And worst of all, the whole thing was her own fault.

If she hadn't made her deal with the fairy godmother, none of them would be in the labyrinth, nobody would have to sacrifice themselves for her. But they wouldn't leave her to go on alone. Paxton wanted to save Rory, too. And Leandra's job was to protect the Prince Consort.

Eventually, in another square marked by an archway entrance, they found their second challenge—as if all the strange habitats they'd battled through to reach it hadn't been challenge enough.

The path ahead was blocked, and another stone slab fell to block the passageway behind them, just as it had the first time. They were trapped again.

In the middle of another shantytown sat a square of nine tiles in a three by three grid, each large enough for a single person to stand upon. To the left of the square stood five of the strange little goblins, all wearing top hats with an X on the front. On the right was another row of five with Os upon their hats.

"Is this our test of strategy then?" Leandra asked.

"I know this game," Paxton murmured. "The aim is to get three of your pieces in a row in any direction. It's impossible to win."

The first goblin in the row of Xs ran to the tile in the middle of the grid. As one, the Os turned to look at Paxton.

"You," he said, pointing to the first one. "Over there."

The goblin ran to the corner square the Prince had pointed to.

Another X ran onto the board. Paxton countered. They took turns until the grid was full. Neither set of goblins had made a complete row. No one had won.

The goblins groaned as they cleared the grid, and the Os looked at Paxton expectantly. It was their turn to start.

Paxton didn't take the square in the center of the grid as their opponents had. Instead, he took one of the corners, but the game played out the same with no winner.

"How do we win, then?" Leandra asked as the goblins cleared the grid again.

"We hope they make a mistake before we do."

As the game began again, Ella wandered around the village. Though the huts looked ramshackle, they were carefully constructed, and when she peered through the windows, she spotted neat little furniture, small pots and pans, and even miniature books. The animals in the pens were well fed and cared for. And even the hovels that were stuck to walls, when she hoisted herself up to look inside, were like cozy nests.

These were the goblins' homes. They probably would've been quite happy here, if the demands of their so-called king didn't mean they had to engage with anyone who attempted to pass by.

He was a bully just like every other man with a skerrick of power.

Ella turned and watched another game fail to find a winner.

This was meant to be a test of strategy, but it seemed like the only way to win was for the other player to make a mistake. There was more patience and hope required than strategy. And she felt bad for the poor goblins who had to play game after game when they didn't seem to be enjoying it.

A better game wouldn't require a winner but would allow the players to have fun.

And that seemed like an excellent strategy to her.

"Wait," she called, as an X was about to run onto the grid. "How about we play a different game?"

All ten goblins turned to peer at her.

The only problem was that her childhood hadn't been filled with games. The only one she'd ever played was weaving through the crowded dining room of the tavern, avoiding the hands of grabby patrons while carrying four flagons of ale and not spilling a drop.

It would have to do.

"All of you, line up on this side." She gestured to where the X goblins were standing, and the Os rushed to join them, making an disorderly line in front of the huts. "You too," she said to Leandra and Paxton.

Once everyone was ready, she explained the rules.

"All you have to do is run to the other side. But if I tag you, you have to join me in the middle and help tag people during the next run. Any questions?"

One goblin, with swamp-green skin and spiky, black hair, raised his hand. His voice came out deeper than Ella expected. "What's it called?"

"Um ... goblin rush." Her answer seemed to please the goblins immensely. "Ready?" she called. "Rush!"

The goblins—and humans—broke into a panicked sprint. Ella set her gaze on the goblin directly in front of her, who was trying to angle to her left. Ella shuffled sideways to intercept her, lunged, and tagged her on the shoulder.

The diminutive creature let out a howl of outrage but dutifully joined Ella in the middle.

"Ready?" she called again. "Rush!"

This time she managed to tag two goblins who, in their panic, tripped over each other. The goblin at her side took out one of her old teammates in a tackle a pig-catcher would've been proud of.

Now that they were five versus seven, it became harder for the runners to sneak between the grabby hands, and only Prince Paxton reached the far side unscathed.

Ella clapped her hands. "Well done. You win. Now you get to start in the middle."

Paxton forced a smile and said, "How delightful."

They played another round, and the goblins became more vicious in their play. When they ran, they attempted to sacrifice each other to save themselves. When they had to join the grabbers, they took each other out like wild animals defending their territory.

"Look," Leandra murmured, as they lined up to begin the third round, facing off against the goblin who had won the previous game.

Across the village, the stone slab blocking the exit started to rise. By the time the third game was complete, the slab had reached the top of the archway.

"Time to go," Leandra said, nudging Ella toward the exit.

Ella twisted out of her way and turned to the goblins. "Thank you so much for playing with us. Maybe we'll see you again soon."

"Not too soon, I hope," Paxton muttered as he passed Ella on his way to the exit.

But as soon as the goblins dispersed, the stone slab crashed back down to the ground. Leandra darted forward, but she was far too late to do anything, even if she'd been strong enough to hold it up.

"But it worked," Ella groaned.

"While we were playing," Paxton said.

Leandra glanced back at the goblins. "We have to keep playing."

"That means one of us has to stay."

Ella shook her head. "No. We're already down to three. How many more can we lose?"

Leandra cursed. "It has to be me, doesn't it? As loath as I am to leave you, Your Highness, this is your quest, not mine."

Paxton's expression twisted, as if he had smelled something foul. "Unfortunately, I think these challenges have been designed to whittle down our numbers. Once we're through, try to make your way back to the entrance. See if you can find the others. We'll meet you back at the carriage once we've completed our mission."

Leandra took a deep breath, as if steeling herself, then turned back to the goblins. "Who's up for another round?"

The goblins let out cheers and chortles of pleasure and assembled into their line. Ella and Paxton joined on the end. As they participated in each rush, the stone slab rose, and they edged closer and closer to it. When a fight broke out between two goblins over whether tripping was allowed, Ella caught Paxton's hand and together they sprinted through the gap.

Paxton spared a glance back at Leandra, but the guard nodded and gestured for them to continue without her. No one was happy, but they all knew they had no choice.

The path changed to another long, curved section, and then shorter, straight ones that zig-zagged around in a way that reminded Ella of the route to the Grand Prince's palace. They passed some small reptilian creatures who were baiting a large bear with sharp sticks; edged around a pit full of snapping crocodiles; and crept between a dozen rusted suits of armor who urged them to turn back, like the statues had.

"We must be almost there," Paxton said, and his tone suggested that he was reassuring himself as much as her.

But, truly, neither of them could be certain. They'd been walking for almost three hours, and although they could have completed a circuit around the outside of the labyrinth by now, the path twisted back around on itself so often that there was no way to judge how long it actually was.

Overhead, the sky darkened with storm clouds, and wind barreled down the passageway toward them, tossing cold rain at them like a child playing in the surf, adding soaked clothing to their sore feet and frayed nerves.

"There's something up ahead," Paxton said, peering between his fingers. "Perhaps we can take shelter until the storm passes."

Ella raised her hand to shield her face, grateful that she no longer had hair that would get tangled from such treatment, and squinted against the fierce wind to see what he was pointing at. Her heart stuttered.

Leaning against one of the walls, as if it had always been there, was the fishwife's hut.

CHAPTER EIGHT

Ella couldn't move; it was as if she'd stepped into quicksand.

"What is it?" Paxton asked, coming back to stand beside her, his shoulders hunched against the weather.

Despite the rain on her face, Ella's throat was parched, and she had to swallow twice before she could speak. "That's the old fishwife's hut, from my village."

"The fairy godmother?" Paxton stared at the hut, a frown marring his features. "What's she doing here?"

Fear threatened to drown her, but she refused to let it. Instead, she stoked the flickering rage in her stomach, encouraging it to spread. When the red mist tainted her vision, she flicked a new dagger into her hand. "I'm about to find out."

When she stepped toward the hut, Paxton moved with her.

"No, Your Highness." Ella held out her hand to stop him. "Leandra will throttle me if you get hurt. It's better if you wait out here."

His eyebrows rose as if he were unused to people giving him commands, but he must have seen the wisdom in her words because he stepped aside to shelter as best he could against the wall.

Ella pulled the indignation around her and stared through her marred vision like a visor on a suit of armor. She pushed the door of the hut open without knocking and stepped inside. It looked the same it always did, and the old fishwife was standing over the cooking fire, brewing tea, as was her habit. Ella was assailed by a quick jab of longing for a past she couldn't return to.

She fended off the assault.

Her past was nothing to long for. She hadn't been loved. She hadn't been happy. She hadn't been free.

As much as she'd made a huge mistake in promising to give Rory's heart to the fishwife, at least she was in control of her destiny. It was worth fighting to fix that wrong.

"If you're here to remind me once again of our bargain, there's no need. I haven't forgotten. But I know you tricked me. I know it's Rory's heart you want."

The fishwife turned slowly. "Tea?" She offered Ella a mug, but Ella had no urge to drink anything on offer.

"I have no interest in *tea*."

The door slammed shut behind her, and Ella flinched. But there was no one else in the hut with them, and she told herself it was just the wind.

"You used to be such a nice girl," the fishwife said absently. "You came and spent time with me though I had little to offer you in return. Now it's all rush, rush, rush."

"Drop this guise and speak to me plainly so I can get on with my task."

The fishwife sighed, straightened, and drank from the mug herself. Her voice lost its waver. "If that is what you desire." She strode across the small room, and Ella shifted her weight and tightened her grip on her dagger, though she doubted the woman would attack her.

"I'm not here to nag you," the fishwife said. "The opposite, in fact. I came to help. First, a warning: beware the Prince, for he shall be your downfall."

"What prince?" Ella demanded. "Paxton? Rory? The Grand Prince?"

The fishwife continued as if Ella hadn't spoken. "Second: you may attempt to weasel your way out of our bargain, you may spend your days searching for a loophole, but you'll know your time has run out when Huxford's Folly comes to life."

"That makes no sense," Ella growled. "What's Huxford's Folly?"

"I've said my piece," the fishwife said. "Leave me now."

"No, I'm done with your games." Ella's fury grew, churning and burning. "I know what you did to Rory, how you treated him. It's not right, and it's not fair."

"Fair? I saved the boy's life."

"And kept him prisoner for five years. And when he was about to escape your clutches, you tricked him into staying."

"That *is* what I do." The fishwife spread her arms wide and made a mocking bow. "But tell me, if I had healed him and sent him on his way, do you think the two of you would have ever met?"

Her words sent Ella reeling, as if she'd been slapped, because they implied the fishwife had kept Rory prisoner just so she could meet him. But she refused to fall for the woman's trickery.

She gathered her courage, her anger, and her guilt, and put them to good use. "I'm not going to kill Rory for you. I'd rather kill you instead." Then she fired her dagger across the room, where it buried itself in the fishwife's stomach.

The old fishwife let out a howl of pain and dropped her mug. As it shattered against the floor, she transformed into the beautiful younger woman. She grasped the handle and slid the dagger out of her gut.

As blood spread through the fabric of her gown, she gave Ella a vicious look. "This is my favorite dress, you impertinent whelp."

All Ella's courage fled and her stomach shriveled with fear. She skittered back toward the door, but the fairy godmother strode across the room, caught her wrist, and squeezed it painfully.

"You think you can break a bargain with me?" The witch's face darkened. She twisted Ella's wrist, and agony forced Ella to her knees. "I made you a deal in good faith. I have delivered. If you don't hold up your end, I will collect in ways more painful than you can imagine."

She bent Ella's arm further, pushing her back toward the door.

"You think giving me Rory's heart is the worst thing I could ask? How about the moment you carve it from his chest, I replace the battered organ and reknit his severed flesh? How about I make you repeat the process hour after hour, day after day, until his mind snaps and yours with it?"

A fierce wind ricocheted around the hut and flung the door open wide.

The witch's voice dropped to a sharp whisper. "How about I tell the poor boy what you have promised? Do you think his love for you will die, or is it so great that he'll choose to sacrifice himself for you?" A cruel smile twisted her features. "I think I know the answer."

The fairy godmother released her hold, but before Ella could fetch another dagger, the wind circled back through the hut, hit her like a runaway horse, and knocked her bodily out of the door. The door slammed shut and the hut collapsed, leaving nothing behind but a collection of wood and iron.

Ella lay on the hard ground, cradling her aching arm and trying to fight back the tears that burned her eyes.

The dagger had pierced the fishwife's flesh, but she'd barely even flinched. Ella couldn't beat her that way, and if she tried to get out of their bargain, Rory would be the one to pay. The witch would see to that.

How could the goblin king aid her against such a malevolent foe? She'd wasted half a day, still hadn't made it to the center of the labyrinth, and wouldn't find what she wanted even when she did.

She curled into a ball and gave in to despair.

WHEN ELLA CAME BACK to herself, she was no longer lying on the hard-packed dirt of the labyrinth. She was instead curled on a fur rug, a soft blanket draped over her. An argument of the most polite nature was going on behind her.

"I must respectfully disagree," Paxton said.

"She did not complete the test of stamina." This second voice was deep and melodious. His words rolled through the air like a boat on the ocean. "She is lying there like a sack of potatoes."

"And yet the tasks were clearly designed for a group. Had Ella entered the labyrinth alone, she couldn't have completed the test of strength."

"Had she entered the labyrinth alone, she would not have been presented with tasks that only a group could complete."

"And yet, I'm still here. So it must've been within my purview to aid her."

"Your logic will not work on me."

Paxton let out a frustrated grunt. "So this whole thing is a trick? We play by the rules, and you change them to suit yourself?"

"Remember, Your Highness, you were not invited into this haven. You've both had your wishes granted already."

Ella pushed herself up, letting the blanket fall aside. She felt groggy, as if she could have slept for a hundred years and it wouldn't have eased her exhaustion. She assumed she was in the goblin king's castle at the center of the labyrinth. It was a vast room with walls made of smooth brick, the ceiling arching high above her, and sunlight streaking through many windows.

She turned toward the voices.

Paxton stood with his back to her, his arms crossed, his shoulders tight with tension. In front of him, on a raised dais, the goblin king sat in a grand throne. He had feathery blond hair, a flouncy white shirt, and tight leather trousers. He sat with one leg slung over the arm of the throne and his head propped up with his hand, as if he found the conversation with Paxton to be tedious. But it was his face that snagged Ella's gaze.

Her heart burst into a furious sprint. She tossed off the blanket and sprang to her feet, her exhaustion forgotten.

"You!" she growled.

The goblin king turned to her, a bored expression on his face. "Ah, the lady awakens."

"You know him?" Paxton asked as she stomped up beside him, rage pulsing through her veins.

"I never told you how I met Rory, did I?" she asked him. When he shook his head, she continued. "He used to come to my father's tavern, and for the first two years, he wasn't alone. He was accompanied by another rogue, an older man." She pointed at the goblin king. "Him."

Paxton's head whipped around to stare at the goblin king, who spread his arms wide, smirked, and said, "Guilty."

"Does he know?" Paxton asked.

"What our dear Rory knows or does not know is no concern of yours."

"He was devastated when you left," Ella said. "How could you?"

"How could *I*?" The goblin king rose to his feet.

Paxton touched Ella's arm in an attempt to move her back or rein her in, but she had no interest in cowering before this self-proclaimed king who mistreated his subjects.

"I did exactly what I needed to do. I taught him what he needed to learn. And the vacancy I left in Rory's life was quickly filled by someone else." The goblin king's gaze shifted to Paxton and back. "And you, Ella, if you recall, were quite happy to fill the hole *he* left."

"That's not the point." Ella shook her head as she felt herself blush. "Are you telling me that after all those years you spent with him, you won't help us save Rory's life?"

The goblin king paused. Something changed. His appearance didn't transform in the way the fishwife's had when she grew younger, but his flouncy shirt grew tighter, the flamboyant cuffs shrinking and the material thickening into sturdy cotton, and his hair lost its bounce to hang around his face. He swept a lock behind his ear. "Come with me."

He jogged down from the dais, led them out the back of the throne room, down a set of stairs, along a passageway, and finally into a room that was barely larger than a closet. The goblin king boosted himself up to sit upon an oak wine barrel. Paxton squeezed in beside a column of animal skulls attached to the wall, bearing a variety of horns and antlers. And Ella perched on top of a wooden crate next to a teetering pile of clothing. The whole room was full of odds and ends and arranged so messily that it reminded Ella of the cupboard in the tavern where her father threw everything that didn't have a home in the otherwise well-organized kitchen.

"What has Helene done?"

"Helene?" Paxton asked.

"The fairy godmother."

Ella didn't mean to ignore the goblin king's question, but her gaze snagged on a bright blue piece of fabric in the pile beside her. Something drew her hand to it. The material felt soft and velvety under her fingers. She tugged.

"Oh, I wouldn't—"

Before the goblin king could finish his warning, Ella pulled harder, the fabric popped free, and the tower of clothing toppled over. It was a vest with golden buttons and matching thread embroidered around the hems, and a long gash split the front, where it was stained almost black.

"Is this—"

"Yes," the goblin king said softly.

Ella looked up. The pain in his eyes doused the anger she'd felt at his betrayal. "Why keep it?"

He swept his arm to encompass the contents of the room. "I've tried to get rid of this—all of this—many times. Burned it. Buried it. Abandoned it. It always finds its way back to me. So I keep it here. Locked away. Out of sight. Out of mind. Until I need to remind myself ... who I was ... who I am ... how I came to be." A flicker of a smile passed over his lips, and he thumped his heel against the wood. "Better than carrying it all on my back. These whiskey barrels are heavy." After an awkward pause where Ella could think of nothing to say, he continued, "Helene?"

"She tricked me," Ella said. She twisted her hands in the tattered remnants of the vest that had once been Rory's, that he'd been wearing when his cousin stabbed him. "I wished for skill with a blade and in return she demanded the Dead Prince's heart. I didn't know the Dead Prince was still alive. I didn't know it was Rory."

The goblin king took a deep breath and seemed to deflate as he exhaled. He scrubbed at his face. "What did she say exactly? Be precise."

Ella cast her mind back to that night in the fishwife's hut. "She said: 'I'll grant your wish, but I want something in return.' I asked her if she was a witch, if she could grant wishes and predict futures, and she said: 'it depends' and then: 'You have to hunt down the Dead Prince and bring me his heart.'"

"Predict futures?" Paxton asked.

Ella looked at him and jumped. The way he was standing, with an animal skull behind him, made it look as if *he* was the one with antlers. "She warned me Rory wouldn't meet me, that I would become the liege of a grand manor, and that I would win the heart of a prince. So far, only the first one has come true."

"Likely a coincidence, then."

"Hmm ..." The goblin king stroked his chin, thinking, then a smile played at his lips. He let out a faint, "Ha," and jumped down from the barrel. When he hit the ground, the guise of the goblin king was back in all its glory. "I cannot undo what she has done. I'm sorry. I'm very fond of Rory, but I cannot save him from this." He took hold of Ella's arm with one hand and Paxton's with the other, and pulled them toward the door. "You had better get moving if you want to make it out of the labyrinth before dark."

Ella lurched off the crate she was sitting on, and the vest on her lap tumbled to the floor. "So that's it? A moment of regret, but tough luck? You won't help us, and Rory is doomed?"

He shrugged as he kept walking, leading them back down the passageway. "Better luck next time."

"But we haven't achieved what we desire," Paxton said. "The sign told us in order to reach the center of the labyrinth we had to pass three tests. We reached the center, which means we must have passed."

"It's only a sign." The goblin king tossed the words over his shoulder as if there was nothing to be done about it. But he wasn't just the goblin king. Ella was sure of it. The goblin king and the rogue were guises, just like the old fishwife. He was a fairy godfather, a wicked witch, a beautiful enchanter. He could save Rory if he wanted to. He could help them.

He clearly didn't want to.

And why would he? Nothing Ella knew about him made her think he would be just or fair.

"If you won't help us," she snapped, as fingers of red mist swept across her vision, "I'll figure it out myself."

They reached the staircase, and the goblin king turned around to smirk at her. "And how can a poor peasant girl beat the fairy godmother? Please, do tell me how working in that tavern for eighteen years prepared you for this."

He danced backward up the stairs, not glancing down even once to check his footing.

Ella stormed up after him and followed him into the throne room. "At least I'm trying to save him."

"As well you should, since it was your bargain that got him into this mess. Though, you are not the first." The goblin king's gaze slid to Paxton.

Ella had no answer to that, so she muttered a curse, stalked past him, and aimed for the exit.

She'd barely stepped outside the throne room, Paxton striding along beside her, when the goblin king's voice stopped her. "I have to say, I was impressed by how you passed my test of strategy. Changing the game was a stroke of genius."

Ella took three deep breaths in an attempt to chase away the red mist. It receded, slightly, but kept licking around the edges of her vision. "Please," she said, turning back to face him, "there must be something you can do to help us."

He waved his hands as if he were helpless. "I've done all I can. The rest is up to you."

Before she could reply, the doors swung shut, locking them out. She stamped her foot in frustration.

"I'm sorry," Paxton said. "This was my idea, but we lost Leandra and Kerr and your wolf, and we're no closer to saving Rory. He was no help at all."

Ella stared at the doors, an idea sparking in the back of her mind. "Maybe he was."

"What do you mean?"

"All this time, I've felt trapped by the fishwife's bargain. I was fool enough to agree when I didn't fully understand the rules, but what if we change the game, like I did with the test of strategy?"

"How?"

Ella threw her hands up. "Well I don't know. I haven't figured that part out yet."

"Maybe this wasn't such a waste, after all." Paxton led her across the courtyard that surrounded the castle and into the second half of the labyrinth. "When I made my deal with the fairy godmother, she told me I had to poison Rory but couldn't kill him. I dallied for months because the more I got to know him, the less I wanted to leave him with a poison's debilitating after-effects. I thought ..." He paused, gazing distractedly down the passageway. "I thought marrying a prince would save Juliana and solve my family's money problems. And it certainly helped. Rickett gifted me that beautiful estate, I moved my entire family in, and we were able to sell our old one and settle our debts. But what secured our future was Rory teaching me to cook."

Ella studied him, but he seemed to be talking more to himself than to her.

"The first time he returned to the haven with a wound, I was able to use my cooking skills to make a simple poultice. I moved on to balms and tinctures and elixirs. It turned out I was quite adept at the medicinal arts, and when I returned home I was able to pass that knowledge on to my family. We now have a steady income, and our wealth isn't tied to the land and the tenant farmers. Dexter's hoping to move into a home of his own soon."

"That's nice," Ella said, unsure what else to say, or how his reminiscence helped their situation.

"It was also what helped me solve my dilemma. I was poring over some old alchemy texts and found a definition of 'poison' which meant 'to reduce the activity of.' I gave him a sleeping potion. When the fairy godmother arrived, I was terrified she wouldn't accept my explanation, but she seemed almost impressed that I'd outwitted her."

Finally, Ella understood the point of his story. "She tricked me when she set the terms of our bargain. I need to find some way to trick her in return."

"But still satisfy the deal."

That would be the tricky part.

As they took another turn deeper into the labyrinth, Paxton asked, "What happened in that strange little hut? Was the fairy godmother there?"

"She was, and I'm afraid of what will happen if I cannot find some way to outwit her. I stabbed her, and she brushed it off as if it were no more effective than a wasp's sting." Ella shivered at the memory. "She also gave me a vague warning that my time would run out when someone's folly came to life."

"Whose folly?" Paxton asked sharply.

Ella strained to remember the unfamiliar name. "Hackden? No, Haxton? It definitely started with an H."

"Huxford? Huxford's Folly?"

"You know of it?"

"Huxford was the prince Juliana was meant to marry. He was rich and powerful and a great source of gossip amongst the nobles. He had a vast estate at the northern border, and rumors spread that he spent a great deal of money creating an elaborate garden, and an even greater amount keeping all the exotic plants alive. That's why they started calling it Huxford's Folly." Paxton paused and shook his head. "My parents received a letter stating the wedding was off. I think they would have been incensed except it arrived on the very same day I returned from my long captivity with Prince Rickett at my side. Since Juliana no longer needed to marry to solve our money problems, they promptly forgot all about him."

"What happened to him?"

Paxton gave a very unprincelike shrug. "I presume he found someone else to marry."

"What about the garden?"

"Unless he continued to pour money into them, the plants probably died."

That would make sense if the fishwife's warning was true. The garden would have to be dead in order to come to life.

They turned another corner and passed under another archway. The way forward was blocked by another stone slab and two strange-looking guards. Their faces resembled those of deer, with long snouts, wide-set eyes, and protruding ears. They stood upright on long legs, carried a spear and a shield in their thin arms, and wore uniforms in a black and white harlequin pattern.

"Who goes there?" the one on the left asked.

"Do you suppose," Paxton said quietly, "that we have to complete another set of challenges to escape?"

"Can't we just ask to leave, like those statues told us?"

"Or are we still caught in the test of stamina?"

Ella groaned. "I'm sick of these games and trickery."

"No games here," the guard on the right said.

"Only a simple task," the other one added.

"Ask one of us to open the door."

"And it will either lead you to the exit ..."

"Or turn you back to the center."

"But here's the trick ..."

Ella glared at the guards. She'd known there would be a trick somewhere.

"One of us only tells the truth ..."

"And the other one only lies ..."

"Ha!" Paxton cried with glee. "I know this one."

"What?" the guard on the left gasped.

"I've got two older brothers, and they loved to torment me with puzzles such as this." He turned to the guard on the left. "If I were to ask your companion if he controlled the way forward, what would he say?"

"Are you sure about this?" Ella hissed.

"Trust me."

The guards glanced at each other. The left one frowned. The right one shrugged. Finally, the left one said, "He would say yes."

"That means he *doesn't* control the way forward, so *you* need to open the door."

"How did you work that out?" Ella asked.

"It's simple really. If the one on the right lies and his way leads forward, he would lie and say 'no,' and the one on the left would truthfully report that. If, on the other hand, the one on the right told the truth, he would say 'yes,' but the liar would lie and say 'no.'"

"Oh ..." Ella's head swam as she tried to follow his logic.

"Inversely, if the way led back, the liar would lie and say 'yes,' and the truthteller would answer 'yes.' Or the truthteller would say 'no,' but the liar would lie and say 'yes.'"

"So, yes means no and no means yes?"

"Exactly!"

"Is that your final decision?" the guard on the left asked.

"Absolutely."

"All right, then ..." The guard touched the stone slab and it slid up, revealing the passageway beyond.

It *looked* like it carried on forward, but who knew if it was merely going to double back on itself eventually.

Paxton grinned and offered Ella his arm. "Shall we proceed, Miss Ella?" he asked.

Ella's stomach squirmed, but as far as she could tell, his logic was sound. She took his hand, and they stepped beneath the stone slab together. And when the ground opened beneath their feet, they fell together, too. Ella screamed as her hand clamped onto Paxton's. She threw out her other hand and caught the edge of the hole into which they had fallen. She slammed against the smooth stone side, and pain shot through her shoulder, hip, and knee. A moment later, Paxton's full weight wrenched on her other arm, and she let out a cry.

The guards' voices echoed down to her.

"Why do they always fall for it?" one of them said.

"One of us always lies and the other always tells the truth!" the other chortled. "What nonsense."

"We ... both ... lie ..." the first one called out, his words barely distinguishable between gasps of laughter.

Ella grunted with the strain of holding Paxton. Her fingers barely clung to the edge of the hole. She glanced down. She couldn't see the bottom, only darkness. "Can you climb?"

"The wall is smooth." Paxton's voice was strained. "There's nothing to hold."

"What if you climb up me?"

Paxton's free hand grabbed her ankle, and he braced his feet against the wall.

Ella's fingertips slid closer to the edge, and fear pulled another shriek from her throat.

Paxton released her ankle. "Ella," he said, his voice eerily calm. "You need to let me go."

"What? No!" She stared down at him. "I'm not letting you go. I'm stronger than I look. I just don't have a very good grip."

"Ella." His voice was firmer, his gaze resolute. "If you let me go, you can get both hands on the edge to pull yourself up."

"No," she said again. She barely knew Paxton, and though she'd resented him at first, he'd been kind to her. He'd carried her when she'd collapsed, and she couldn't imagine facing his family and admitting she'd sacrificed him to save herself. "Try dropping your pack."

"Ella," he said again, and she was starting to hate her new name. "Either you escape or neither of us do. It was my mistake that led us here. You shouldn't pay for that."

"No!" Tears filled her eyes and his visage blurred. "It was a trick. It didn't matter which guard opened the door, we would still have fallen into this trap."

The fishwife's words came back to her. *Beware the prince for he shall be your downfall.*

Well, that had certainly come true.

Her fingertips slid even closer to the edge. Paxton's hand shifted in hers.

"Ella," Paxton said one more time. "If you see my family or my husband, tell them I love them. And when you find a way to save Rory, make sure you don't waste a moment of your life together."

Then he wrenched his fingers from hers and dropped into the darkness.

Given gave a set of three termite mounds a wide berth as he ran down a curved path after Ella and Paxton. He couldn't be far behind them; their scent trail was still strong. Leandra's had disappeared at the last village he'd passed through, one marked with two archways and a grid on the ground. He'd been worried he would face a challenge he couldn't pass alone, but there had been no stone slab blocking his way.

He gave another set of three termite mounds a wide berth as he kept on around the curve. He was still coated in the mucky swamp water, a wound on his nose where the first goblin had hit him with her cane stung, and the last thing he needed was to accidentally invade the termites' territory and find they came armed with tiny swords.

A feeling of unease settled over him as he passed a third set of termite mounds, and he slowed to a halt. Their structure and position seemed so familiar. He shook off the feeling and kept moving.

When he passed the termite mounds for the fourth time, he knew he wasn't imagining their similarity. He scratched at the dirt with his paw, drawing an arrow, then continued on along the curve. When he came upon the mounds again, he checked the ground and there was his sign.

Somehow, the walls of the labyrinth had shifted to trap him in a complete circle.

He ran his nose along the walls, using scent and touch to ensure his eyes weren't fooling him, making him miss a fork in the path. He even sniffed carefully at the termite mounds and pawed at the wall behind them to check they weren't blocking the way.

He couldn't fathom what sort of test this was. Stamina? Strategy? Or survival, like the swamp?

He flopped to the ground to give himself time to rest and think.

He hadn't come up with a solution when the faint scent of fish wafted past on the breeze. He scrambled to his feet, followed his nose around the curve, and found the scent was emanating from a ramshackle hut that hadn't been there the last three times he'd passed this way. He approached hesitantly, sniffing to see if he could pick up the scent of anyone—or anything—inside. A familiar perfume invaded his nostrils. Rosewater.

The door of the hut opened, and an arm reached out of the gloom to beckon him inside.

His hackles rose, but he forced his paws to carry him forward.

A fire burned in the middle of the floor, sending a thick layer of smoke up to the ceiling, where it took its time escaping out a narrow chimney. Nets and ropes hung from the walls, and the odor of fish oozed from every surface, overwhelming the rosewater.

The enchantress sat at a small wooden table, her beauty out of place against her surroundings. "Tea?" she asked, raising a delicate cup to her lips.

Given let out a low growl.

"There's no need for that," the enchantress said. "I don't hold a grudge."

She paused, as if expecting him to contribute to the conversation. When, of course, he didn't, she continued. "I must admit I'm curious." She set down her cup, leaned forward to set her elbows on the table, and rested her chin in her hands. "Why are you still a wolf?"

Given let out a confused, "Ro?"

"Come now, we both know you broke the curse on the last new moon." Her lips twitched as if she were attempting to contain a smile. "Or are you still trying to pretend that didn't happen?"

The day of the new moon still burned bright in his memory—his conflicted feelings as the sun set without the familiar tingle coating his skin; his desperation to turn back into a wolf. He'd dismissed the possibility that he'd broken the curse, but if what the witch was saying was true—and he didn't immediately rule out that this was a trick—then he *did* love Ella. And she loved him in return. But not in the way he'd assumed the witch meant. Not romantically. Ella had Rory for that. And Given had never needed it.

No. He'd been right. He was fond of Ella, but more than that, he'd do anything for her. And that was, perhaps, the greatest love he'd ever felt for anyone.

"I warned you, did I not, that if you took too long, you would remain a wolf?" The enchantress made no attempt to conceal her grin this time, and there was such menace behind it, that Given worried he'd fallen from a cooking pot into the fire. "Poor Ella will certainly benefit from having a loyal, dependable wolf companion ..." Her lips pouted with fake concern. "Though, if you want to save her from the trouble she's about to succumb to, you will need opposable thumbs."

The enchantress smirked as dread settled over Given's haunches.

"Run along now," she said, "and you might just make it in time."

Fear for Ella's safety made Given scramble out of the hut at breakneck speed. No longer trapped in the circular path, he chewed up the ground and soon burst into the open area in the center of the labyrinth. A vast castle rose above the walls, and Given aimed for it.

But Ella's scent—fainter now and tightly entwined with Paxton's—was overlaid by another, stronger one.

They'd gone into the castle, but they'd already come out again.

Given spun around to follow the fresher scent trail, which headed into the labyrinth once more. The passageways looped around and doubled back until he burst through another archway. Two deer-like creatures with shields and spears stood beside the exit. One was doubled over with laughter. The other was collapsed back against the wall, his face lifted to the sky.

Through the opening, Given could see a large pit. A pair of hands gripped the edge. Ella's scent was so strong that he knew exactly whose hands they were.

The enchantress was right. A wolf couldn't help in this situation.

And he had no time to waste on doubt.

He needed to be a man, and he needed to be one *now*.

The familiar tingle ran over his skin.

The guard who was still upright gasped in surprise when Given snatched his spear on his way past.

He skidded to a halt, dropped to his stomach, and leaned into the pit. He clamped one hand around Ella's wrist and buried the spear into the wall as far down as he could reach, about level with her shoulder.

"Hold on," he growled. "I've got you."

Ella let out a sob that was half fear, half relief.

Given didn't have any experience rescuing people who were dangling on the edge of a pit, but he didn't think he'd be able to pull her up while lying on his stomach. But if he got to his knees, there was a chance she would merely pull him into the pit with her.

Either way, he had to take some sort of action, as he didn't know how much longer she could hold on before *her* strength gave out.

"I'm going to try to lift you high enough to use that spear as a step, all right?"

She nodded, her gaze locked on his.

"But you'll have to let go of the edge."

She let out a whimper—definitely fear—but swallowed it down and nodded again.

He pushed up onto his knees then grasped her other wrist. "Now."

She loosed her right hand and clamped his wrist then repeated the action with her left. Her weight dragged on his human form in a way he wasn't used to. He gritted his teeth and heaved. She braced her feet against the wall of the pit, her face twisted with determination. He heaved again, moving her higher. She got one foot on the spear, which groaned under her weight.

Given rocked back onto his toes. "Now!"

He threw himself backward, Ella thrust herself upwards, and the spear snapped.

She let out a curse as she hit the edge and her legs tumbled back into the pit. Given grasped her arms tighter and dragged her closer. She found the ground with her knee then scrambled forward and collapsed down beside him.

Given lay panting for a moment, relief flooding his system, before he realized that his state of undress, which was perfectly acceptable as a wolf, was entirely inappropriate as a man. He rolled sideways and hunched against the wall, as there was nothing for him to hide behind.

With a groan, Ella pushed to her knees. "Given?" she called, but rather than glancing around for the wolf, she stared straight at him. When he didn't respond, she repeated his name and began to crawl toward him.

He held up his hand to warn her off. "Stay back, Miss Ella, I'm not attired."

"I can fix that." Her eyes narrowed and she flicked a dagger into her hand before stalking back through the archway, where the guards were still laughing. A moment later, their laughter died, and not long after that, Ella returned with one set of the guard's clothing and offered them to Given. He pulled them on gratefully and rose to his feet.

He was surprised to find he wasn't much taller than her.

She lunged at him. He threw himself backward until he hit the wall, scared she was going to stab him.

She did not stab him.

Instead, she wrapped her arms around him and buried her face in his neck.

"Miss Ella ..." he said.

"I thought I'd lost you."

"Ella?"

She pulled back. Her cheeks were damp with tears, but she was smiling. "I know it's you." She reached up, ran her fingers through his straggly beard, and scratched under his chin as she had done so many times before.

"How did you know?"

"Your eyes are the same." She let out a contented sigh and snuggled in against him again.

"You're not surprised that I'm a man?"

"Well, I would've been less surprised if you'd let Rory tell me what a demi-wolf *actually* was, but I knew you weren't a normal wolf."

No matter how many times she had hugged him, he'd never been able to hug her back. This time, he could and he did.

"Where's Paxton?" he finally asked. "His scent trail accompanied yours all the way here."

Ella's face twisted with shame and despair. She glanced at the pit.

Given's stomach dropped, and he dropped to his knees at the edge of the hole. "Your Highness?" he called. "Prince Paxton?"

He listened as well he could with his human ears, but there was no reply.

"I didn't die," he said gently, rising once again. "We can only hope he survived too."

"What about Leandra? We had to leave her. Did you see her?"

Given shook his head. "Maybe she did what the statues suggested and asked for an exit?"

"Maybe," she said, but she didn't sound convinced.

"Do we have any choice but to keep moving forward?"

Ella shook her head, slipped her hand into his, and gripped tight. "Let's go."

ELLA TRIED NOT TO stare, but she couldn't stop her gaze from drifting repeatedly to Given. With his dark, straggly hair, stolen clothes, and coating of swamp sludge, it was difficult to gauge how old he was, but she was fairly certain he was closer to her father's age than her own.

He was a little taller than her, with long, lean limbs. The way he loped along reminded her so much of his wolf form that she had to suppress a giggle. His large hand wrapped around hers, his grip was firm and warm, and despite all they had been through, despite losing their companions, she felt safe with him.

"Who are you?" she asked, unable to hold back the questions that had hounded her since they'd met or the ones she'd only thought of since discovering he was human. "Where did you come from? How did you end up in the dogfighter's pit? Do you have a family?"

"That's a lot of questions."

"I'm sorry, but you haven't been able to talk before." Then a thought hit her. "Will you turn back? Can you control it?"

"I never used to be able to," he said. "We shall see if I truly can now."

"Why didn't you show yourself to me earlier?"

He glanced at her, and his eyes—the wonderful deep brown eyes that were so familiar—pinched. "I wasn't sure how you'd react." He cleared his throat. "You seem to have a strong aversion to older men."

"You can't be that old." Ella laughed, but when Given didn't join in, her lightheartedness was replaced with shame. "I only dislike cruel men. Are you cruel?"

"I wasn't always particularly kind," he said gently.

She swallowed hard, trying to shove her emotions aside, trying to stop them from taking her over. "At least tell me this: were you a man who was turned into a wolf, or a wolf who turned into a man?"

"I was a fool of a man who made a terrible mistake."

"Did you accidentally promise to give the heart of someone you love to a witch, or repeatedly give in to the righteous indignation that fuels your talent with a blade?"

Given's eyebrows bounced, but he gave her a sympathetic smile. "We'll find a way to save Rory. Was the goblin king any help?"

Ella recounted the story of meeting the goblin king and her suspicion that she somehow had to change the game the old fishwife was playing. "We just have to figure out how. And do it before Huxford's Folly comes to life, though I don't—"

"Before what?" Given asked, his voice sharp.

"The fishwife warned me that my time would be up when Huxford's Folly came to life. And Paxton told me Huxford was some old prince, and his folly was a garden full of exotic plants that all died when he disappeared. But I never got to ask him where the prince lived, so I'm not sure how we're going to know when the garden comes to life."

Given closed his eyes while he let out a wavering breath. "I know where Huxford lived. And so do you."

"No, I don't."

"Yes, you do. The manor house we've been staying in belongs to Prince Huxford."

"What?" Ella gasped. It seemed like too much of a coincidence, but maybe that was why the fishwife had chosen the garden to be the sign.

"Why was it empty? What happened to the prince?"

Given glanced at their clasped hands. "He disappeared three years ago. No one has seen him since."

"That's so sad." Ella shook her head. "And unfair. He put all that effort into his garden then never got to enjoy it."

Though there were many questions she wanted to ask Given, he hadn't answered her first ones, and she didn't want to bombard him with more. If she was lucky, they would have plenty of time to discuss everything.

After walking for another couple of hours, they turned a corner and found themselves in a straight section that stretched as far as they could see.

Ella almost didn't want to risk giving voice to her hope, in case it proved wrong, but she said, "Are we back in the same passageway where we started?"

"We can only hope."

Ella's footsteps slowed. She pulled Given to a stop.

"How am I going to tell Paxton's family what happened? How am I going to tell the Grand Prince? What if he hurts Rory out of grief and rage?"

"I can't say how the Grand Prince will react. All we can do is soften the blow as best we can."

Ella's grip tightened on his. "You won't leave me, will you?"

He shook his head. "Never."

She walked with a heavy heart until they reached the large archway that led out of the labyrinth. When she stepped outside the walls, she spotted Kerr leaning casually against the carriage, chatting with the coachman.

Ella gasped in surprise. "You made it out safely!"

Kerr snapped to attention and called, "She's here," before his gaze drifted to Given and his hand went to his sword.

Ella dropped Given's hand so she could hold her own out in front of him. "That isn't necessary."

Before she could explain, the carriage door opened and Paxton jumped down the steps. Then Leandra appeared from the far side of the carriage.

"You're all here!" Ella couldn't hold back tears of joy as she sprinted forward to hug Paxton. "I thought you were dead."

He gave her a brief squeeze before stepping back. "I thought I was too."

"How did you survive?"

"A net was strung across the pit to catch me, and a goblin was waiting to show me the exit, which somehow brought me directly to this outer passage."

"Your Highness," Kerr warned, drawing the Prince's attention to Given, who was loitering by the entrance to the labyrinth.

Paxton tensed. "Who is your companion, Miss Ella?"

Ella ran back to her friend, caught his hand, and dragged him forward. "This is Given. He was turned into a wolf, but now he's a man again."

"Is *that* what Rory meant by a demi-wolf?"

"Yes, but don't ask me how he knew." She glanced at Given. "How did he know?"

Given winced, and Ella delighted in seeing the familiar expression on his new face. "For as long as I've been a demi-wolf, I have turned back into a man during each new moon. I believe Rory saw me transform."

Paxton eyed Given and let out a thoughtful, "Hmm."

Given dropped his gaze under the Prince's scrutiny. "I mean no harm, Your Highness."

"He's my friend," Ella told the Prince, "and he saved me from succumbing to the pit as you did."

Paxton cleared his throat. "Well, of course you're welcome in whatever form you come. Let's return to my estate where we can sate our hunger and wash away today's troubles."

Though the Prince's words were generous, there was an undercurrent to them that Ella didn't understand and couldn't easily dismiss. He might have been suspicious of Given because he didn't believe the man and the wolf were one and the same, or it could have been because he didn't trust someone who had undergone such a transformation, but Ella couldn't help thinking it was more than that, as if Paxton for some reason held a grudge against him.

But how could that be when they'd never met before? What could Given have done as a wolf that Paxton would hold against him as a man?

CHAPTER NINE

Given enjoyed a luxurious bath, dressed in a fine set of borrowed clothes, brushed the tangles from his hair and secured it with a ribbon, and braided his beard. But when a maid came to invite him and Ella to dinner, he demurred.

"I've been a wolf for a long time," he told Ella. "I'm afraid my manners will appear beastly."

Ella took his hand. She touched him a lot as a wolf, but there was always a layer of fur between them. He wasn't yet used to feeling her skin on his.

"You can't leave me to face Paxton's family alone, after all I put him through."

"That wasn't your fault. It was Paxton's idea to go to the goblin king."

"But it was my bargain with the fishwife that made him suggest it." Her face set. "If you won't come to the dining room then we'll dine here together. It will give you time to tell me how you became a wolf and who you were before."

Though Given intended to tell her eventually, it didn't feel right doing so here, in Paxton's house. "That would be ruder, I think, after they have been so kind to us." He forced a smile. "Let's go down. I'll do my best not to eat directly from my bowl."

The whole family was already present in the dining room, and silence descended when they entered.

Given was so used to the fact that nobody remembered Prince Huxford that he'd been startled when Paxton looked at him with a flash of recognition. Now that the curse was broken, he'd have to get used to being recognized. He only wished he didn't have to start with a family he had wronged.

Ella clearly sensed the tension in the room though she couldn't know its cause. "Don't be startled," she said. "It turns out my wolf is a man."

It was Serafina who broke the silence. She stepped forward to scrutinize him before finally declaring, "You still look like a wolf."

Given ran his hand over his beard. "Thank you?"

"You sound like a wolf, too."

To his relief, Given found himself seated near the foot end of the table between Ella and Serafina, but that didn't stop the baron from asking, "What shall we call you now?" which seemed like a particularly pointed question.

"Given is as fine a name as any," he replied.

The baron let out a faint harrumph and shared a look with his wife before changing the subject. "I'm sorry the goblin king didn't provide any assistance."

"I'm sorry it wasted a whole day," Ella replied.

Paxton had warned them he had no intention of telling his family the details of the trials they had faced in the labyrinth, so as not to worry them. Although, Given was no longer sure how much risk they'd really faced. Once they'd passed through the test of strength, the goblins had stopped attacking Kerr. And once the others had left Leandra, she'd no longer been required to play the game with the goblins. Like Paxton, both had been shown a magical exit in the wall that had taken them back to the entrance.

Even the skeletons hadn't really hurt them. Apart from a few superficial cuts and bruises—and Given's near-drowning—they had all escaped unharmed. Ella may have felt like the journey had been a failure, but at least she had a clue to chew over.

"What will you do now?" the baroness asked.

Ella glanced at Given. "I suppose we'll return to the manor house and try to find a solution before the garden comes to life."

"You own a manor house?"

Ella let out a light laugh. "Oh no, it was one we found abandoned. Apparently it belonged to a prince who built a fantastic garden then disappeared."

"What prince?" the baron asked.

"Prince Huxford."

"Never heard of him," the baron said.

Across the table, Juliana gasped.

"You've never heard of him?" Paxton asked, exchanging a look with his sister.

"No. Should I have?"

"I guess not."

If they still couldn't remember Prince Huxford, then Given had read the tension in the room incorrectly, but he was certain Paxton, at least, knew who he was.

"We'll leave in the morning," Paxton continued. "I'm sorry I can't stay longer."

The meal passed without providing any further answers. Once the dessert dishes had been cleared, Ella excused herself, claiming exhaustion.

"I'll be up soon," Given said. "I'd like to stretch my legs before I settle. I am, after all, not used to having only two."

Her brows dipped briefly before she nodded and headed for the stairs.

Given slipped through the house, out the back door, and into a large courtyard. It wasn't long before he had company.

Juliana stepped up beside him. Paxton arrived a moment later. Kerr trailed discreetly behind them.

"Prince Huxford?" Juliana asked, studying him carefully.

Given turned to face the young woman. "I really do prefer Given now, if you don't mind."

"What happened to you?"

"I incurred the wrath of a witch and she turned me into a wolf."

"When?"

"Three years ago. Just before I was going to send for you."

Paxton let out tight groan. "I believe that may have been my fault."

"I assure you, Your Highness, I accomplished it perfectly well on my own."

"I'm not certain you did."

"Pax," Juliana said. "Are you sure about this?"

"It's too much of a coincidence." Paxton's expression was torn between shame and irritation. "I didn't want you to marry him and look what happened."

"It wasn't your fault," Given said. "You may have set things in motion with your wish, but the fairy godmother came to me and offered me a way out. I was too stubborn to see it for what it was and refused. I thought ..." He paused and turned back to Juliana. "I thought you would be the perfect bride, but I never asked your opinion on the matter. You were too young. I was too self-serving. And your parents were too eager. For that, I'm truly sorry."

Juliana gave him a soft, forgiving smile.

"No, I'm sorry," Paxton said. "When I wished to marry a prince in Juliana's stead, I didn't consider there might be consequences for you. I didn't question how the fairy godmother would get you to rescind your proposal, and I never imagined that her methods would involve bodily transformation."

"No need to apologize, Your Highness. I believe I'm a better man for being a wolf."

"But why don't our parents remember you?" Juliana asked.

"I cannot answer except to say *no one* remembers me except you two. My servants forgot me the moment they left my estate, my tenant farmers have no memory of their lord, and even the Grand Prince doesn't recall I own the border lands."

"Did your absence allow Caveline to invade?" Paxton asked.

"Caveline hasn't invaded."

"Prince Rickett thinks they have. All the High Council does."

"It's as if whatever curse the enchantress placed on me has skewed their memories. But, I must admit I'm confused. I thought now that the curse has broken, everyone's memories would return."

"Has it, though?" Juliana asked.

"I'm a man, and the moon is not new."

"If it was indeed the fairy godmother who cursed you," Paxton said, "she doesn't play idly. Maybe the curse runs deeper than you think."

A shiver ran down Given's spine. The enchantress had warned him twice that if he didn't break the curse quickly enough, he would remain a wolf. Yet, here he was.

He closed his eyes, let out a long breath, and urged himself to be the wolf. The tingle ran over his skin and within a moment, his clothes were draped awkwardly over his lupine form. He concentrated again, and once more stood between Paxton and Juliana as a man.

He straightened his trousers and smoothed his shirt.

"Should you still be able to do that?" Juliana asked.

"I'm still a demi-wolf," he murmured.

But he couldn't make sense of that. Hadn't he solved the mystery? He loved Ella, and she loved him. And why could he change at will when he'd never been able to before?

"If the Grand Prince still can't remember that I own the border lands, will he believe the Cavelian Queen when she tells him she hasn't invaded?"

Paxton shook his head slowly. "In his current state of mind, I'm not certain."

"If I can truly break the curse, his memory of me should return. It will head off the war."

"Then how do we break the curse?" Juliana asked.

Given shrugged helplessly. "I'm afraid I do not know."

THEY LEFT THE NEXT morning after breakfast. Ella didn't enjoy the bumpy carriage ride any more than she had the other times, but at least Given sat beside her instead of roaming along the road.

Paxton still seemed suspicious of Given, and the tension in the carriage made Ella want to throw open a window and hang her head out. Given, for his part, spoke about as much as he did in his wolf form, which is to say he barely said anything at all.

She'd tried to stay awake last night, waiting for him, but he'd stretched his legs too long and she'd fallen asleep before he'd returned. And when she awoke, she found him asleep in an adjoining room.

An ache had formed in her chest. As much as she was happy that he'd found his human form and broken whatever spell had been placed upon him, she missed her pet wolf.

When they stopped at an inn that night, Paxton paid for separate rooms for each of them. Ella lay awake in the dark alone, shivering in her cold bed. Given had been her constant companion for weeks. She didn't understand why that had to change now that he was human.

As she twisted and turned, her thoughts did the same.

He'd understood the motivation behind her acts of vengeance before she'd told him. When she'd asked if he was cruel, he hadn't answered plainly. He'd said he hadn't always been kind, but she'd only ever seen kindness from him.

She knotted her hands in the blankets—hands stained by the blood of the men she'd hurt, hands that would never be clean again.

No wonder there was a distance between them.

As a wolf, Given had probably stayed with her because she had a pair of hands, convenient for opening doors and lighting fires. She could buy supplies at the village to save him the effort of hunting.

Now that he was human again, her worth to him had lessened. He was likely to send her—and her problems—away as soon as they arrived at the manor.

She would have to return to the palace with Paxton and wait for her time to run out.

She wouldn't be able to find a way to save Rory on her own.

She would lose both of them.

She would be alone again.

Unloved.

No one had ever loved her, and she didn't know why she'd expected that would change.

She threw back the covers, pulled on her cloak and boots, and stepped into the hallway. Leandra, who was standing guard outside the Prince's room, snapped to attention.

Ella had forgotten for a moment that she was still the Grand Prince's prisoner.

"I can't sleep," she said. "A nighttime walk usually helps."

Leandra knocked on a door across the hallway, and when Kerr poked his head out, she said, "I'm taking Miss Ella to stretch her legs."

Kerr nodded, wiped the sleep from his eyes, and took up the guard's position by the door. Ella wondered how either of them functioned after staying awake half the night.

They slipped out the back door of the inn, and Ella felt like she could finally breathe.

The scent of the ocean was missing, but otherwise this night was like any she'd spent in Leyton. The sky was speckled with stars, the waxing moon sat low on the horizon, and a light breeze played across her skin.

Finally, Ella could breathe.

Leandra walked silently beside her, and Ella appreciated the fact that she didn't feel obliged to talk. All the worries that had plagued her in bed didn't seem half as bad out here. Surely, once they returned to Huxford's manor, things between her and Given would return to normal, and they would be able to work together to save Rory.

The inn wasn't part of a village—it was but a convenient stop for travelers, nothing more. The only other building on the road was a two-story barn surrounded by farmland.

As they drew closer, a flicker of light caught Ella's eye, and voices drifted on the breeze. Leandra held her hand out in warning. Ella slowed her pace but didn't stop as she strained to see.

Two silhouettes appeared against the light of an oil lamp. One was tall and burly, the other short and slight. As Ella's heart rate picked up, she watched the taller one—a man, she was certain—give the shorter one a vigorous shake.

Another father abusing his daughter, or a master abusing his servant, or a husband abusing his young wife.

Ella's night vision deepened to red almost immediately, and she broke past Leandra and launched into a sprint. After all the injustices she'd had to ignore in the labyrinth, here was one she could do something about.

She flicked a dagger out of the bracer and yelled, "You! Unhand her!"

Both the figures turned. She was close enough for the light to show the surprise on the man's face, shock at being caught in his misdeed.

Ella slammed into him, breaking his grip on the girl. The impact was so great that it threw the man to the ground and sent the oil lamp sailing out of his hand. Ella pounced on top of him and pressed her dagger to his throat.

He let out a whimper of fear and held his hands wide in surrender. Satisfaction pulsed through Ella's veins. These bullies were always cowards underneath.

"How does it feel," she snarled, "to be treated as you treat others?"

"What do you mean?" the man babbled. "I haven't treated any-one—"

"The girl. Is she your daughter? A servant? Why do you think you have the right to lay your hands upon her?"

"That girl?" Some strength returned to the man's voice. "She's a thief."

"A what?" Ella's pulse turned sluggish.

"Ella ..." Leandra called from her behind her, tension lacing her voice.

"I brew ale," the man continued. "And that girl has been stealing from me for months. How am I meant to make a living when I can't fulfill the inn's order? When my day's work is taken by someone who's never worked a day in her life? I have wife, I have children to feed. Why aren't you holding a dagger to *her* throat for stealing food from my babies' mouths?"

Nausea twisted Ella's stomach, and she pulled her blade away.

She was wrong. Completely wrong. She'd misinterpreted the situation, jumped to conclusions, and attacked an innocent man. He didn't deserve her vengeance. He deserved an apology, yet the words tasted bitter on her tongue and she couldn't force them out. She blinked hard, trying to clear her vision, but she couldn't rid herself of the red mist.

"Ella!" Leandra cried again.

Ella's gaze snapped up. The oil lamp had hit the side of the barn, and flames were licking over the wood.

The man let out a strangled cry and shoved Ella off him. He ran into the burning building, calling, "Mara! Mara!"

Leandra sprinted after him.

Ella scrambled backward, horrified. She knew the right thing to do. She should get to her feet, find some water, help to extinguish the fire before the whole barn caught alight. But the red mist thickened and dripped down her vision in rivulets of blood, making it difficult to see clearly.

"Thanks for the distraction," the thief said.

Ella turned to stare at the girl, who was partially obscured by the red curtain. She gave Ella a mocking salute and slipped away into the darkness.

The fire had spread up the wall of the barn, and the heat pricked at her skin. The shame of what she'd done choked her worse than the thick, black smoke rolling off the building.

She pushed to her feet and wiped at her eyes while she ran, but nothing offered relief from the thick red mist or from her disgust at herself.

GIVEN WOKE TO SOME sort of commotion in the inn. He pushed back the covers of his bed, which had been both too large and too cold. Perhaps he should have changed back into the wolf and slept on the foot of Ella's bed as he had done so many times before. Most likely they would both have been happier.

He pulled on his borrowed clothes and boots, and padded down the stairs.

The inn's dining room was in chaos. It was full of people, adults and children alike. Two of the children were sobbing, and a woman was cradling a crying baby, tears streaking the soot on both their cheeks. All their clothes were charred, and the scent of smoke burned his nostrils.

Paxton was crouched in front of Leandra, tending a wound on her arm. Kerr stood across the room, pouring a jug of water over a man's hands.

"By the stars," Given muttered. "What happened here?"

Leandra lifted her gaze to meet his, her face tight with pain. "Fire."

"Fire? Where? What can I do to help?"

"Do you have any nursing skills?" Leandra asked, her words cutting.

"Hush," Paxton murmured. "This isn't his fault." He twisted around to look at Given. "Can you fetch more water? There's a well out the back."

Given nodded and headed out into the dark night. He returned with two full buckets.

Paxton worked his way around the room, tending one injury after another, applying salves and bandages and directing judicious applications of water. Given helped where he could but felt generally useless. The innkeeper handed around mugs of warm tea and gave sweet treats to the children.

When everyone had been tended, Paxton finally took a seat, accepted a mug of tea, and asked Leandra what had happened.

Leandra shot Given a vicious look, though he couldn't fathom what he'd done to deserve it.

"Ella said she couldn't sleep and wanted to go for a walk. Foolishly, I indulged the girl."

The hair on the back of Given's neck stood to attention, and he glanced around. In his urgency, he hadn't noticed Ella's absence.

"We came upon this brewer's house." Leandra stabbed her thumb toward the man with the burned hands. "He was in the middle of an altercation with a thief, but Ella didn't wait to hear the circumstances."

Dread settled in Given's gut. He could imagine what had happened next without Leandra giving him the details.

"She attacked the brewer as if he were the aggressor and not the victim. In the chaos, an oil lamp spilled and set the barn alight. As we were saving his family from the flames, both Ella and the thief escaped."

Given thudded heavily into a chair. "Was everyone saved at least?"

Surely if someone had been lost, the family's grief would have filled the room.

"Only my livelihood," the brewer croaked.

"Don't fear for your livelihood," Paxton said, his voice reassuring and warm. "I'll give you a grant to re-establish your brewery."

"You've been so kind to us, sir," the woman said, still gently rocking her baby. "Yet we don't even know your name."

The Prince drew a short breath before saying, "You may call me Paxton."

What color was left in the woman's face drained away. "Your Highness, I—" She swallowed hard. "Thank you."

Given turned to Leandra. "Where did Ella go?"

"I don't know. I was too busy to notice her flee, and even then, my priority was to bring the family here, not chase down a rogue prisoner."

"You probably have a better idea of where she would go than we do," Paxton said lightly, as if he wasn't asking Given to betray his friend.

But when the anger took Ella over, she was a different person. Maybe she needed to be hunted down.

Not to be punished, but to be saved.

And the best person to approach her wasn't a person at all.

Given stood up. "She's likely to return to my estate." He gave Paxton a grim look. "I'll meet you there."

He shrugged off his jacket and hung it on the back of his chair as Leandra said, "I'm not letting another prisoner escape."

Given toed off his boots. "Technically I'm neither a prisoner nor am I escaping." He peeled off his shirt and turned back to Paxton. "You know where we'll be."

Paxton nodded, granting him permission.

Given waited until he was outside before he dropped his trousers, transformed into the wolf, and loped into the night.

ELLA RAN UNTIL HER lungs screamed and her legs burned. She ran until the glow from the burning barn disappeared behind her. She ran until the horror of her actions started to fade.

Then she walked.

She didn't know where she was, or how to get back to Huxford's manor, but that was the only place she could think to go. But they'd been headed along a wide road, which she assumed was going in the right direction, so she continued along it. If she eventually reached the river that separated Bretland from Caveline, she was sure she would be able to find her way from there.

Ella studied her hands in the watery morning light. She could still feel the hilt of her dagger against her palm, could still see the blade pressed against the man's throat, could still smell the sharp tang of his fear.

She'd been so sure of the situation. A large man and a young girl, what else could have been happening but the same abuse she'd suffered all her life? But the red mist had distorted her vision, led her astray.

How many other times had she made the same mistake?

Not many, surely.

She had definitely been in the right with the dogfighter. Saving Given had been her most important act. And that innkeeper shouldn't have hit the young waitress for dropping the tray of glasses. And the girl selling flowers had been wronged by the man who'd tried to take her coins ... but Ella also hadn't needed to punish him so cruelly.

And this latest man, the brewer ... how close had Ella come to doing something she couldn't undo? He'd said he had a family. Were they in the barn when it had caught alight? He'd run inside, calling to someone. And Leandra had followed him.

And what had Ella done? Attacked a man who didn't deserve it. Let a thief go free. Ran away from the consequences of her actions.

Her fingernails dug into her palms.

She wasn't a hero. She was a villain. It would be better for everyone if she returned to the manor and locked herself up until she found some way to control her vengeful urges.

She walked through the day, avoiding any people or clusters of buildings, and eventually came to a village she recognized. From there it was simple enough to find her way back to the manor.

Huxford's Folly.

She wondered about this prince who had put such effort into making those intricate gardens. What had spurred him to do such a thing? Was it simply the urge to be surrounded by beauty? Had it been to impress visitors?

Ella looked carefully as she headed through the gardens in the near darkness, wondering when they would come to life. She paused in the rose garden, where she had first picked a bloom that had somehow survived the onset of winter.

Most of the plants looked well dead to her, but she knew little enough about gardening. Did they die off in winter and grow anew in spring? The warmer days weren't far off, so if that were the case, she didn't have much time to save Rory. And the fishwife had been very clear in her threats. If Ella didn't deliver his heart, he would be the one to suffer.

She let herself into the manor as despair as dark as the encroaching night settled upon her.

Given was sitting in the middle of the kitchens. Upon seeing his familiar wolf's face, she let out a sob, dropped to her knees in front of him, and buried her face in his fur.

He was warm, and solid, and smelled reassuringly *right*.

She pulled back, stroked his furry cheeks, and pressed her forehead to his.

"What happened?" she asked. "Why are you a wolf again? No, don't tell me. I don't care. I'm just so glad you're here."

As a wolf he couldn't probe her with questions, scold her actions, or disparage her mistakes.

Seeing him drove the red mist to the very edges of her vision, but it still didn't fade completely.

"Shall we find something to eat?" she asked, making her voice bright and perky before turning to search through their store of supplies.

The night passed like many of the others they'd spent in the manor. They ate a light supper then settled down to sleep. Given hopped up beside Ella on the bed, and she snuggled in close against him, hoping his presence would keep the despair and rage away.

Early the next morning, she left Given sleeping and headed into Riverlea to buy fresh produce and replenish their supplies so she wouldn't have to leave the manor again for a long time. She grew wary as she approached, but she was determined to keep her indignation under control and the red mist at bay. She pulled up the hood of her cloak, avoided the village green, and made a quick circuit of the butcher's, the baker's, and the greengrocer's.

As she headed back through the village, Ella was relieved no incidents had occurred, and she was burdened only by the heavy bags on her shoulders rather than guilt or anger.

Then a voice behind her cried, "That's her!"

Her stomach dropped to her feet, and she spun around.

The man she had assaulted was standing with an older woman, and was flanked by another two villagers with sashes slung across their chests.

"She's the one who did this to me!" He pointed at his cheek, where a nasty scab had formed over the flower Ella had carved there.

The older woman stepped forward. "My name is Frida. I'm the reeve of this village, responsible for keeping the peace. What's your name, girl?"

Ella glanced desperately around. People had stopped their tasks and were eying her curiously. "I'm Ella."

"Ella," Frida said, speaking her name as if it were some sort of spell. She gestured to the man beside her. "Is it true that you attacked Brandon?"

Ella backed up a step. "He was assaulting a young girl."

"Imogina, yes. For stealing his flowers."

"They weren't his to be stolen." She glanced at Brandon, and he stared smugly back. Now that he wasn't facing her alone, he wasn't scared and blubbering.

"Brandon says they were. So why did you take it upon yourself to permanently scar him?"

Ella took another step back. Despite what he'd done, she hadn't meant to go that far. "That was a mistake. He lunged at me, I got angry. I shouldn't have done it."

"We practice restorative justice in this village. How will you make up for what you've done?"

Ella shook her head. It was as if the reeve hadn't heard her, or didn't care. Tendrils of red licked hungrily around the edges of her vision. "What about him? Will he repay his debt to the girl? Will he pick replacement flowers and help her sell them?"

"Imogina hasn't come forth to defend herself against his accusations. Her absence implies guilt."

So that was how justice worked in this village. Bloviators got what they wanted by shouting their lies so loud as to drown out the truth.

The tendrils thickened and spread, turning everything red. The crowd had grown, encircling them. If she wanted to leave, she would have to fight her way through the circle. Her argument wasn't with any of the curious villagers, but if they refused to stand up for what was right, that made them no better than the rest.

She turned back to the reeve. "I don't recognize your authority."

"And yet I am the authority here." Frida regarded her for a moment, her eyes narrowing. "My judgment is this: blood must have blood. You cut Brandon; you will be cut in return."

"You can't do that." Anger frothed in Ella's stomach, over-flowing in a stream of words. "Why are you the one who gets to decide who's right and who's wrong? How can you be so bloated with self-confidence that you make a snap decision without hearing from anyone else? He filled your head with lies, and you came here with your mind already made up, yet you dare to call it justice. You're corrupt, poisoned by power, full of thriftless ambition—"

Frida's expression turned fierce. "No, *you* are the one who can't do whatever they want. If you saw Imogina being assaulted, you should have called for the constables to resolve the situation. You do not come to our village and exact your own justice. If we let everyone do whatever they wanted, our village would descend into chaos. If justice is to be done, it will be carried out by the constables, not vigilantes."

She gestured to the two villagers behind her—the constables, Ella assumed—and they stepped forward. One of them drew a long dagger from the sheath at his waist.

Ella dropped her heavy bags to the ground as the circle tightened around her. The villagers might not have been baying for blood, but they were eager to see justice done.

But this wasn't justice, and Ella wouldn't submit.

She flicked a dagger from her bracer, tossed it to her other hand, and produced another. She turned to face the constables, who spread out as they approached her.

"Stay back," Ella warned them. "I will not be held responsible for what I do."

"Oh yes you will," the reeve said in a stern voice.

It was Ella's own fault for ending up in this situation. She shouldn't have returned to the village. But why should she be punished if Brandon was not?

She fired one dagger toward the constable on her left. It flew true and pierced the woman's boot. She cried out in pain and dropped to her knee. Ella fired another dagger into the second constable's shoulder. He let out a curse and grabbed at the wound.

Ella spun around to face the crowd as she released two more daggers. "Let me through. I have enough daggers for all of you."

"Ella, stop." Given appeared through the crowd. He was in his human form, and was dressed in a worn pair of trousers, a thin shirt, and no boots. "This is not you."

Ella pointed a dagger at him. "You agree with this travesty?"

Given's expression tightened. "I think further discussion is warranted, but I saw you attack that man, and what you did went far beyond protecting the girl. You humiliated him, and you enjoyed it. I'm worried about what's happening to you."

Ella snorted. "You're worried about me? At least Rory stepped in to save me from being whipped. All you're doing is keeping me from escaping."

"And didn't you tell Rory that you weren't his responsibility? If I protect you from the consequences of your actions, will that help you? This curse the fairy godmother laid upon you may have given you the ability to protect yourself, but it also unleashed a darkness in you."

Ella glanced at Brandon, at the crusty scab on his cheek.

Saving the girl, Imogina, had been the right thing to do, but attacking Brandon, *taunting* him, *scarring* him, had been wrong.

She'd attacked the brewer seeking justice for a perceived slight, and it had led to terrible consequences. She hadn't wanted to sacrifice her companions to reach the center of the labyrinth, but in the end, she'd done it willingly enough.

She'd lost control and was losing herself in the process.

She didn't want to be a cruel, vengeful person, didn't want to get to a point where she decided that keeping her skill with a blade was worth sacrificing Rory.

"You're right," she said. She aimed her next words at Brandon. "I was wrong to attack you, just as you were wrong to attack Imogina." She turned to encompass the whole crowd. "Just as all of you were wrong to sit by while she was attacked, and sit back now while lies are told about her." She turned to Frida. "Brandon hasn't made amends for his actions, and I won't let you lay your hands on me when yours are just as stained as mine."

She lifted her dagger, pressed it to her temple, and ran it down to her jaw in one swift stroke.

"Ella, no!" Given cried, but he was far too late.

Pain flared in her cheek. A howl ripped from her throat. Her dagger fell from her fingers.

Given darted forward, took her in his arms, and pressed something soft against her face. Agony spread its claws out from her cheek through her entire body, and she clung to him. The red in her vision crystallized then shattered, and the pain, the anger, *everything* faded to black.

CHAPTER TEN

Given hugged Ella's slumped form and pressed his bunched shirt against her cheek. Blood, thick and warm, oozed between his fingers. The image of her slicing her own cheek would not clear from his mind's eye. He had reacted too slowly to stop her, and he feared his words had led to her actions.

"Are you satisfied?" he heard Frida ask.

"I suppose so," Brandon replied.

Given turned a baleful glare on them. "How could you witness that travesty and not express an iota of remorse?"

Brandon's expression tightened. "After what she did to me? I'm not going to spare any pity for her."

"She's trapped by a curse that's causing her behavior. What's your excuse?"

"We were simply enforcing the laws of our land," Frida said, stepping forward. "Who are you to come here and judge us?"

"Who am I?" Given wanted to stand up tall, loom over Frida, and see her tremble. But he was dressed in only a pair of trousers, his hair was unkempt, and he couldn't stand up without letting go of Ella. He had no power, no wealth, no servants. He was not in a position to intimidate anyone, but he tried his best. "I am your lord."

Frida snorted. "We have no lord. We are the free people of River-lea."

"Does no one remember?" He glanced around the gathered crowd but found only hostile stares.

"We used to have a lord. And a lady," someone called out. "Years ago. But when they died, we never got a new one, and we're all the better for it."

"They were my parents," Given tried. "Surely someone remembers me. I've lived in that manor house all my life. I took over running the estate from my parents when I was only a boy. In return for a tithe I ..." He trailed off.

He wasn't certain what he'd done in exchange for their taxes. He hadn't presided over disputes or helped the farmers when spring storms hit. He hadn't ensured fishing rights were fairly distributed or laws were obeyed. All they got for their money was to be left alone.

He hadn't been such a great lord at all.

"We're happy without a lord," Frida said. "And we certainly don't need some grubby drifter coming here and telling us our business."

The crowd moved closer, and the air thickened with tension.

He'd made a terrible mistake.

"Where's this manor of yours?" Frida asked.

Given didn't think she was planning to arrive on his doorstep with a gift basket of baked goods. More likely they would arrive with pitchforks.

He pulled Ella closer to him. He had no weapons, and even if he did, he couldn't fight while holding her. All he wanted was to flee, and his wolf form was much better for running, but he couldn't carry Ella without arms.

Panic made his skin tingle with the urge to change.

Man or wolf? Wolf or man? Which was better? He couldn't decide. All he knew was he needed to run *and* he needed to keep Ella safe.

He gave in to the change, pushed to his feet, and let out a blood-curdling howl.

FEVERED DREAMS TORMENTED ELLA. Jolts of pain shot through her body, as if a giant jellyfish had made a home in her chest and spread its stinging tentacles into every limb.

She dreamed of herself as she was now. Short hair, leather clothing, a dagger in each hand. Spitting hateful words and slashing at anyone who did wrong in her eyes.

She dreamed of herself as she had been. Tangled curls, ill-fitting dress, a flagon of ale in each hand. Barely saying a word and dodging the groping hands of the tavern's customers.

She dreamed of Rory, sitting beside her at the table, a book open in front of him, his heart displayed on a silver platter.

She dreamed of Given. One moment a wolf, the next a man, both of them disappointed by who she'd become.

She dreamed of her father, berating her for a mistake she couldn't remember making, his fist constantly raised but the blow never falling.

When she awoke, the memories of the dreams clung to her in the way the scent of ale used to permeate her clothes. Her cheek felt like it was on fire. She lifted her hand to it, but found her face covered by a thick, sticky bandage. A hand closed around hers.

"Don't play with it." Given's voice sounded as if he had a mouthful of rocks. "Paxton has sutured the wound and applied a poultice."

She forced her eyes open and turned to face him. They were back home, in the cook's quarters behind the kitchens.

Given's hand fell away as he drew back. "Don't be afraid. It's still me."

She stared at the beast sitting in the chair beside her bed. Given was no longer a man, but he wasn't a wolf, either. He was roughly human-shaped but taller, with massive shoulders and powerful limbs. His muzzle was long like wolf's and his ears flicked nervously on top of his head. The same soft gray fur covered his body, hidden though it was by a lavishly embroidered dressing gown, and his eyes were still his eyes.

"I know it's you." She let out a hiss as her skin pulled and pain flared in her cheek. She pressed her hand against the bandage. "What happened?"

"You cut yourself. Do you not remember?"

Ella winced at the memory and shook her head. "I meant what happened to *you*?"

"You were in danger. I couldn't decide which form was best and ended up like this. A true demi-wolf." Given shifted from the chair to sit on the edge of the bed and took her hand in his again. "If you need, Paxton can give you some tea for the pain."

Fully conscious now, she realized that was the second time he had mentioned the Prince. "Paxton found us?"

Given's gaze softened. "I told him where we would be."

"Given!"

"I ..." He looked away then back. "I didn't want you to suffer like this, but I knew it was time you took some responsibility for your actions. Hurting that man on the village green was bad enough, but misreading a situation so badly as to attack an innocent party and, through carelessness, burn down a family's home was too much."

"I know. I'm sorry." Ella dropped her gaze. Fear raked over her, and she tried to shrink against the wall. Given wasn't frothing at the mouth like her father did when he was angry, spit flying as he yelled at her, his face turning red, but she knew he was angry just the same. But she couldn't face it. Not from him. And her indignation didn't come to save her. It couldn't. Because she deserved it. So she fell back into old habits. Her timidness had never saved her from her father's wrath, but she couldn't help babbling the words. "Please don't hurt me. I won't do it again."

Given dropped her hand. "Hurt you?"

"I'll go," she said. "I'll leave. Hide myself away somewhere so I won't hurt anyone else. Maybe the Grand Prince can lock me back in his dungeon."

"Oh, Ella. I don't know what sort of life you've led, but I know it wasn't good. You didn't target men who were abusing young girls for no reason, did you?"

She pressed further back, as if the wall could swallow her like the statues in the labyrinth. Tears blurred her vision.

"I would never hurt you," he said. "You're brave, and caring, and full of joy despite what has happened to you in the past. And if that makes it sound like you have to behave in a certain way to be safe from me, be assured that isn't the case. I will never lay a hand on you."

Tears streaked down Ella's cheeks, and she raised her hands to cover them. She couldn't bear to let him see her as such a pathetic wretch, not when he'd been her constant companion, her kind, caring rock.

His voice continued softly. "The curse broke on the day of the last new moon, the day of that incident in Riverlea, but I refused to let it go. I made the choice to become the wolf again, because I knew you needed me as your pet dog, and I doubted you would want me as a man. But that was a mistake. You didn't need a friend who would stand by silently while you lost control. In forcing myself to remain the wolf, I've prolonged my curse, let you lose control, pushed Bretland to the verge of war, and left my people without a lord." He shook his head. "Even after all these years, I was still being selfish, still putting myself first. I can't do that anymore."

Although her fear still wrapped her like a blanket, Ella was brave enough to lower her hands and look at him, desperate enough to ask, "Are you leaving?"

"No. Never." His large, furry hand reached forward to grasp hers again. She didn't pull away this time. "You mean everything to me. You're the daughter I always wanted. But if I want to be the father you deserve, I cannot always be your friend. I need to step back and tell you when you're heading down a bad road."

His words made Ella's chest ache. He thought of her as his daughter? She couldn't comprehend it. Her own father had never wanted her, had treated her worse than a servant, had willingly sold her off, and here was someone who had shown her nothing but kindness, who had risked himself for her, who was offering her everything she'd never had.

Before she could put voice to her thoughts, he continued. "I don't expect that means you will always take my advice," he said, with a faint rumble that Ella realized was a self-deprecating laugh, "but I expect you to at least listen. That being the case"—he sat up straighter, and his expression became stern—"if you would like to continue living here with me, and I very much hope you do, there will have to be some rules. You cannot continue to let this darkness overcome you, and I cannot continue to let you get away with it. You must learn to control it. And I'll help you in any way that I can."

Ella carefully wiped her sodden cheeks and nodded, her throat too thick to speak.

"Oh." Given looked somewhat taken aback. "I expected you to argue. In that case, while we work on your control, we'll do our best to make amends for your past actions. And that includes saving Rory's heart."

Ella nodded again, more furiously. There was nothing she wanted more.

"Then you'll stay?" he asked, his furry eyebrows dipping.

Ella pushed herself up and threw her arms around him. "Of course I'll stay."

His strong arms hugged her tight. "I love you, dear girl."

Ella froze. More hot tears filled her eyes, spilled over her cheeks, and soaked into her bandage. She had never heard those words. Not from anyone. Ever.

But she knew he meant them. She felt the truth of them. She'd seen it in his actions. And deep in her heart, she heard the answering cry. It wasn't the instant, intoxicating infatuation she'd felt with Rory. It came bubbling up from a hole that she'd lived with for so long that she'd stopped noticing it. She loved him too. In any form. The wolf, the man, the beast. He was her Given. And she wanted nothing more than to live in this crumbling manor with him. As a family.

She pressed her forehead into the thick fur of his neck. "Thank you," she said, her words muffled, "for saving me."

"Nonsense," he said with another soft, rumbly laugh. "You saved me, remember?"

"Given?" Paxton called softly, sticking his head into the room. "I don't mean to disturb you, but—oh, is she awake?"

"She is. What do you need?" Given replied, glancing over his shoulder at the Prince.

Paxton ignored the question and stepped back out of the room. He returned a short while later with a steaming mug, and came to sit beside them on the chair Given had set beside the bed.

"Here, Ella, drink this." He offered her the mug. "It's a tea to help the pain."

Ella shifted on the cot to lean more comfortably against the wall before taking the mug and sipping at it.

"How do you feel?"

She kept her gaze downcast. "Sore. And ashamed. Are you here to drag me back to the palace? Am I to be punished for attacking that brewer, for burning down his barn?"

Paxton sat up straighter and took on a more regal air. "You should count yourself lucky that none of the family died. They have wounds that will leave scars, and not all of them visible. But I have offered them a grant to rebuild. I will ensure they do not suffer for their loss."

"I have a little money," Ella said. "I'm sure it won't be enough, but I'll give all I have if it will help."

"I'm certain they would appreciate some reparation. And we shall call that the end of the matter." He shook his head. "But this cannot happen again. Building a new barn doesn't undo the burning down of the old one."

"I understand."

Given watched her carefully. He truly hoped that she got control of her rages, because he didn't want to see her take another misstep and hurt someone else. He couldn't help her with that, but he could certainly help her make amends. Money and power were things he had plenty of.

"What did you need, Your Highness?" he asked.

"How good is your night vision in your current form?"

"Excellent."

"Then come with me."

Ella came too, slipping her hand into Given's massive, furry one as they ascended to the second floor of the manor house. Paxton led them into a vast sitting room, where Kerr was standing by an open balcony door.

The sun had not long set, and hints of gray still hugged the horizon, but the gardens in front of the house were cloaked in darkness.

"If I'm not mistaken," Kerr said, "the garden is moving."

A flicker of movement outside caught Given's eye. Then another. It did indeed seem as if the plants were moving, creeping forward in short bursts toward the house.

"Has the garden come to life?" Ella asked, her voice tight with worry.

"No," Given said. "But the villagers have found us."

During all these years when everyone had forgotten about him, the manor had lain abandoned. No one remembered him, no one had come looking, and certainly no one had hunted him down. Until now.

"They're here for me," Ella murmured.

"I think not," Given replied. "As unjust as it may have seemed, they wanted reparation, not vengeance."

"Then why have they come?"

Another flicker of movement caught his eye as a villager darted closer. Given eased away from the window to stand beside Ella.

"I told them I was their lord, I reminded them I'd taken a tithe from them in exchange for nothing much at all, and then I turned into a ferocious, snarling beast before their eyes."

"You're not ferocious." Ella stroked his arm.

"How much time do we have before they attack?" Given asked Kerr.

"Attack?" Paxton's head whipped around. "Surely that's not inevitable? If I go down and speak to them—"

"You are *not* leaving this house, Your Highness. We're severely outnumbered. Our only advantage is they aren't trained soldiers, and they don't know how many of us there are." Kerr's gaze slid to Given. "Or how many of us are like *you*. But uncertainty won't hold them back forever."

"Is it only the two of you?" Ella asked. "Where's Leandra?"

"I sent her after Prince Rickett," Paxton said. "To update him on my current situation. She'll return, but not for a few days."

Without hope of reinforcements, they headed down the stairs and ran from room to room, closing the shutters on the windows, bolting the doors, and stacking the furniture to make barricades.

"Do you have a cache of weapons?" Kerr asked Given. "Bows and arrows? Spears? Shields?"

Both the guard and the Prince had their own swords, and Ella had her endless supply of daggers. Prior to the curse, Given had never been in the habit of carrying a weapon, as he'd always had a retainer to do that for him. And afterwards, there had been no point, as he'd spent so much of his time as a wolf.

"If there are bows, they'll be out in the groundskeeper's hut. They were only ever used to hunt small animals, and they've lain neglected for years. I have a pair of swords in my study, but they're ceremonial." He held up his hands, showing his claws. "These will most likely serve me better."

"Get the swords anyway," Kerr said. "We may have need of them."

Given left them busying themselves in the kitchens and headed upstairs to his study. He took the two swords from the wall, but as he turned around, he paused beside his desk.

He'd last sat here on the morning he'd written the letter to Juliana.

He set the swords down, sat gingerly in the chair, and opened his desk drawer. The letter was still there, faded but legible.

He tore it in two, laid the two halves together, and tore them the other way.

Then he took out two new pieces of parchment, scribbled a note on each, and headed back downstairs.

Paxton and Ella were standing side by side at the workbench. They were wrapping a sticky mixture into bandages, half-rotted clothing, and torn-up sheets.

"I know you're busy," Given said, "but if I can beg your indulgence, Your Highness, this cannot wait."

"Of course," Paxton said, without a trace of irritation in his voice, though he must have been at least slightly vexed at being interrupted. "What do you need?"

"In your role as Prince Consort, can you witness a document for me?"

Paxton's gaze rose. The look in his eyes suggested that he'd guessed what the document was. "Let me wash my hands." Before he turned away, he murmured to Ella, "Keep going, you're doing a fine job."

He washed his hands quickly but thoroughly and dried them as he walked back across the room. Given laid one piece of parchment on a clear spot of the workbench for Paxton to read.

"Are you sure about this?" the Prince asked.

Given nodded and handed him the fine brush. "If anything should happen to me, will you ensure my wishes are carried out?"

Paxton signed the parchment, let the ink dry, then tucked both pieces into the pocket of his jacket. "I will."

WHEN THEY'D RUN OUT of ingredients for Paxton's sticky bundles, they retreated upstairs and barricaded themselves in the sitting room. Ella felt sick at the prospect of what was to come.

"It's fully dark now," Kerr murmured from where he stood on the balcony. "Why haven't they attacked?"

"You said it yourself: they're simple villagers," Given mused, stepping up beside the guard, "and I'm a fearsome beast."

"Who has the best arm?" Paxton asked as he lifted one of his bundles.

"That would be me." Given took the bundle, and Paxton held a flaming oil lamp against the long, dangling tail.

They all watched in silence as the flame caught and hungrily snaked up toward Given's hand. Tension wrapped Ella's shoulders.

Before the fire reached his fur, he flung the bundle into the courtyard. It arched through the night like a shooting star and hit the ground with a wet splat. The flames roared high as they feasted on the contents.

"Well, they know we're ready for them," Kerr said.

As they prepared a second bundle, Ella stared out into the night. With a bright spot on her left, it was hard to make anything out, but a streak of movement caught her eye. A shadowy figure moved through the night.

"There," she cried, pointing.

Given twisted and aimed his flaming bundle to the right. As it sailed through the air, the figure spun to the right and kept running. The firelight played against the runner's hair, bringing out the auburn highlights

"Another," Given cried.

"No." Ella grabbed his arm to stay his actions. "That isn't a villager." She darted to the far side of the balcony and leaned over to watch, the men crowding in behind her.

The figure threw himself directly at the wall, found a toehold on a windowsill, and boosted himself higher. He caught the edge of the balcony with his fingertips and hoisted himself up in a flurry of frenzied activity that left Ella breathless.

"Well," the new arrival said, from where he casually perched upon the balustrade. "Being bombarded with fire is not the worst welcome I've ever received."

"Rory!" Ella pounced on him, almost knocking him backward. He let out a squawk of surprise and grabbed her tightly in return. "Sorry," she said, holding him carefully while he hopped onto the balcony beside her. He was still wearing his usual black trousers, but he'd changed into a cream shirt and a padded tunic that were much too large and might have belonged to one of Prince Rickett's guards.

"What happened?" he asked, cradling her face. "Who hurt you?"

For a moment she regretted the fact that her bandages prevented her from feeling his skin against hers. Then shame overcame her and she dropped her gaze. She found she couldn't answer, didn't want to see his disgust with what she'd done to herself.

"I'd hardly call a single projectile a bombardment," Given said, his voice unusually jovial as he filled the awkward silence.

Rory reluctantly removed his hands from Ella's face as he looked at Given. His brow furrowed, but he seemed otherwise unsurprised at Given's beastly appearance. "Are you speaking Brettish or can I speak Demi-Wolf?"

"Brettish. Wait. Is there a Demi-Wolf language?"

"Not that I've heard of," Rory said with a shrug, "but that's never stopped me before."

"Could we save this conversation for later?" Paxton asked in an exasperated tone.

"Have I vexed you, my lord?" Rory asked.

"Perpetually." Paxton clapped his hand on Rory's shoulder. "But I'm glad you're here."

Ella felt a thin stab of jealously at the fondness of the gesture, but she spat it out like a fish bone. She had no need for it. More concerning was the look on the Prince Consort's face. This was the first time he'd seen Rory since he'd learned his heart was in peril, and he looked like he'd already lost all hope. It made her own guilt surge back to life.

But she still had time. She'd figure out how to save him. Once they'd dealt with the immediate threat.

While Given threw more flaming bundles, lighting up the courtyard, they filled Rory in on Given's transformation into his current form.

"They're quite spread out," Rory said of the villagers, "but I would guess no more than thirty are hidden in the gardens. They've disguised themselves with branches, leaves, and vines, but I was able to pick them out easily enough as I slipped between them."

"They didn't see you?" Kerr asked.

"I'm very good at sneaking, and they weren't looking." Rory stood beside Ella as he spoke, leaning back against the balustrade. She let her hand rest next to his, and his fingers slipped between hers "They're not hardened fighters. They're carrying rakes and hoes." His gaze shifted to Paxton. "Someone once told me that winning a fight is better than losing, but avoiding a fight is best of all. Could we not avoid this fight by talking to them?"

"I did suggest that," Paxton murmured.

"I don't believe we can avoid this one," Given said, casually tossing another flaming bundle into a large gap between two others, completing a near-perfect semi-circle in front of the manor. "Unless I can figure out how to break the curse, for good this time." He paused. "It's me they're after. None of you need to stay."

Ella reached forward and took his hand. "I'm not leaving."

Rory's fingers tightened on hers. "Me neither."

"Your Highness?" Kerr asked.

Paxton shook his head. "We'll see it through."

"Thank you," Given murmured. "All of you."

Ella turned to watch the courtyard. One figure dashed out, highlighted cruelly by the flames. They hooked the burning bundle with their rake and swept it aside. It made a short arc through the air, broke apart as it hit the ground, and quickly extinguished.

She didn't want to hurt any of these people, but she wouldn't let them to hurt Given, either.

"Here they come," she said, flicking a dagger into her hand. She had just enough indignation to control the daggers, but not enough to *lose* control.

Her vision was clear.

Rory stepped up beside her and attempted to do the same, but his dagger caught in his sleeve, and he let out a curse.

"May I borrow that?" He plucked the dagger from her fingers and made quick work of slicing through his sleeves and tearing them free. He handed her dagger back before flicking another one into his hand. "Much better."

"If you want to break the curse," Paxton said, "now would be an excellent time."

Given threw his arms in the air. "But that's the problem. I figured it out, but it didn't work. Instead of breaking the curse, I *broke* the curse." His gaze locked on to Ella. "It was you. You were the answer. I had to learn to love, and I did, but ..."

Ella's heart ached for him. "You said you thought I wouldn't want you as a man, that you forced yourself to be the wolf for me. Is that the problem?"

Given nodded. "I caught tight to the tail of the curse and refused to let go."

Rory let out a low whistle. "That's impressive."

Ella smacked his shoulder, appalled at his rudeness, but he caught her hand.

"I'm not mocking." He turned to Given. "You took control of the spell Godmother cast on you. You bent it to your will. You out-witched the witch."

"Did I? Or was this her plan all along?"

Rory shook his head. "She is conniving, but she cursed you to be a demi-wolf and this"—he waved his hand to encompass Given's beastly form—"is all you."

"Then how do I rid myself of it?"

Rory let out a sigh. "As someone who spent five years avoiding the one thing that would have solved my problems, might I respectfully suggest you start with the most obvious solution?"

Ella braced herself. It felt like he was announcing a punishment.

"If you're holding on for Ella's sake, I assume you need to let go. Wolf or man. Choose one. Not both."

Given's dark gaze bored into her. "Which would you prefer, Ella?"

She shook her head. "Don't ask me that."

"I was never much of a man," Given said. "I was much better as your wolf."

Ella slipped her hand out of Rory's, stepped up to Given, and cupped his long jaw. "That's not what I meant. I don't have a preference. I can't. You're both. You are and you will always be my Given, whether you're a wolf or a man."

He placed his hands over hers then brought them to his lips and planted a wet kiss on her knuckles. Tears pooled in his eyes, and Ella's burned as she tried to hold back her own.

"In case I no longer have a voice to tell you my thoughts, know that I love you, I'm proud to call you my friend and my daughter, and if you ever decide to ask that rogue for his hand, I heartily approve. He truly is a gentleman."

Behind her, Rory inhaled sharply.

Ella pushed up on her toes, kissed Given on his nose, and turned to rain daggers on their foes.

CHAPTER ELEVEN

GIVEN PACED THE BALCONY, thinking, trying to decide.

"Why can't we hurt them?" Rory asked from behind him.

"Because they're our people, not the enemy," Paxton answered.

"I'm fairly certain they won't show us the same courtesy."

Ella inhaled sharply, and Given glanced around in time to see Rory catch a fist-sized rock that had sailed out of the darkness directly toward her face. He fired it back into the crowd below, and someone let out a sharp cry of pain.

"My apologies," he called after it in a half-hearted way. "Does anyone have any other ideas about how to buy us some time?"

Given turned away. They didn't need any other ideas. They knew what needed to happen. And it was up to him.

He had to decide.

He had to let go of the curse.

That was the only way to ensure the safety of not only the people on the balcony, but also the ones attempting to break down the door.

But he didn't know how.

He had spent too long as the wolf, searching for an answer to a question that, when it had revealed itself, had been almost too simple. When the witch had told him he had to learn to love, he'd assumed she'd meant romantically. But he'd loved Ella platonically almost since the moment they'd met, and it had only grown with time. And it was clear, now, that she loved him in return.

And she would continue to love him in whichever form he chose.

He liked being both the wolf and the man, he liked being the silent companion when Ella required it, but she also needed to hear advice he could only deliver when he had a voice. But he also liked the power of being able to switch between them as he pleased. Neither the wolf nor the man could have saved her in the village. His beast form had arrived at exactly the right time.

And that was the problem.

Although he had framed his thoughts around what *she* needed, he was still thinking of himself.

He enjoyed his life too much to want to give up any part of it.

Yet he had to.

For her.

For all of them.

And for himself.

The sitting room door splintered as the head of an axe broke through the heavy wood.

They all ran in from the balcony, and Ella stopped in front of Given as if to shield him with her body. "Stay behind me, Given."

Rory stepped up beside her. "How about you stay behind me?"

She shook her head. "It's not your job to protect me, remember?"

Rory's expression was set, his gaze intense, and only a slight tremble in his hand as he laid it upon Ella's shoulder gave away his true feelings about their life-threatening situation. "Remind me which of us has greater talent for close combat and which of us is better working from a distance?"

Ella winced. "Fine. I'll stay behind you."

Another axe swing took out a chunk of the door, and an angry face peered through. Three more whacks, and the door broke down completely.

"Here we go," Kerr muttered. He was standing in front of the Prince, his sword ready to defend them both.

Three burly constables—two men and one woman—pushed their way inside, shoving aside the barricaded furniture. Unlike the villagers who were carrying farm tools, the constables had daggers at their waists and wooden cudgels in their hands. Frida stepped in behind them. She surveyed the group as the promise of violence swirled around her.

"We're here for the beast," she said, her voice cool. "The rest of you are of no interest to us."

"If you plan to break the curse," Paxton said, "now would be an excellent time." He directed his next words at Frida. "You cannot have him."

"Who are you to come here and tell us our business?"

"He's the Prince Consort," Kerr growled, "and you'd do well to respect that."

Frida's face twisted. "We have no need of a prince here." She made a quick gesture with her hand, and the constables moved to attack.

Given took a step backward, but Rory darted forward to meet them. He ducked low and thrust a dagger into the first man's knee, spun to the side and swept his blade across the next man's arm so he dropped his cudgel, and when the remaining constable drew her dagger, Rory buried his blade in her armpit. Then he danced back beside Ella.

"Rory!" she snapped. "You're not meant to hurt them."

"I apologize, my lady," he said. His breathing was somewhat fractured, though it didn't appear to be from the exertion. "In my defense, I'm very good at inflicting minimal damage for maximum reward."

Indeed, the three constables had been incapacitated, but none of the wounds appeared to be fatal. Hope flared in Given's chest like one of Paxton's sticky bundles catching alight. Perhaps he didn't have to choose. Perhaps they could fight their way out of this.

But more villagers forced their way into the room, spreading out to present a force that Given doubted even Rory's skills could overcome.

"Are we allowed to hurt them, then?" Kerr grunted, fending off blows from a man wielding a pitchfork. "Because that'll make my job a lot easier."

"No," Paxton shot back, as two women attempted to back him into a corner. He struck with the flat of his blade to send one sprawling to the ground, but the other swung her sickle, and he had to throw himself out of the way.

Ella stood directly in front of Given, edging him backward as she fired her blades into the floor, making the villages dodge to save their toes.

And Rory danced through the crowd, striking with the handles of his daggers where he could, only using the blades when he had no choice.

But it didn't take long for the number of villagers to overwhelm and separate them all.

Ella let out a surprised cry as the sharp edge of a hoe caught her arm. Rory turned to search for her in the melee, and his moment's distraction allowed one of the remaining constables to strike a lucky blow with his cudgel.

Rory dropped.

Ella screamed.

"Stop!" Given bellowed, his voice booming around the room. The fighting ceased, and all eyes turned to him. He met Frida's gaze. "Leave my friends in peace, and I'll come with you."

She eyed him coldly then stepped aside to invite him through the wrecked door.

"Given, no," Ella croaked.

"It's for the best," he said. This was his fault. He couldn't decide, couldn't break the curse, and he should be the one to pay, not them. If he let the villagers take him away, his friends would be safe.

He stepped past Ella, giving her shoulder a squeeze. But before he made it through the door, the crowd closed in around him, a villager swung her rake, and the tines bit into his shoulder.

Given let out a howl of pain and dropped to his knees.

Ella screamed again.

More blows followed as tools usually reserved for farm work became weapons of hatred and fear. They pounded his flesh as he lay on the ground, curled in a ball. They cut into his skin until his fur ran thick with blood. They spewed hateful words as they attempted to destroy him.

He could not let them.

If he didn't let go of the curse, there would be nothing left of him, and that would hurt Ella more than if he made the wrong choice between wolf and man.

He didn't focus on any particular form, he merely willed the curse to shape him as it would. And as the familiar tingle ran over his skin, he succumbed to darkness and pain.

ELLA SCREAMED UNTIL SHE thought she would go hoarse, but the red mist didn't come. The villagers swarmed Given, beating him with their makeshift weapons, but she didn't let her fury convince her that their lives were forfeit.

When the first wave of anger had subsided and clarity took hold, she aimed her daggers carefully. They found homes in weak spots that made the villagers drop their weapons and crumple to the ground. Kerr darted forward to catch a hoe before the villager could strike. Rory had somehow found his feet and was hauling people away from the back of the crowd, disabling each efficiently before moving onto the next.

The villagers were not battle-hardened soldiers. Even the constables cared more about their own wounds than they did about continuing to inflict them upon Given.

Then Given's fur started to sparkle, a sight that reminded Ella of when the fishwife had used magic to replace her tattered clothing.

As one, the villagers fell silent and still, and those that weren't writhing in pain looked to Frida.

"What are we doing here?" she asked, confusion twisting her features as she stared down at Given. "What have we done?"

Ella forced her heavy feet to move, and fought her way through the crowd. Given lay on the floor, coated in blood, a wolf once more. Ella's knees gave out and she dropped beside him. "Is it finally broken?" she asked through numb lips.

But the answer was obvious on the faces of the villagers. They may not have realized that it was their lord who was lying bloody in front of them, but they did remember they'd once had one.

"A wolf ..." someone mumbled to her left. "A wolf broke into the house and killed our lord."

"We must finish the animal off before he claims another life," Frida said, but there was no venom in her words, no enthusiasm for the task.

"No," Ella said, trying to keep her voice steady as she looked up at the people still crowded around, at the injuries they'd sustained. "He's not a threat."

Paxton squeezed in beside her. "By the stars," he muttered. "Rory, hot water and as many bandages as you can find."

The sitting room became a makeshift infirmary. Due to the way the fight had unfolded, only a dozen of the villagers had been injured, but those were bad enough. Though both Ella and Rory had been careful with their blades, a dagger wound was still a brutal thing to see.

Rory had a welt on his temple, and although he assured Ella he was fine, he occasionally spoke in a language she couldn't understand, without seeming to realize what he was saying.

Luckily, Paxton wasn't the only one familiar with healing. As peasants, the villagers were used to sustaining the occasional injury from manual labor, and the uninjured ones set about tending the others while Paxton focused on Given.

When Ella was free, she came to kneel beside him. She didn't offer to help, as her own experience was limited to dealing with the cuts and burns her father sustained in the kitchens. Neither did she ask what Given's outlook was. She'd never seen someone beaten so brutally, and she was afraid of what Paxton would say.

Eventually, he lifted his gaze to hers. His face was haggard, as if he'd aged fifty years. "I've staunched the bleeding and done my best to clean and bandage his wounds."

Ella held her breath as she waited for the bad news that was sure to come.

"What concerns me is his shoulder. I fear the bones are shattered. I have little enough experience treating that sort of injury in humans; I have none at all with wolves." He paused to wipe his brow with the back of his hand. "All we can do is make him comfortable, wait, and hope."

None of the villagers had any better ideas for Given's treatment, and the look on Frida's face suggested an animal with that type of injury would be put out of its misery.

Given let out small whimpers of protest but didn't wake as they removed the tattered remnants of his dressing gown and carefully lifted him onto a makeshift bed beside the fireplace. The villagers left in twos or threes, the strong assisting the injured, until only Frida and one of her constables remained.

Her expression was still unfocused as she asked, "What will happen now that our lord is dead?"

Ella was about to protest that he wasn't dead yet, until she remembered that as far as they knew, he'd died three years ago.

"Lady Ella is your liege now," Paxton said simply. "Go about your lives, and she'll summon you when she's ready."

Frida nodded politely before leaving the room.

"Why did you tell her I'm their liege now?" she asked.

Paxton gave her a sympathetic look. "Because that's what Given wanted." He took two pieces of parchment from his jacket pocket and handed them to her.

Ella carefully unfolded them and started to read.

My dear Ella,

If you're reading this, I'm no longer with you. I hoped there would be time to explain everything in person, but a hastily drafted letter will have to do.

I haven't been honest with you.

When I told you this manor used to belong to Prince Huxford, you asked me what happened to him, and I told you he disappeared. What I should have said was he turned into a wolf. I'm sorry I kept the truth from you. I left Huxford behind me a long time ago, and when you named me Given, I knew I never needed to go back to being who I was.

"Given's a prince?" Ella asked.

"Yes," Paxton replied, from where he had collapsed into a chair.

She turned to gaze at Rory, where he and Kerr were trying to clear the broken door. "Rory's a prince."

"Indeed he is."

"Is everyone a prince in disguise?" she asked.

Paxton let out a tired laugh.

She turned back to the letter.

I'm prepared for this night to not go well. The villagers are here for me, and if it's required, I'll sacrifice myself to save the rest of you. I know you'll find that unacceptable, which is why I'm taking the coward's route and not telling you in advance.

With that in mind, I have chosen you as my heir. If I die, you will inherit my lands, my fortune, and my title.

Ella swallowed hard. "I'm the liege of a grand manor?"

"Yes," Paxton murmured wearily. "Congratulations."

The letter fell from her numb fingers. "No, no, no. Why would he do that?"

"Because he loves you."

The fairy godmother was right. She'd been right about everything. Ella had become the liege of a grand manor. Rory hadn't come. The Prince had been her downfall.

But how could she have a happy ending if Given died?

A long night stretched ahead of them, and Ella was unsure what hope the dawn would bring.

ELLA SLEPT POORLY, CURLED on the carpet next to Given, even after Rory tucked a blanket around her. She gave up trying when the first hint of dawn turned the night sky gray.

Rory was standing out on the balcony, surveying the gardens.

Ella slipped out to lean against the balustrade beside him, wrapping herself up in her blanket.

"Where's Kerr?" she asked. Her cheek ached as she talked, only slightly more than the wound on her arm where the hoe had clipped her. She would need to track down some of Paxton's pain-relieving tea before long.

"Checking the grounds."

"Have you been out here all night?"

"I watched you sleep for a while," he said, and she couldn't tell from his tone if his words were in jest, "but I didn't fancy getting a dagger sent my way if you caught me."

She relaxed. It was his attempt at levity.

"I want to assure you he'll survive," he continued, his voice tight, "but I need to stop making promises I cannot keep."

Ella rested her head against his shoulder. "It's not your job to assure me. I am, apparently, the lady of the manor."

Rory leaned heavily on the balustrade, his hands knotted together. "I believe I have done you wrong, Ella, and without my father here to confirm my suspicions, I fear I have to ask your opinion."

She thought about the familiarity that existed between him and Paxton, that maybe her flare of jealously hadn't been misplaced, that maybe seeing the Prince again had reminded Rory of his feelings.

She drew away from him. "I appreciate you coming to help save Given, but now the danger is past, you're free to leave."

"You're releasing me? If only it were that easy." He lifted his gaze to the fading stars and let out a long breath. "The first time I attempted to make a grand gesture of my feelings toward someone, he poisoned me and left without saying goodbye. The second time, she didn't wait for me to escape from a dungeon and come to her. I think it's better for everyone if I stop trying to make grand gestures and simply state my feelings plain."

He turned to face her, and she steeled herself for rejection.

"Ella, if you don't want me, I'll leave, but know this: I have nowhere else to go and nowhere I would rather be. I didn't mean to fall in love with you, not given the situation I was in, and certainly not after things with Paxton went so poorly." His gaze dipped before returning to meet hers. "But I seem to have done so against my best intentions."

"You're in love with me?" she murmured as a stillness swept over her.

"In my defense, it came upon me slowly." Pink flared in his cheeks, reflecting the dawn on the horizon. "And it's mostly Esme's fault for making me realize it and giving me hope for a life where I was free of Godmother's tyranny."

Ella's breath caught. In the chaos of last night, she'd forgotten her own bargain with the fairy godmother. "Oh, Rory."

"I apologize," he said as he turned back to survey the gardens. "It seems as if I've swapped grand gestures for dramatic speeches. Stop me if I descend into rhyme."

"No, that's not—"

"I'll leave once the sun is fully up. At least the view will be pleasant."

She was about to tell him to be quiet and listen, but his words sent a chill down her spine and she turned to gaze over the gardens. As the sun crested the horizon, it spread its golden light over blossoms and buds and leaves.

Huxford's Folly had come to life.

BEFORE ELLA COULD GRAB Rory or tell him to flee or do *anything*, he straightened and his eyes narrowed.

"You appear to have your first guests," he said.

Ella scanned the gardens, her heart thrashing, searching for signs of the old fishwife. But instead there was a troop of people on horseback coming up the wide driveway.

They headed back inside the sitting room, where Rory nudged Paxton awake. The Prince jerked upright before scrubbing some color back into his face.

"Apologies for waking you, my lord," Rory murmured, "but your prince has come."

Delight then apprehension crossed Paxton's face. "I never asked how you came to be here."

"I'm afraid we don't have long for explanations, but we never made it into Caveline. Something happened to the Grand Prince when we got close to the border. He seemed perplexed that we'd seen no sign of Cavelian troops, and we stopped to search. We were still there when your guard arrived, telling of your journey here, so I escaped and made my way as quickly as I could."

"You escaped?" Paxton blinked. "Just like that?"

"Indeed, my lord. I imagine the Grand Prince will be none too pleased with me."

"Unless the lifting of the curse has returned him to the man he ought to be."

"We can only hope."

Hope did indeed fill Paxton's face as he fled from the sitting room.

"Will you be all right to stay with Given while I go to my fate?" Rory asked.

Ella wanted to say no, to tell him that it wasn't the Grand Prince who held his fate in his hands, to burst out with the horrible truth before she lost her nerve. But she couldn't force it upon him when he was already facing up to one problem she'd caused him.

"Of course," she said. "I'll be here."

She watched him head stiffly through the broken door before sitting beside Given to monitor the rise and fall of his chest.

"He's going to be so very upset when you finally tell him, don't you think?" the fishwife said from behind her.

Ella jumped to her feet.

The old fishwife was standing beside the balcony doors, as if she'd come in from outside. "Your time is up," she said. "I've come to collect my due."

"You tricked me," Ella said.

"And you were fool enough to fall for it." She shuffled across the room, her steps unsteady, her feet dragging across the rug as she approached Given's prone form.

"You leave him alone." Ella moved to step between them, but the fishwife held up one withered hand, and Ella froze, as if her body had been turned to stone.

"I won't hurt him." She let out a series of groans as she lowered her ancient body onto the floor beside the wolf. "My business with him is complete." She stroked her hand across his fur. Panic ran through Ella's body, but she couldn't break free of the fishwife's spell. She need not have feared, though. Given didn't let out even a single whimper of pain. The fishwife's touch was more gentle than Ella would have thought possible, and her voice came out low and almost tender. "I warned you, didn't I? If you took too long, you might remain this way forever. Looks like I was right once again."

She heaved herself to her feet and turned to Ella. "You have until sunset to deliver me the Dead Prince's heart. If you do not—"

"No," Ella said. Her body may be frozen, but she could still speak.

The fishwife's eyebrows rose. "No?"

"No. I won't give you Rory's heart."

The fishwife stood up taller and crossed her arms. Her hair began to darken and her wrinkles smoothed out as she transformed into the beautiful enchantress.

"Do I need to remind you of the tortures I have dreamed up for our dear Rory?" She took a step closer, and every instinct told Ella to flee, but she still couldn't move. "You do not get to renegotiate the terms of our bargain. You have already agreed. Not only have I granted you skill with a blade, I have gifted you predictions of the future at no extra cost. Did I mislead you? Have they not come true? Are you not satisfied?"

She stepped so close that Ella could feel every angry breath as it rushed out of the witch's nose.

"Whatever price you demand for Rory's life, I will pay it. Me. Not him."

The fishwife's gaze drifted over her, as if evaluating her worth. "Curious," she said, in a way that sounded more threatening than her actual threats. "I'll be back at sunset to collect what's mine. Use your time wisely. Maybe say a goodbye or two."

The enchantress disappeared in a blast of acrid smoke that sent Ella stumbling back into the easy chair.

All was lost.

If she hadn't managed to come up with a solution to her mistake after all this time, what good was one more day? And the fishwife still hadn't agreed to punish her instead of Rory.

Given jumped to his feet, spun around frantically as if searching for something, and let out a curious yip.

Ella launched herself out of her chair but fear made her hesitate. She'd never been scared of Given before, but then he'd never been a normal wolf. Due to the curse, he'd always been a man in lupine form. Now he'd broken it, he could be a wolf in mind as well as body. "Given? Are you still *you*? Do you understand me?"

Given plopped down onto his rump and batted his tail against the rug in a very un-Given-like way.

Ella eased down on her knees in front of him, but didn't hug him as she normally would have. Instead, she reached out her hand somewhat tentatively. He stretched forward to sniff her fingers then swiped his tongue over her palm. She laughed even as her heart broke. Her Given was gone, but she had a friendly pet wolf in his place, and he would have a home with her for as long as he wanted.

"How are you standing?" she murmured, gently stroking his shoulder. "Are you in pain?"

There was no comprehension in his eyes; he simply wagged his tail more enthusiastically.

Ella peeled his bandages off one by one, murmuring in surprise each time she revealed not open wounds but healed scars.

"She healed you," she murmured. "Why would she heal you?"

He gave no answer, but when she eased forward to hug him, he let her. She buried her face in his fur. He felt the same, he smelt the same, but he wasn't the same.

She pulled back. It seemed no stranger to speak to him now than it ever had, even if he couldn't understand her. "I don't know why she showed you kindness, but she won't do the same for me." She pushed to her feet. "Come. I have something to show you."

He followed her out onto the balcony, and when she leaned on the balustrade, he leaped up to rest his forefeet beside her. Now the sun was fully up, it was clear that spring had sprung in the gardens. There were flower buds of pink and white and yellow, tender leaves of every shade of green, and tiny berries in rich reds and brilliant blues.

"I have until sundown to give her Rory's heart. I don't know what I'm going to do, because she'll punish *him* if I break our bargain." Her hand drifted over to smooch Given's ears. "I don't suppose you could tell Rory for me?"

"Tell me what?" Rory asked. He stood in the balcony doorway, his arms folded loosely across his chest. "Perhaps what price Godmother demanded when you made your deal?"

Ella's throat closed up.

"Ella ..."

"Your heart."

"My what?"

"She wants the Dead Prince of Caveline's heart." Ella wanted to run to him, to hold him, to protect him from her words. But she knew she'd crushed any love he felt for her, and she would be the last person he wanted comfort from. "I didn't know *you* were the Dead Prince. I thought the Dead Prince would be *dead*, that I was simply tasked with retrieving some gruesome relic—"

"How does she want it?" Rory asked, his expression tense. "Please say still beating in my chest."

"She didn't specify."

Why had she never thought to ask the question that had been first to Rory's lips? The fishwife hadn't told her to kill Rory, she hadn't requested Ella carve his heart from between his ribs, she hadn't demanded it be presented on a silver platter.

The flicker of hope that still lived in Ella, which the fishwife had attempted to extinguish with her threats of torture and torment, raged back to life.

Rory let out a low groan and retreated inside to collapse into the chair by the fireplace. Given laid his head on Rory's lap, and the rogue scratched absently between his ears, apparently too distracted by his dire predicament to notice the wolf was healed.

"I knew it was too good to be true," Rory muttered. "Esme played her at her own game and won, but Godmother sets the rules. She always wins in the end. She wanted me indebted to her and now my life is forfeit once again."

Ella crouched in front of him, fighting back her own shame. "Rory, please, I'm sorry for what I did—"

"It's not your fault." The love and forgiveness in his gaze hurt her more than angry words would have. "You're but a pawn in her game. For some reason, I'm always the prize. I have no doubt she'll offer me a deal. Ten tasks for my life."

"No, I won't let her take you. I'll ..." Her voice trailed off as Rory's words swirled in her head.

It was all a game. And if they wanted to beat the fairy godmother, they had to play.

"No," she said.

Rory blinked. "No?"

"I'm sorry," she said, her voice coming out hard, "but you don't get to give up. I'm not going to give her your heart, and you're not going to be her prisoner. Do you expect me to wait around while you work off some unspecified debt? I have a manor to run, and I can't do it alone."

"Would you?" he asked, his voice catching.

"Would I what?"

"Wait. For me?"

Ella smiled softly at him. "Well, you may have had the pleasure of love growing on you slowly, but I, unfortunately, got hit like a sudden storm when you first walked into the tavern with that aloof expression on your face."

"I wasn't aloof."

"Not only aloof, but painfully handsome, and dressed in that outfit ..." She caught her lip between her teeth at the memory.

He took a breath. "Please tell me you have an idea because hope has never been my friend."

"Nope, none at all. But we have a day to figure one out." She pushed to her feet and offered him her hand. "Come on."

Ella dragged Rory through the broken door, down the stairs, and out into the courtyard where Paxton, the Grand Prince, and all their guards were still loitering. The princes were embracing, as if they'd been apart for years instead of mere days.

They turned at the sound of her approach, and she skidded to a halt with Rory beside her and Given on her heels. It was only now that she remembered that she was still the Grand Prince's prisoner.

"Forgive me, Your Highness," she said, dropping an awkward curtsy before turning to Rory. "Um ... what happened? You're not in chains. No guards came for me."

"All is forgiven."

"Oh. Good." Ella turned back to the Grand Prince. "In that case, could I borrow Pax—the Prince Consort for a moment?"

The Grand Prince's face, which had always carried a cold or cruel expression, softened. "Of course, Lady Ella."

"It's just Ella, really, and thank you."

Paxton stepped forward then around her to where Given was standing. "How are you on your feet?"

"The fairy godmother healed him."

"Godmother?" Rory gasped.

"Why?" Paxton asked.

"I don't know, and, truly that question is not so pressing." She took hold of Paxton's hands. "Please remind me how you fulfilled your bargain with the fairy godmother."

Paxton stiffened. "We've talked about this, Lady Ella, it's not common knowledge."

"Please, Rory's life depends upon it."

Paxton sighed and sent a hesitant look first to his husband and then to Rory. "I agreed to poison Rory to save my sister from marrying a man she didn't want to wed."

"*That* was your deal?" Rory said. "Why me?"

"I don't claim to know the fairy godmother's motivation, but I wasn't overly keen to comply once I'd met you. Unfortunately, she was rather insistent." He cleared his throat. "Eventually, with time running out, I discovered that poisoning can mean 'to reduce the activity of.' So I gave you a sleeping potion, and by no small stroke of luck, she accepted my explanation."

Ella nodded sharply and turned to Rory. "What about your deal?"

"Which one?"

"Which one?" she echoed. "How many did you make?"

"Two."

"Didn't you learn from the first time?"

Rory winced. "I was trapped in a dungeon, and I really didn't want to be the Twice Dead Prince. And in my defense, they were tied together anyway."

"How so?" Ella asked with a frown.

"Firstly, I promised ten tasks in exchange for Godmother banishing my father's ghost."

"What?" Paxton croaked.

"And then, although I'd done my part of the deal but she hadn't, I agreed to complete another ten tasks if she got me out of the dungeon alive."

"And she did?" Ella guessed.

"But here's the thing," Rory continued. "She didn't banish my father. I avenged his death and he left of his own accord before she could. Fool that I am, I would have completed the ten additional tasks had Esme not pointed out that Godmother was in danger of breaking our original agreement, and she offset one debt against the other."

The Grand Prince stepped up beside Paxton. "But why would your father need avenging? I heard he died of food poisoning."

"As I was gored by a boar, Your Highness."

"Then who killed him?"

"My uncle, his brother."

"Then *you* were the one who killed King Wybert?"

Rory let out an awkward cough. "He was found with my cousin Abigail's dagger in his chest. You may draw your own conclusion as to who was responsible for his demise. But remember, Prince Gregory died five years ago, so it couldn't have been him."

Ella smacked Rory in the stomach, and he flinched. "Can you please focus? I'm trying to save you."

"I apologize, my lady."

"What are you thinking, Lady Ella?" Paxton asked.

"We all know that the fairy godmother likes to play games. You won when you found another definition of poison. Esme won when she traded one of Rory's debts for another. I just need to figure out how to change the game so I can win."

"Win Rory's heart?" Paxton asked.

A memory hit Ella like a hurricane, and for a moment her lungs hurt so much she couldn't breathe.

Win the heart of a prince.

That was exactly what she needed to do.

CHAPTER TWELVE

ELLA'S EXPERIENCE WAITING TABLES came in useful as she delivered plate after plate of food to the Grand Prince's soldiers.

"The manor liege doesn't usually serve people," Rory said as he relieved her of two plates.

"Until I get some servants, there's no one else," she replied, before turning to collect two more. And considering the Prince Consort was the one cooking, she felt she could do no less.

Once the soldiers had been fed, and the Grand Prince had left their commander with instructions, Ella served herself and the four princes in the kitchens. Prince Rickett glanced around the hot, work-worn kitchens before resignedly taking a seat beside Paxton at the small table.

Ella set a plate on the floor for Given, and he feasted hungrily. She stroked him absently, her heart aching. No matter how many times she'd spoken to him since he'd turned back into a wolf, he'd never looked at her with any understanding in his eyes. It seemed he was truly a wolf and nothing more.

"I think the idea has been there all along," Ella said. "Even in the labyrinth, the goblin king—"

"You've met the goblin king?" Rory broke in.

Ella winced as she remembered that he didn't know the goblin king's other identity. "So have you."

"No." Rory shook his head. "He never deigned to grant me an audience."

"He didn't have to."

Rory frowned, and Ella reached over to squeeze his hand. "The older rogue who would accompany you to the tavern …"

"Bernard? What of him?" The color drained from Rory's face before she could answer. "No."

"Bernard is the goblin king."

Rory shook his head again. "No. It cannot be. All that time? Godmother treated him as cruelly as she did me."

"It was an act," Ella said, as gently as she could. "A role. Just as the fairy godmother can be the old fishwife or the beautiful enchantress. Bernard can be the goblin king or the charming rogue."

Rory groaned and rubbed at his brow. "No wonder he never answered my requests." His head snapped up. "How did you manage it?"

"We fought our way through the labyrinth," Paxton said, "though little good it did us."

Rory's jaw sagged open. "You fought your way through the labyrinth?"

"Of course. We were desperate for a solution, and he was the only one I knew of who might equal the fairy godmother's magic. How else were we to see him?"

"Make the wish!" Rory said, as if it should have been obvious.

"What wish?" Paxton shot back.

Rory groaned. "Though any wish may summon the fairy god-mother, there is only one that can summon the goblin king. It never worked for me, despite how often I said, 'I wish the goblin king would come and take me away.'"

"You called?" a familiar melodious voice drawled from behind them.

Rory flinched so hard, he half fell from his chair, and only his quick reflexes saved him from hitting the ground.

The goblin king stood beside the oven, leaning casually against the warm bricks.

"*Now* you show up!" Rory growled. "After all this time?"

He shoved up from his chair and strode across the room, his fists clenched at his sides. Ella scrambled after him, trying to stop him before he succumbed to his own rage and did something careless like attacking the goblin king and getting himself hurt.

Rory reached the goblin king first, but he didn't strike him or attempt to slip a dagger between his ribs. He stood frozen for a moment, as if he were under the fairy godmother's spell, then sprang forward and clenched the goblin king in a tight embrace.

The goblin king let out a contented sigh, patted Rory's shoulder, and said, "I missed you, too."

"I thought I'd never see you again." Rory pulled back enough to gaze up at the goblin king, who was a head taller. "I thought she'd have you killed or worse. And all this time, you were on her side?"

"Not exactly." The goblin king's gaze drifted to the table, where Prince Rickett had risen to his feet, and gently extricated him-self from Rory's grasp. "Perhaps you could introduce me to your friends, dear boy."

Although Ella and Paxton had already met the goblin king, Rory formally introduced them all.

"And what, exactly, are you king of?" Prince Rickett asked.

The goblin king, not appearing to take offense, replied, "A pocket of land, measuring little more than one square mile, and all the creatures contained within."

"And your *kingdom* is within my principality?"

"Indeed it is."

Ella shifted uncomfortably as tension built in the room, and Given, maybe picking up on her unease, planted himself between her and the goblin king and let out a low growl.

"He's not here to start a fight, Your Highness," Rory said. "Are you?"

"Of course not." The goblin king shook his head, and as he did, his pretense fell away. His hair flattened and pulled itself back into a stubby ponytail. His flouncy white shirt dissolved into a black vest identical to the one Rory usually wore. When he spoke, his voice had lost its resonance, and he was merely the rogue. "I came because our Rory summoned me, and if no one objects, I'll join you for breakfast." He gave Ella the friendly smile she'd seen so many times at the tavern. "That is, if you have a plate going spare."

"Of course," she said.

Before she could move, Given let out a loud string of barks. Bernard stepped around Rory and bent over to stroke Given's head.

"I didn't hurt her in the labyrinth," he murmured. "I won't hurt her now."

"He's just a normal wolf, now," Ella said.

"Really? How curious."

Given flopped to the floor, seemingly deciding this stranger was no threat, and Ella hurried to fill another plate.

When everyone had settled warily back into their seats, and Ella had watched Bernard eat three mouthfuls, she forced herself to ask. "How do I save Rory?"

Bernard picked at something in his teeth. "You don't need me to answer that. You already know."

"Change the game?"

"It worked in the labyrinth, did it not?"

"But how? The fairy godmother won't let me change our deal. She's been very clear with her threats."

"What threats?" Rory asked. "No. Don't tell me. I'd rather not know."

Ella felt no closer to coming up with a solution, and it was clear that even in this guise, Bernard wouldn't answer any questions directly. This was *her* challenge. If she wanted to prove herself worthy, she had to figure it out on her own.

"Tell me this, at least," she demanded. "If I find a way to turn her tricks back upon her, will she finally let Rory go?"

"If you pull this off," Bernard replied, taking another mouthful, "I'll do my best to ensure she does. She may be fond of you," he said to Rory, "but we have plenty of other ways to amuse ourselves."

Rory's expression pinched. This wasn't a fondness he desired. But Ella could save him. And she would.

When Bernard had finished eating, he pushed to his feet and turned to Ella. "Thank you for your hospitality." His eyes narrowed slightly as he studied her. She blushed under his scrutiny and ducked her head, knowing her bandages made her look slightly ridiculous.

He reached out to lift her chin. "Good luck ... and don't worry about your appearance, it's going to scar beautifully." Then he clapped his hand on Rory's shoulder. "You know how to call me, if you should need me."

"If I should need you?" Rory echoed.

Bernard smiled tenderly. "I'm sure it won't come to that." As he strode back toward the oven, a bubble of light formed around him.

"I needed you three years ago," Rory called after him.

Bernard gazed back at him softly. "I'd taught you all I could."

"That wasn't why I needed you." The pain in Rory's voice made Ella reach for his hand. He clung tightly to her fingers.

Bernard regarded him a moment longer then the bubble of light blinked out. "I suppose I could stay for dessert."

"Oh," Ella said, confused, as they didn't have dessert with breakfast in her village. "We didn't make any."

"Really?" Bernard cocked his head as the intoxicating aroma of baked apples filled the room. "Because I think it's ready."

Ella found an apple pie in the oven and a jug of fresh cream on the work bench, which she quickly shared out, and Bernard seated himself back at the table.

They ate in silence until Paxton cleared his throat and said, "That outfit is a uniform, then?"

"I certainly did not choose it," Rory replied absently.

"And yet you still wear it."

Rory turned to study him, and even though any conversation was better than none, Ella wasn't keen to listen to their bickering. "There wasn't much choice in the haven. I made the best of what I had."

Bernard sucked in a breath through his teeth. "You really should have said goodbye."

Paxton's jaw dropped. "Is *that* why you're vexed at me?"

Rory's jaw twitched. "I thought we were friends."

"We were."

"You *poisoned* me."

"As I've pointed out, I had no choice."

"I didn't know that. By Godmother's gown, if you'd told me, I could've helped. I wish everyone would stop keeping secrets." Rory clapped his hand over his mouth, and everyone froze, waiting to see if the fairy godmother answered his accidental call.

Eventually, Paxton shifted in his seat. "I'm sorry I didn't say good-bye, Rory. I couldn't face it."

Rory dropped his gaze.

Prince Rickett laid his hand over Paxton's. "Forgive me, my love, but I thought he kidnapped you."

"Oh, he did, but he was also my friend. Without his company, the six months I spent in the tower would have been very lonely indeed."

"In that case," Prince Rickett said, turning to Rory, "as sorry as I am for your misfortune, I'm also grateful for it."

"It all worked out for the best, Your Highness." Rory shot Ella a troubled look, and she smiled back as reassuringly as she could. "And we're still friends, Pax. People I dislike don't vex me this much."

Bernard stared rather smugly around the table as he lifted a spoonful of apple pie from his bowl. "There, isn't it better to get that out in the open?"

Indignation flared in Ella's chest. "You're as bad as she is, aren't you? Making Rory lay himself bare for your amusement? Haven't you hurt him enough? You two bring nothing but pain and suffering."

Bernard arched his eyebrows, but before he could speak, Paxton murmured, "And happiness."

Ella shot him a startled look. Surely he couldn't mean that.

Paxton held up his hand to forestall her denial. "It's hard to believe, because you've seen the worst of it, but it's true. If not for the fairy godmother, Juliana would have married a man she didn't love, and I wouldn't have met the one I do."

Rory's hand slid along Ella's thigh, and the warmth of his touch was reassuring. "I'm the last to defend her, but it's true. There were others who were quite happy with their bargains in the end. Though a roll of a dice may decide which ending you receive."

Ella sat back in her seat as the conversation drifted to lighter topics. Prince Rickett gently yet firmly questioned Bernard about his tiny kingdom and his intentions. Paxton and Rory shared stories of their months together in the fairy godmother's tower. And Rory recounted how his sister had come from obscurity to be the Queen of Caveline.

Meanwhile, Rory's last comment turned over in Ella's mind. Given laid his head in her lap and stared up at her with his dark eyes as she stroked his soft fur.

If she was going to win Rory's heart, she couldn't leave it to chance. She needed certainty, and the roll of a dice wouldn't give her that.

She pushed to her feet. "I'm going to get some air."

"Would you like some company?" Rory asked.

"Thank you, but no. If you lot would like to be useful, you could clean up this mess." She pointed to the work bench, still covered with the detritus of meal preparation, before she realized that she'd ordered three princes and a king to be little more than scullery maids.

But Rory had already risen and taken her plate. "Of course, my lady."

Even Prince Rickett was rolling up his sleeves.

"You don't have to, Your Highness," she said quickly.

"Nonsense. If I can't clean up this mess, how can I expect to sort out the one I made with my High Council?"

Paxton struggled to hide his amusement as he said, "I shall aid you, my love."

"Excellent." Prince Rickett gave him a tender look. "Because I have no idea how to start."

Ella let her hand brush against Rory's then she beckoned to Given and headed out the door.

It was clear to Ella that Given loved being out in the garden. He ran from one walled section to another, skidded to a stop, doubled back to Ella, and paused to chase down every sweet scent of spring.

The gardens may have been his folly, but she didn't believe he regretted them. And she was certainly glad of them now, because the last of her indignation fell off her shoulders as she strolled between the plants, inhaling the fragrant scents.

"How am I going to beat her?" Ella said absently. "I can't change the terms of the deal. I need to trick her somehow, but if I get it wrong, she'll take her fury out on Rory."

Even if he'd been able to understand her, Given could voice no answers.

A chill wind whipped around them, ruffling Given's fur and making Ella hug herself. Storm clouds darkened overhead, and a fat raindrop splattered on her cheek. Then another.

"Maybe a walk wasn't such a good idea."

She shot a look back toward the manor house, but they were so far through the maze of gardens it would be quicker to keep moving forward. As the rain intensified, she ran into the rose garden, and there, between the blooms, was the fishwife's hut.

Given let out a low growl of warning, but there was no point. If the fairy godmother had decided to linger here until sundown, there was nowhere they would be safe. But that didn't mean Ella had to act like a simpering victim again.

She strode through the downpour to the hut, threw the door open, and yelled, "I'm not afraid of you."

But only the crackling of the fire answered her. The hut was empty.

She crept inside one step at a time, stripped off her wet coat, and stood by the fire to warm herself. Given whined pitifully as he pressed against her hip, his tail tucked between his legs.

"It's fine," she murmured as she retrieved a thin blanket from beside the bed. "She's not here, and we may as well wait where it's dry."

As she toweled the wolf's wet fur, the door slammed shut. They both jumped, but still no one was there.

"On second thought, let's brave the rain."

She shrugged her coat back on and pulled the door open again, but it no longer led into the rain-swept gardens. They were back in Leyton, night had fallen, and a bright moon reflected on a rhythmic sea.

Ella sucked in a ragged breath. "Is this real, or some sort of waking dream?"

They headed away from the salt-scented shore and through the village. It was late enough that the streets were empty, but the tavern was full. Oil lamps flickered, patrons ate and chatted, and a young version of Ella—wearing a worn dress and with a tangle of long curls cascading over her shoulders—weaved between the tables.

Ella stroked her hand between Given's shoulders. "A dream then," she murmured.

The wolf padded to the nearest table and sniffed around the customers. They didn't look at him, not even when he jumped his front feet upon the table and nosed at their plates of chowder.

"Show yourself," Ella demanded, but still the fairy godmother didn't appear. If this was some trick, surely she would eventually come to gloat.

Ella moved to the center of the room, watching her younger self collect four flagons of ale from the bar.

She'd always been stronger than she looked.

She'd had to be. Not only physically, so she could spend hours on her feet, but mentally, to cope with her wretched life.

The younger Ella lofted the flagons high as she weaved between the tables and dodged the reaching hands of the patrons, all without spilling a drop.

And then she had the solution.

It took most of the day to prepare. Prince Rickett's soldiers were a great help, going to the village for supplies and providing muscle.

Once the sun started to sink toward the horizon, everyone crowded into the grand dining room on the ground floor of the manor, and their hard work was rewarded with food and ale.

Ella couldn't eat. Her stomach felt worse than it had after she'd drunk all that wine. Instead she retreated to the cook's quarters to change into the simple skirt and peasant blouse that Leandra had bought for her in Riverlea. But she kept on her sturdy boots. Her bandages were in a terrible state after getting soaked in the rain and then neglected for most of the day, so she found a looking glass, carefully untied the knot, and unwound the ribbons of fabric. As she peeled away the sticky poultice, she stared in disbelief. Paxton's careful stitches were gone. The wound had healed into a fine white line. She gently traced her fingertips over her skin, as if her reflection was deceiving her, and then she remembered how Bernard had told her it would scar beautifully.

He'd healed her, the same way the old fishwife had healed Given.

She would have to thank him the next time she saw him.

Pulling on a guise of confidence, she returned to the grand dining room. Rory was waiting by the door and caught her hand as she entered. Somewhere, in one of the wardrobes, he'd found a black vest identical to the one he'd left at the Grand Prince's palace, and it was both comforting and troubling to see him back in the role of the fairy godmother's rogue.

"Your face," he murmured, pressing his palm to her cheek.

She placed her hand over his. "I'll explain later."

"Magic?"

"Magic."

He nodded and freed his hand from hers. "In case things don't go our way ..." He reached inside the collar of his vest, caught the leather cord around his neck, and slipped it over his head. He twisted the cord around his fingers and showed her the ring which dangled from it. The silver shone with an intricate design of a shield surrounded by a two-headed eagle, a panther, and a crown. "This was my father's ring. It's all I have of my life before. If you ever need Esme's help, and normal diplomatic means cannot get you an audience, use this."

He didn't meet her gaze as he pressed the ring into her hand.

Ella's throat was tight as her fingers closed around it. "Thank you," she murmured, "but I won't need it. Remember, I had no trouble meeting the Grand Prince."

Rory let out a short laugh at her attempt to lighten the mood.

Ella slipped the cord around her neck, tucked the ring inside her shirt, and leaned forward to press her forehead against his. "I know you're scared," she said, keeping her voice low, just for him, "but I'm going to save you. It's my turn to make a grand gesture."

Rory stiffened a moment before the fairy godmother said, "That's sweet, but the time for grand gestures has passed."

Ella took a breath before she turned around.

The fairy godmother stood as tall and imposing as ever in her beautiful enchantress guise, her arms crossed, her expression cold. It would have been appropriate if her arrival had sent silence spilling across the crowded room, but the soldiers had been plied with enough food and ale that they didn't even notice.

"My side of our bargain is complete," Ella said, as she slipped her hand against Rory's lower back and gently urged him forward. "I hope you don't mind the packaging."

As the fairy godmother reached her hand toward him, her polished fingernails like claws aiming for his heart, Ella proclaimed, "I challenge you for the Dead Prince of Caveline's heart."

Now silence fell like a dropped plate.

The fairy godmother blinked and her hand dropped. "Excuse me?"

Ella stood up taller. "I, Lady Ella of Huxford's Gift, challenge you, the fairy godmother, the evil witch, the beautiful enchantress, to a single contest for permanent possession of the Dead Prince of Caveline's heart."

The fairy godmother's cheeks sucked in. "You dare challenge me?"

"I do. Do you dare accept? Do you think you can beat me without magic? Or do you only make bargains when you know you can cheat?"

Rory shot her a panicked look, and she hoped she hadn't gone too far, but everything she knew about the fairy godmother told her that she loved to be challenged, loved to play games. But this time, Ella was setting the rules.

She held her breath. Everything hinged on this moment. If she was wrong and the fairy godmother refused to play, Rory was lost.

But she wasn't wrong. She *knew* she wasn't.

The fairy godmother regained some of her composure. "Of course I accept your challenge. Even in this limited mortal form, what competition could you propose that would give you any chance of besting me?"

Ella swept her hand to encompass the room. "The only thing I'm good at."

The long dining table had been replaced by a dozen smaller ones where the soldiers and some brave villagers sat, eating and drinking. At one end of the room, before the fireplace, stood two large basins. At the other, on a makeshift bar, were two barrels of ale and a row of flagons.

"You never came to the tavern, did you?" Ella asked. "In this form you would've stood out like a shark fin in the bay. And as the old fishwife, my father would've turned you away."

"What concern of that is mine?"

"Here is my challenge: using the flagons, transfer the ale from this barrel into the basin at the other end of the room. The first one to fill their basin wins Rory's heart."

The fairy godmother's nostrils flared, as if Ella had insulted her with such a simple game. "I won't need magic to beat you at this."

Rory caught Ella's hand and kissed her knuckles before retreating to the side of the room where Paxton, Prince Rickett, and Given were seated. Ella and the fairy godmother took their places in front of the barrel. Each one had already been tapped, ready to pour.

Ella closed her eyes briefly, let out a steadying breath, and murmured, "Let's begin."

She grabbed her first flagon, turned the tap, and watched the golden ale flow.

Beside her, the fairy godmother did the same. But she didn't know the correct angle to hold the flagon so the ale didn't form a thick head, so by the time it was full, it was half foam. She set it aside and moved on to her second. When that one was full, she shut off her tap, picked up both flagons, and turned to weave between the tables.

Ella couldn't see the witch, but she could hear the jeers of the soldiers as they grabbed for the flagons, the grunts of irritation as the fairy godmother attempted to dodge, and the splashes as ale slopped over the side of the flagons and hit the floor.

When Ella's second flagon was full, she filled a third and then a fourth. Then she caught two in each hand and hoisted them to shoulder height, as she had done so many times before. No matter how many people reached for them—or her—she merely lifted the flagons higher and twisted out of the way without spilling a drop.

When she poured the ale into her basin, it was a quarter full.

As Ella made her way back, the fairy godmother was already on her second trip, and she gave Ella a filthy look. Her perfect hair had started to frizz, and a wet stain soaked the front of her beautiful gown. "What magic is this?" she demanded.

Ella only shrugged. "You're the one with magic, not me."

She filled another four flagons as the fairy godmother battled her way through the crowd again. No one dared touch her, but their hands reaching for the flagons made enough of an obstacle. As she spilled more ale in her attempts to avoid them, the floor became slick, and she couldn't move as quickly without the risk of slipping over.

Meanwhile, Ella danced around the tables and dodged the grabby hands with ease. Her basin was half then three-quarters full.

She hummed as she filled her last set of flagons.

The fairy godmother returned to her own barrel, her hair disheveled, her cheeks flushed from exertion, her gown reeking of ale.

Ella lifted her flagons and turned to make her final trip.

The fairy godmother didn't attempt to compete. She was too far behind, her basin not yet half full, and she couldn't win by playing fair. Instead, she turned to face the crowded room. With a sweep of her hand, the tables pulled together into a tight mass of chairs and people, plates and mugs.

There was no way through.

But Ella wasn't disheartened. She simply hummed louder, stepped up onto a chair, and then skipped across the table tops.

The fairy godmother let out a howl of rage, and the table under Ella's feet collapsed. She hit the ground, bent her knees to keep her balance, and kept walking.

She was four steps from the basin. Three. Two.

The fairy godmother appeared in front of her, holding Rory by the scruff of his neck.

"Do not take another step," the fairy godmother said.

Ella hesitated. Her arms were starting to ache from the weight of the ale. Rory's gray eyes bored into hers, but she only saw encouragement there. Belief. Trust. He didn't ask her to stop.

The fairy godmother traced her finger across Rory's chest, over his heart. "Are you sure about this? Once it's done, it cannot be undone. His heart will be yours forever. Are you prepared for that?"

Ella shrugged and said, "It's only fair. He has mine." Then she stepped forward and dumped her four flagons of ale into the basin. The golden liquid rose to the brim and overflowed.

She'd won.

The fairy godmother dropped Rory. He fell to his hands and knees, sucked in a breath, and let out a choking cough. No. A laugh. He was laughing.

Ella braced herself for an attack, but the fairy godmother simply ran her fingers through her hair, returning it to its shining glory, and over her gown, removing the stains.

"Congratulations," she said. "I hope you two will be perfectly happy together."

Ella shivered. The words sounded more like a threat than a benediction, but before she could think of an appropriate response, the fairy godmother snapped her fingers and disappeared.

Ella crouched down beside Rory and caught his shoulders. He was still laughing, and she realized she'd never heard him laugh before. It was slightly hysterical.

"You saved me," he said, lifting his gaze to meet hers.

"I had to. I got you into that mess."

"No." He shook his head. His laughter subsided but his face still glowed. "I got myself into that mess when I made my wish five years ago. She never wanted to let me go. Esme tricked her into loosening her grip, but *you* made her withdraw her hand in defeat."

Ella didn't know what to say to that, except, "I have money and excellent prospects. If I made my life here, would you stay with me?"

"You think I'd choose otherwise?"

"I wouldn't make you stay against your will. I wouldn't trap you as she did. I wouldn't—"

She didn't get to finish declaring what she wouldn't do because Rory cupped her face in his hands and pressed his lips to hers.

He kissed her in a way she had only ever dreamed of, a way that made her feel as if she were dreaming now, a way that made her never want to wake.

When he pulled back, she sat intoxicated for a moment before saying, "Does that mean yes?"

Rory smiled. "Yes."

IT TOOK SOME TIME to set the dining room mostly to rights before they all collapsed into chairs and raised a flagon to the stresses of the day.

"I won't forget that for as long as I live," Leandra called from where she was sitting across the room. "Can you give us another demonstration of how you skipped along the tables?"

"I don't think I could do it now," Ella replied. "The magic has gone."

The soldiers, disappointed but content enough, turned back to their drinks.

"It truly was an impressive display," Prince Rickett said. "If and when you come to court, you'll make a grand impression."

Ella smiled politely at him, though she had no interest in royal politics. And she doubted it would be wise for Rory to show his face in the palace where someone might recognize him as the Dead Prince.

"But tell me, how did you know you could beat her?"

"Because she told me so." Ella cradled her flagon in her lap. She'd never had the taste for ale, and she wasn't keen to start now. "Back when this all started, when I thought she was just an old fishwife, she made some predictions for the future." She counted them off on her fingers. "Rory wouldn't show up to save me. I would become the liege of a grand manor. I would win the heart of a prince. And I would have my happy ending. The first two had already come true—"

"I was trapped in a dungeon!" Rory protested. His cheeks were flushed, maybe from the ale, maybe because his foot kept brushing against hers underneath the table.

Paxton shushed him. "Continue, Lady Ella."

"The goblin king told me to change the game, and whether she meant to or not, the fairy godmother herself reminded me who I really was. I may have inherited this fancy title from Given, but I'm really just a timid waitress who was only ever good at dodging grabby patrons to deliver food and ale."

Prince Rickett let out a low whistle. "That was quite a gamble."

"I couldn't lose, Your Highness, because she'd told me I wouldn't."

"But she could have—" The effects of the ale meant Paxton's words were slightly slurred and his gaze heavy as it slid to Rory.

Rory stared into his own drink as he said, "Ripped my heart from my chest?"

"But *that* wouldn't have been a very happy ending, would it?" Ella reached down to stroke Given, who was dozing half under her chair.

The only way her ending could've been happier was if he had come back to himself.

"Why must you stare at me?" Rory asked in exasperation.

Ella looked up, but of course he wasn't talking to her.

Paxton had lazed across the table, his head propped on his hand. "First, I'm pleased you're alive. Second, since neither of you are from this realm, I can only assume you aren't familiar with our customs, and that means I get inform you that since it's Lady Ella who carries the liege's title, you shall henceforth be known as Lord Consort." He paused then added in a smug tone, "My lord."

Rory winced. "I suppose anything is better than being the Dead Prince."

"I can think of no one better to inhabit our border lands," Prince Rickett said, "than an adopted daughter of Bretland and a son of Caveline." His tone turned serious. "I assume I'll be able to count on both of you should relations with our neighbors become strained."

Rory tensed, and Ella slid her hand under the table to squeeze his knee. She was too unfamiliar with politics to know whether to take the Grand Prince's words as a threat or a request for aid, but she knew which one she hoped it was, and she knew what sort of man she hoped the Grand Prince would be now he wasn't bewitched.

"Of course, Your Highness," she said. "Would it aid relations with Caveline if you and the Queen could meet during an informal gathering?"

"Such as?"

Ella took a tiny sip of her ale and avoided looking at Rory as she said, "A wedding, perhaps?"

Paxton snorted with laughter then whispered hoarsely behind his hand, "I like her a lot."

Rory let out an aggrieved sigh but couldn't hide a smile as he replied, "Me too, Your Highness."

Chapter Thirteen

THE GARDENS WERE SO lovely that they decided two weeks was plenty of time to return the manor to its former glory, hire servants, plan a feast, and arrange accommodation for a long list of guests.

Given padded around the house, getting underfoot and feeling about as useful as a wolf without opposable thumbs could feel.

He was delighted for Ella, of course. Proud that she'd outwitted the fairy godmother and set everything to rights. And pleased that she and Rory had chosen each other.

Paxton offered the Lady and soon-to-be Lord Consort advice and his own head of household to help them get established, as Ella had no idea how to run a manor, and being a lord sat awkwardly between Rory's twin experiences of being a prince and a rogue.

Given would have been the perfect person to help them learn, and it pained him not to be able to help. It pained him more to let Ella keep thinking he was merely a normal wolf.

But it was better this way.

If she knew he was still a man trapped in a wolf's body, she would either be overcome with pity for him, or pledge to look for a way to turn him back. But there was no turning back. He was a wolf now, forever. The curse was broken, and this was the form he was stuck with.

The beautiful enchantress had warned him, after all.

It seemed unfair, though he knew the fault was his alone, that he'd found his daughter so late and had spent such a short time with her. Not that he would exchange those wonderful days for anything. And being her pet wolf wasn't so bad.

So he spent his days roaming the gardens and hunting rabbits in the woods, and at night he would slink back to the house, bound up to Ella and Rory's bed chamber—the room that had once been his—and scratch at the door until they let him in to sleep on the foot of the bed.

The two weeks passed in a flurry of activity, and finally the night before the big day arrived, and the manor house was packed full of important guests until it overflowed, and more were sequestered in the surrounding villages.

Given retired early to avoid scaring people and was already on the bed when the young couple arrived in what was clearly an enthusiastic rush.

They stopped short when they spotted him.

Rory gave Ella a tender kiss on her scarred cheek. "Would you like to use the washroom first?"

"Yes, thank you, *my lord*," she murmured before taking her nightgown and slipping into the small room.

Rory stood beside the bed as he changed into his nightshirt. He no longer wore the black rogue's outfit unless he went traveling. Instead, he spent his days in soft white shirts and fine woolen trousers, as was appropriate for his status as a lord.

"I find myself in an awkward position." Rory spoke far too softly for Ella to hear in the other room. "Please don't take offense if I ask if you're aware what day tomorrow is."

When Given glanced around to see who Rory was talking to, the room was otherwise empty, and Rory was looking directly at him.

Surely he didn't know.

Given did his best to look like an innocent wolf.

"I haven't told her," Rory continued. "I've been trying to avoid making promises I can't keep. And I haven't wanted to kick you out—you do an excellent job of keeping Ella's feet warm—but, fair warning, tomorrow is another story."

Given settled down, puzzling over Rory's words. He supposed it was only right. He couldn't keep sleeping on their bed once they were married and desired privacy. He supposed he'd have to make a nest in one of the other rooms, near a fireplace, where he would be warm even if alone.

He woke the next morning with Rory whispering his name.

"Quickly," Rory said. "Would you like to tell her now or surprise her at the ceremony?"

Given blinked the sleep out of his eyes. Rory was seated on the bed beside him, holding out a dressing gown. When he didn't respond, Rory merely threw the gown over him.

"It pains me that my own parents aren't alive to attend my wedding," Rory said, still whispering, his brow knotted, "and I would save Ella from that pain if I could, but Prince Huxford can't show up when everyone thinks he's dead. Luckily, *that* is something I have a lot of experience in." He pushed to his feet. "Are there any clothes in your wardrobe that would work as a disguise?"

When Given remained unresponsive, Rory crossed the room to the wardrobe.

Why would he need clothes? Surely a wolf in human clothing would stand out more.

Unless …

He closed his eyes. He dared not look.

He looked.

His hand was a hand not a paw.

He was human.

Beside him, Ella stretched, yawned, and sat up. Her eyes fell upon him, and she let out a shriek of joy and launched herself at him.

"You're here!"

"I am," he said, his voice rough. "I don't know how."

Rory came out of the wardrobe in a rush, carrying a bundle of clothes. He stopped short when his gaze fell upon Ella. "Good morning, my love."

"Did you know?" she demanded.

"I suspected, though he did an excellent job of acting like a wolf. And … I didn't want to let you down again if I was wrong."

Her expression softened. "Is that why you insisted we get married so soon? So the day would coincide with Given's turning?"

A blush flooded Rory's cheeks. "It was the only gift I could give you."

"Thank you." Ella's voice hitched. She squeezed Given tighter then pulled back and smacked his shoulder. "You let me think you were just a wolf."

"I thought I was trapped in that form, and I didn't want you to be sad."

"Are *you* sad?"

Was he sad? He'd wanted nothing more than to be her wolf since the day she'd rescued him from the dogfighter's. "No."

"Then neither am I. If one day a month is all you get in this form, I won't waste it in tears."

The day passed faster than he wanted.

Ella dressed in traditional Brettish style, wearing flowing trousers and a matching floor-length jacket of the finest burgundy silk embroidered with golden thread; Rory looked every bit the prince he was in subtle gray; and they exchanged vows in the garden surrounded by rose buds and concentric layers of royals, nobles, and peasants.

Given hung at the back, wearing the black rogue's outfit that Rory had found in his wardrobe. It fitted him perfectly, as if by magic, and he tried not to think too hard about how it had gotten there. He'd thought dressing in black at such a celebration would draw attention to him instead of away, but Rory had assured him no one's gaze ever lingered on rogues for long, and he'd been right.

As the newly-weds leaned in to seal their vows with a kiss, Bernard, in his guise of the charming rogue, stepped up beside Given. He hadn't been seen since breakfast on the day Ella had won Rory's heart, and Given stiffened.

"Nice day for a wedding," Bernard said.

"If you're here to cause trouble, I have to inform you I'll do everything in my power to prevent it."

"Me?" Bernard shrugged. "No. I don't like to interfere."

"Then why are you here?"

"I wouldn't miss our dear Rory's nuptials."

"And is *she* here too?"

"Helene? No. I believe she's still licking her wounds."

A sigh of relief escaped Given.

"She doesn't like to lose, but a happy ending was promised and earned, and she doesn't break her bargains." Bernard clapped him on the shoulder then started to move away. "Give the happy couple my congratulations."

"Are we truly free of her?" Given called after him.

Bernard gazed into the distance, thinking, before shaking his head. "Helene has always had some plan in mind for our Rory, and she may yet give him a nudge if he strays from her path."

"What plan? Why Rory?"

"Now *that* I do not know." A bubble of light formed around Bernard as he headed through the garden.

"Wait!" Given chased after him, and the man who flicked an impatient glance back over his shoulder was no longer the rogue but the goblin king. Given blanched but rushed on. "You'll do your best to keep him safe?"

"I always have, and I see no reason for that to change, though he may resent me for it." Then the bubble of light popped, and Bernard was gone.

A shiver ran over Given, and he rubbed the goosebumps from his bare arms.

He turned and followed the crowd, which was slowly making its way to the house for the wedding feast. There was eating and drinking, dancing and speaking. It pained him to hang back, to forgo his chance to speak as the father of the bride. With his parents dead, Rory had no one to speak for him either. But they made do. The Grand Prince spoke, succinctly avoiding the story of how he'd met

Ella, and the Queen of Caveline spoke, artfully omitting the fact that Rory was her supposedly dead brother.

As the sun began to set, and the feast gave way to revels, Given slipped away. He headed to his study, which had a nice fireplace and a comfortable rug. He left the door ajar, hoped nobody entered at an inopportune moment, stripped off his clothes, and set them neatly folded on a chair.

As he settled his lupine form in front of the fireplace, he thought back to the day the fairy godmother had cursed him.

You will stay in this form until you learn to love and to be loved, she had told him. *I hope it doesn't take you too long, or you might remain this way forever.*

Her words had sounded like a threat that he wouldn't break the curse, but he knew now they were a promise that he could keep this form when he did.

He may have been looking for a wife, but that had merely been a means to an end. What he'd really yearned for was heirs. Someone to carry on his line, to inherit his estate, to benefit from all his hard work. But what he'd found in Ella, and through her, Rory, was better than he could have dreamed.

He'd done what the fairy godmother had demanded of him. He'd learned to love, and he was loved in return.

And that was a lesson worth getting his head around.

BERNARD RETURNED TO THE goblin king's castle with a contented heart. Rory was safe and happy and loved. He could not ask for more.

He avoided the grand hall where the goblins would surely be carousing as they did every day, and instead headed up the stairs to his bed chamber.

Helene was standing on the balcony, gazing out over the labyrinth.

"You missed a lovely ceremony," he said as he shrugged out of his vest. It was simpler, of course, to change his clothes with magic, but there was something comforting in these small, human moments.

"What do I care for human foibles?" Helene asked, her voice bitter.

Bernard didn't pause to pull on a shirt. He joined her on the balcony, stepped up behind her, and slipped his arms around her waist.

"You don't always have to be the evil fairy, you know," he murmured, brushing his lips against her ear.

"And go back to the days when they would summon me on a whim, wishing for this, wishing for that? Have you forgotten what happened?"

No, he hadn't forgotten.

He ran his fingers over her stomach. Even with her gown in the way, he knew there was no scar from where Ella had stabbed her. It would take more than a simple blade to injure her. No matter how often they tried. "You should have more faith in them."

"If I left them to it, things would work out even worse."

"You could have come to the wedding." He planted a kiss under her ear. "Hid at the back with me. It would have been a fitting way to say goodbye."

She twisted around in his arms, planted her palms on his chest, but didn't push him away. He leaned in to kiss her, but she turned her head aside, and he stopped short.

"What do you mean by goodbye?" she asked icily.

He sighed and let his hands drop. "You need to leave our Rory alone now."

"I *need* to, do I?"

"You've tormented the boy enough."

She held his gaze for a long time before dropping hers. "I suppose you're right." She ran her hand down his chest, and though it sounded as if he'd won, he suspected there were more battles yet to come.

"Shall I set you another challenge, then? What wishes have you heard lately?"

"I could do with something lighter. A dessert after a heavy meal. I'm bored of royal intrigue and talk of war."

Bernard slipped into the guise of the goblin king, who never took things quite as seriously as the tenderhearted rogue. "I'm always up for trying something different," he purred.

But Helene eased out of his arms, distracted. "I haven't checked on the twins in a while."

Bernard stiffened.

She swept toward the doors, the hem of her gown whispering across the stones, her heels clicking. The sound stopped as she paused. Bernard glanced over his shoulder at her.

"Were they happy?" she asked without turning to face him.

"It was their wedding day. Of course they were happy."

"Good," she said. "I did promise Ella her happily ever after, and I don't want anyone to claim I do not keep my promises."

She swept from the room, leaving him alone with his unease. He moved to lean heavily on the balustrade. Not a moment after he'd finally removed Rory from Helene's field of view, she'd settled on a new—old—target.

He didn't know what trickery she had planned for the twins or what trouble she would make them cause, but he did know a pre-emptive strike might be his best chance to beat her. And it seemed that after all these years, the time was finally right.

He didn't like to interfere, but that didn't mean he couldn't nudge and poke and prod people to interfere for him. His fingers tightened on the railing as he assessed his options and came up with only one solution.

He could only hope Rory wouldn't take it too hard.

But, after all, every married couple deserved a honeymoon, and he had the perfect destination in mind.

About the Author

Amberley Martin is an author from Aotearoa New Zealand.

She enjoys baking cookies and drinking tea and can often be found escaping to fantasy worlds.

You can find out more about Amberley and her writing at www.amberleymartin.com

Books by the Author

The Fairy Godmother Tales

The Rogue and the Peasant
The Demi-Wolf and the Hunter
Mollification For a Giant (novella)
The Spinster and the Free Maid

Short story available exclusively by subscribing to Amberley's newsletter
www.amberleymartin.com/subscribe
Pestilence For a Rogue

CONTENT GUIDE

The Fairy Godmother Tales are meant to be fun reads, but I understand some readers may want to know what they're getting into before they start. Nothing on the list below is particularly gory or graphic.

* Deceased parents
* Parental abandonment and neglect
* Indentured servitude and bullying
* Sexual harassment
* Descriptions of injuries, treatments, burns, and scars
* Descriptions of past trauma (physical injuries and emotional abuse)
* Violence and murder, particularly with bladed weapons
* A house fire
* Bodily transformation
* Strong romantic subplot, some kissing
* Happy ending

www.ingramcontent.com/pod-product-compliance
Lightning Source LLC
Chambersburg PA
CBHW020646120726
47906CB00001B/149